DRAGOON'S HONOR

THE SCIENCE OFFICER
VOLUME 13

BLAZE WARD

KNOTTED ROAD PRESS

Dragoon's Honor
The Science Officer Volume 13
Blaze Ward
Copyright © 2023 Blaze Ward
All rights reserved
Published by Knotted Road Press
www.KnottedRoadPress.com

ISBN: 978-1-64470-391-5

Cover art:
Illustration 112700977 © Marciomauro | Dreamstime.com
Illustration 3641255 © Noel Powell | Dreamstime.com
Illustration 27018144 © Natuska | Dreamstime.com

Cover and interior design copyright © 2023 Knotted Road Press

Reviews
It's true. Reviews help. Even a short one, such as, "Loved it!" So please consider
reviewing this book (and all of the ones you've read) on your favorite retailer site.

Never miss a release!
If you'd like to be notified of new releases, sign up for my newsletter.

http://www.blazeward.com/newsletter/

Buy More!
Did you know that you can buy directly from the Knotted Road Press website?

https://www.KnottedRoadPress.com/shop

ALSO BY BLAZE WARD

The Science Officer Series

Start with: The Science Officer

The Jessica Keller Chronicles

Start with: Auberon

CS-405 (Command Centurion Kosnett, part of Jessica)

Start with: Queen Anne's Revenge

First Centurion Kosnett (sequel to Jessica)

Start with: Encounter at Vilahana

Additional Alexandria Station Stories

Alexandria Station Collection

Handsome Rob (Alexandria Station Universe)

Start with: Can't Shoot Straight Gang

====================

Corsac Fox

Start with: Flight of the Corsac Fox

Operation Marrakesh

Start with: Trial by Leviathan

Captain Daring

Start with: Revoked

The Hunter Bureau

The Gunderson Case Files, Volume 1

Augustus Derlyth, Occult Detective

Start with: Ill Tidings

CONTENTS

KRANIEAFIM

YU'URID

SOVEREIGN NAKHIMOV

GETAWAY

KRANIEAFIM

PART 1

Javier would lie if confronted.

Evade.

Disseminate.

Bullshit with the best of them.

Second nature by now.

He was, however, alone in his quarters, cursing under his breath as he typed things into the search box, rabbit-holed the results, then cursing some more and starting over.

"You could always just ask," Suvi announced over the room's speaker.

He looked up and grinned, wondering how long she'd been looking over his shoulders metaphorically and cursing herself, because he hadn't asked.

Wouldn't, but that was because it had turned into stubbornness by now, and this crew understood how stubborn could get.

Still had that replacement coffee mug he'd had made for him, after he'd sent the original home with 'Mina, all those years ago.

Wardroom gremlins simply couldn't lie and say they thought it belonged to someone else.

Not when it had **THE SCIENCE OFFICER** in *bas relief* block letters down one side.

Not messing around here.

"Are you even listening, or should I send in a medical team?" she sassed him.

"It was before your time, kiddo," Javier finally answered her.

Evading. Disseminating. Bullshitting.

"I'm older than you are, youngster," she fired right back, reminding him that she was his daughter.

Of the soul, if not the flesh. He'd taken her and transformed her from a simple electronic *Concord* Yeoman in command of a Probe/Cutter and turned her into...a pirate.

A dork, really, but also a pirate.

Kinda like him.

And she'd outlive him, as long as her ships survived.

Ships?

Sure. He'd make sure to pour her into something more modern and automated, next time around, but for now, he'd needed the last First-Rate Galleon still in service. Maybe not the firepower equivalent to the most modern Warmasters, but certainly their teacher for sneakiness.

He wondered where she'd gotten it, though, grinning.

"Yeah, but you were still a spit and polish sailor in those days," he said, sighing and leaning back from the screen. Probably would have to ask for help, much as it galled him.

"*Someone* corrupted my databoards, apparently."

He laughed.

It was possible to reprogram a *Sentient* system. You had to have knowledge, patience, tools, and something desperately wrong with your personality to do it.

Fortunately, he'd fit, at least in those days.

And maybe still today, but we don't discuss those things in areas where statutes of limitations might not have run out yet.

"So, what are you looking for?" she practically demanded. "I have fifty-three million books in my datacore at present, including no fewer than twelve thousand encyclopedia sets of various age, region, and accuracy."

Read that: More books than you can even skim in the rest of your life, old man.

He sighed and shrugged, which turned into everything above his kidneys popping loudly.

How long had he been sitting?

Javier looked at the clock. Goggled. Looked again. Stood up.

Too long.

"Hey, where are you going?" she asked sharply. "Come back here."

"Follow me," he said, bending over to touch his toes to pop the rest of things loose.

He'd been down that rabbit-hole for three hours.

"I need something hot to drink," Javier continued. "Meet you in the wardroom. Wanna make me some chai?"

"Gotcha," Suvi replied. "Coming right up."

And the room went that special sort of silent it got when she wasn't present. Only monitoring with a mere shard, instead of a full avatar.

His chai was steeped and steaming when he got there. Middle of the ship's afternoon, though it felt like the middle of the night.

Ships ran around the clock. Even *Sentient* ships, where Suvi controlled just about everything, had to have folks on duty.

She'd just needed a much smaller crew than most warships this size.

And he didn't trust any of those militant bozos one damned lick.

His daughter was special.

And a dork.

Javier considered the wardroom as he sipped his chai, then surrendered to entropy and left again.

"Would you make up your mind?" Suvi exasperated as he traversed a hallway.

"Bethany awake?" he asked. "Might as well only explain this once."

"She is currently cataloging...music from the thirty-fourth century, after we got a big dump of the stuff on *Nausi* at the last stop," Suvi said. "In the library. I'd suggest she might be as bored as you."

He chuckled and kept walking forward.

He liked Bethany. Had recruited her originally on Dorn's recommendation, and she'd finally opened up and relaxed around the crew. Every ship needed a Librarian. *Especially* the *Sentient* ones, who had access to as much data as could be loaded, and no flipping clue what any of it meant.

Which was why he'd reprogrammed Suvi to be a person, instead of a highly responsive decision-tree matrix.

None of those grumps composed music. They could shit out notes, but not tell you what it meant. Or make you cry.

He entered the library and found Bethany already paying attention. Yup, probably bored.

Bethany Marie Durbin. *Bryce* Academy graduate (Class of '79). *Concord* Navy retired. Still tall and lean as thirty got close. Blue eyes. Pretty face. Light brown hair that couldn't decide if it was dirty blond or mousy brown.

Smarter than him, which honestly didn't describe that many people on this ship, though he'd lie if challenged.

Didn't have to bullshit Bethany. Yet another reason he liked having her around.

"And what dreadfully stupid idea has infected our terrible pirate overlord today?" she asked in a voice equally dripping with sass and honey. And a face to match.

Also why he liked her.

Javier couldn't help but give up and smile. Moved to sit across the table from her, because he knew that as soon as he started talk-

6

ing, she'd be diving into the datacores for tidbits as fast as she or Suvi could work.

That was what Librarians did, and she was really the best he'd ever met at it.

Took a long sip of chai, just to torture both women, because the panel by the door lit up with Suvi's face. Her presentation, anyway. Blonde hair with bangs and a French braid. The same sharp, blue eyes as Bethany. The same brains.

The same sass.

"I'm looking for a ghost," Javier began.

PART 2

Javier leaned back and realized that his chai was gone. And his jaw hurt. And he'd been talking for close to an hour, an explanation that had reversed into both women interrogating him within an inch of his sanity.

What there was of it.

"A party barge?" Bethany finally asked. Mostly confirming all those details, then translating them into whatever her matrix of understanding necessitated.

Javier shrugged.

"It's a lot more than that," Javier replied. "But, yeah, you might not be too far off with such an assumption."

"Why?" Bethany asked.

"Because where we are right now triggered something in my head," Javier said. "Some old story I remember from Academy myself, however bloody long ago and that many beers and arrest warrants since. We've been on the road for a year now, and I felt like maybe this was a good time to stop and have some R&R without anybody shooting at us. Plus, if we went this way, I don't have to travel anywhere close to *Neu Berne* or *Da Xing* to deal with either sets of those yahoos."

"Call it twenty-five years, then," Suvi offered. "Maybe twenty-eight. I find a few records of attempts at such an engineering project, but none of them apparently succeeded."

"That's because they were trying to make money," Javier nodded. "Hard to do, when mining on that scale."

"But hollowing out a small, dead moon?" Bethany asked. "Attaching engines and even JumpDrives? Flying it???"

"If you don't care where you're going, you ain't lost," Javier said. "Rune's Rule, and a damned good one for explorers. Or rich folks looking to party. I remember references to them starting a party on board something like four hundred years ago. About the time they had enough space hollowed out inside to install stuff. After that, you keep carving out the walls by boring inwards like a worm inside an apple. If you dump ore after you extract useful metals, it gets lighter over time, which makes it faster, though something like this has the overall speed and maneuverability of an iceberg on a planetary ocean."

Bethany got that thousand-light-year stare in her eyes, so he shut up.

"Suvi, look in the social register," she ordered. "Notes for a traveling caravan or possibly a circus."

"What?" Suvi pipped. "Oh, hey, there's something. Hang on. Gotta unpack some bits and digest it. Ship's name is *Sovereign Nakhimov*. Okay, that's weird. Bethany, coming up on your screen."

Javier nodded.

Suvi thought at something like fifty thousand times the speed of a normal person, when she could focus on something. He'd programmed her verbal tics and delays in such a way that she wasn't offended at having to wait for him to actually finish a sentence before replying.

She'd probably spent half a day of her time reviewing and

cataloging whatever thing she'd just uncovered, in the process of that sentence.

Javier rose and moved around to loom over Bethany's shoulder. She wasn't wearing any scent other than clean and healthy.

Smelled nice.

Fortunately for him, she was focused on the screen.

Megastructure, indeed. Monstrous thing.

Small, as moons went. Only maybe forty kilometers across the equator. Enough mass that it had originally formed into a sphere. Then been kicked out of some planetary system sometime in the distant past instead of being captured.

Long enough that most of the internal heat of radioactive decay had faded, leaving a cool lump of iron and nickel, wrapped in a thin layer of carbon and stuff.

And flying.

"I'd ask how that was possible, but obviously somebody had enough money and pissiness," she observed.

"You haven't been around enough rich people," Javier laughed. "And Behnam doesn't count, because she's the exception to most of those rules."

"How so?" Bethany asked.

"Most of them are men," Javier nodded as she turned to look up at him. "They have ego problems."

"Sound like somebody I know," Suvi offered dryly as color commentary.

"Bad ego problems," he corrected himself, then waited for both women to stop laughing. "Anyway, they have to show off their wealth. That asshole with the Land Leviathan before we stole it. Somebody got the bright idea to do this thing. Paid a stupid amount of money and accomplished it. Nobody else could compete at that point, because they'd be an also-ran, even if they built something bigger and badder. Original guy gets all the credit."

"And to fund it, he built a casino?" Suvi asked from her corner.

"Among other things," Javier nodded, studying the readout on the screen from a purely social standpoint, after the engineer in him was done drooling over the actual work. "I presume that at this stage, they have ships running back and forth to whoever is nearby on a regular basis, hauling exotic goods and consumables. Plus some of the best recycling systems you can manage. Not like space is a problem, unlike most ships."

"Agreed," Suvi said. "Would it be *Sentient*?"

"I don't seem to remember it being so," Javier replied. "But your kind only got really sophisticated in the last century or so, and you're several generations ahead of all your cousins, on top of that. Likely just incredibly smart systems, automated, as though living on the surface of a moon instead of inside it. Eventually, they might even finish hollowing all the stone off the outside, and turn what's left into a giant space station that moves. Several more centuries, I'm guessing."

"At a minimum," Suvi said. "I've read the logs of a ship that visited eighty years ago. They have a ways to go."

"But yes, a moving party," Javier said. "Plus, I need to see the interior."

"I can get you scans that aren't that far out of date," Suvi said, flickering Bethany's screen.

"Social interior, kiddo," Javier replied. "I want to see how resilient the personality systems are in a place like that."

"Why?" Bethany asked, honestly confused now, but her mind worked in logical patterns.

Librarian stuff.

She didn't take enormous leaps of faith without a lot of prodding.

Not like him.

"The Rising Storm," Javier quoted, circling back to Dorn's theory that the galaxy was on the verge of unraveling again.

And soon.

PART 3

Zakhar had learned to sit there with a growly look on his face when Javier got one of those wild hair ideas. Listen without interrupting. Digest. Fire off some pithy one-liner with perfect comedic timing when the man was done in order to deflate whatever pomposity his Science Officer had come up with this time.

Djamila beat him to the punch.

"We going into the casino business?" she asked in that moment when all things serious hung in the air, like the sound of artillery at the top of the arc, just before it started whistling down on you.

Zakhar liked the way Javier's face screwed entirely sideways as his head snapped around to look at her.

They were all seated forward in the main lounge, sipping whatever they preferred. As good a place as any, and they weren't eating, or they might have done this down in the Bistro instead.

Him, Djamila, Afia Burakgazi, Bethany Durbin, Suvi, Javier.

The *Rogue's Gallery*, though he'd deny membership if pressed.

Senior crew council, maybe.

Same thing.

Zakhar let his seriousness melt off into amusement. Javier deserved it.

"What?" Javier demanded.

Demanded might be too strong a word, though.

"Why do we need to stop at this casino?" she asked. "By definition, it fails at the primary purpose of being a self-contained entity that might evade and avoid your coming war. Unless you expected most of the personnel aboard to vacate at some point?"

Man's mouth moved like a fish. Open. Close. Open. Close.

"Maybe," Javier finally managed to say. "It has purely engineering benefits, by being a mobile base, however slowly it might move. Ready source of metals and some minerals, because a thing that big has a tremendous amount of volume, whatever is left to hollow out. Life support might be an issue, but it's easy enough to mine nearby comets and planetary system debris for carbon and oxygen if you don't have what you need immediately at hand. You can usually find it in the form of dirty ice that can be cracked down to elemental components. That's not why I want to see it."

"Why, then?" she asked.

Zakhar smiled. His love could be blunt when she wanted, though the level of personal abuse between those two had long since ended. The teasing, however...

"We need a break," Javier said, leaning back and shrugging. "We're halfway home at this point, give or take, and the crew has been going like hell. Plus, I want to see if these people could maintain the sort of isolated social environment that doesn't turn turbid and ingrown, like most farm worlds cut off tend to."

"*Shangri-La?*" Zakhar asked, just to snap Javier's head back around again to face him.

And get his pupils to dilate while his brain caught up.

"*In Xanadu did Kublai Khan a stately pleasure dome decree...*" Zakhar quoted back at the man, an old joke he still owed Javier.

The Science Officer shivered once, reset, and nodded.

"Yes," he said. "*Shangri-La*, or whatever it might need to be."

"Whole sentences, please?" Afia perked up, getting growly herself.

Pixie Kodiak. Small size. Pure power when she got going. Climb you like a tree then knock you on your ass.

"A mythical utopia," Zakhar filled her in. And the others. "Hidden in the Himalayan Mountains on *Earth* in the distant past, supposedly, where Buddhists could retreat to and hide when things got bad, down in the valleys or the lowlands. Before industrial technology, when you could climb up somewhere and hide."

"Exactly," Javier agreed. "Building a ship to escape might be a good thing, but it would have to be huge, if you wanted to use it to hold an entire civilization, however compact. Bloodlines, food, entertainment, *et cetera*."

"And a generation ship would be even larger," Bethany interjected. "There are records of some from the very early days of starflight, when jumps were short and not all that accurate. Folks still wanted to escape from whatever political, cultural, or economic crap they'd left behind them."

"*Kimmeria*, all over again?" Djamila asked.

"We're kinda out here conducting science," Javier noted, pausing to look around at everyone. "There will be enough war in a generation for everybody to get their fill. I'm trying to find ways to save the future from that sort of stupid shit. *Kimmeria* was a bust, and it wasn't. The concept was solid, but their super-advanced tech wasn't even as good as what we have today. Plus, generation ship, so you have the founder/grandchild problem, as we watched unfold with them. But a traveling casino might make enough money, might draw in enough new blood, might do the things today that mean they could be in a position to go dark and turn left on some future date, riding things out for a decade without letting pirates or enemy warships know they were there."

"Is war inevitable?" Suvi asked.

"You've read Dorn's thesis in every version he's sent me," Javier said to her projection on the near wall. "And I've programmed you to understand those fifty-three million books. I can't imagine a galaxy where somebody doesn't get the bright idea to invade and subjugate some neighbor, in spite of having billions of stars and planets to pick from. Human nature, unfortunately. Other people will push back. You are the only veteran of the Great War I know, Suvi. Have we changed as a people?"

Zakhar watched her face fall, which still astounded him, considering that she was a program. All of those things had been programmed into her, and she used them intentionally to convey emotion and meaning at least as well as any organic being he knew.

"We have not," Zakhar announced. "And I agree with Hetzel that bad things are coming. I'm not sure I agree that it will be worse than the one our great-grandparents dealt with, but I'm willing to be wrong. What does it gain us, to understand these things?"

He had locked eyes with Javier as he spoke, with the others falling silent.

"Behnam might need to build something even bigger than *Shangdu*," Javier replied. "A warship station planetoid that either she and her kids can disappear on, or as a basis of a fleet of such things that could drive off any invasion force on the basis of mounting guns of frightening power, because they were ground-mounts, with cubic kilometers of rock on which to install equipment."

Zakhar nodded.

At least they'd gotten Javier's fears out in the open. Zakhar would be sixty soon. If the timing worked as Hetzel had laid it out, he would be elderly or maybe already dead by the time such a conflagration reached the *Altai* region.

After his time.

So it was incumbent upon him to make sure that those kids were prepared. Javier was the same way. Hell, this entire voyage was intended to find out more about places beyond the space than any of them had visited.

To connect a Silk Road from *Altai* in the far east to the oldest colonies in the far west.

Just in case a war came, and folks needed to know where refugees might flee to.

Or from.

Zakhar studied the faces around him with intensity. All seemed mollified for now, but some of that, he knew, was simply ignorance of the situation.

However, they were good at sailing into something strange and finding the safe way out again.

Look at what the Science Officer had managed, since he had first fast-talked his way into the crew of the old *Storm Gauntlet*.

"I also think a brief vacation from duty would be a lovely thing," Zakhar announced.

The others nodded.

After all, how much trouble could you get into in a casino?

PART 4

Djamila studied her face in the mirror, looking at lines that hadn't been there in the past. At hair coming in gray on the sides. Still mostly brown. Still buzzed short on the sides and faux-hawk on top for working in suits. Sixteen studs in the ears, nine and seven, though none anywhere else.

She'd enlisted at sixteen. Served ten years of active duty and could have stayed another twenty had she wanted, but she'd already been promoted to Leader-3 and there had only been one more rung up the ladder she could have gone, because the *Neu Berne* officer corps was exceedingly jealous of its rank and prerogatives.

And she'd been born on the wrong side of the tracks. Career enlisted, and nothing better, regardless of how good she was.

Now, she was forty, and looking at it in the mirror. Not old. Not even halfway, but no longer that bright-eyed child who had taken the oath, once upon a forever ago.

"You're grumbling," Zakhar mentioned from where he sat in his favorite chair and read.

Djamila blushed. Then blushed worse that she could blush in public.

She turned to one of the loves of her life and shrugged. Fought down a sigh, in spite of the utter privacy of anything said in here.

Even Suvi would honor that. They'd spoken at length on the topic.

"Javier got me to thinking," she said, moving to the bed and sitting on the near edge.

After so many years alone, sleeping with any man, even this one, was still something that took her breath away. However, she was safe here.

Zakhar closed his tablet to set it in the side table, focusing that entire charisma on her in ways that almost knocked her over.

And then he didn't speak. Didn't question. Merely waited for her to continue.

"What do we do after this voyage?" she asked, noting that the *we* was even more complicated, because she had left Farouz back on *Altai*, where he was one of Behnam's top bodyguards.

"What would please you?" he asked.

More breathtaking moments.

She could have opinions that other people would accept. Not like an enlisted trooper, however good she'd been. And she'd been among the very best.

"My mind keeps circling back to this casino Javier wants to find," she said, looking inward but not sure which words were coming out. "Those people mostly don't have to worry about violence and conflict in their lives, except at several removes."

"Alien, isn't it?" he asked, nailing her discomfort squarely.

"Yes," she agreed. "Is that possible for us? Or will we forever be in the thick of things?"

"Depends on what you want," Zakhar said, leaving it to her. "I took this job because Javier shouldn't be in command of that many people, even with Suvi. And it let me do things that didn't necessarily involve going to war with people. Or robbing them."

"We still do," she noted.

He shrugged.

"Of volition," he accepted. "Because we make the galaxy a better place than we found it, in the process of stopping bad people. But yes, at some point we could retire. I can see Javier taking a job teaching at King's College, then just puttering as he and Behnam grow old together. Would you prefer to retire to *Altai* when this is done? Or do I need to buy us a yacht and sail away?"

Djamila blinked, unable to process such a thing.

What did she want?

That was exactly the problem.

She had two amazing men, both madly in love with her and willing to share. A job that let her be the best combat trooper in the galaxy, at least as long as she could maintain her own standards.

And how long was that?

When would she have to admit that she had lost a step? That the total perfection of being that Javier still called the *Ballerina of Death* had finally passed her by?

She was still better than anybody on this ship. The Doctors St. Kitts, Emma and Rainier, saw to it that everyone exercised regularly, and Emma taught various close combat forms that supplemented what Djamila knew.

The men Javier called *The Gunbunnies* were among the best in the galaxy. She was still better.

For how much longer?

"I don't know," she admitted, able to do that here, with him.

Zakhar nodded.

"When you do, we will," he said.

Simple as that.

She stood up and walked over to kiss him.

He would.

She could do anything, with Zakhar and Farouz supporting her.

And she would.

PART 5

Afia had returned to her cabin after talking to Javier and the others.

Something didn't sit right, though. Gnawed on her ankle when she wasn't looking.

"Suvi, got a minute?" she asked the room.

A screen lit up.

"What's up?" Suvi asked.

Afia frequently flashed back to that moment when she'd watched this chick being born into this very ship. When Javier had put all the boards and things in and awakened a most terrible dragon, who had turned out to be a pretty cool babe.

"This casino ship thingee," Afia said. "Javier thinks it is four to five centuries old, right?"

"I have various reports, with dates that don't agree, but all of them start at least four hundred and twenty years ago, yes," Suvi acknowledged.

"And you and your cousins were state of the art, *Concord* technology, when you were born, right?" Afia pressed. "When was that?"

"One hundred and twenty-seven years ago," Suvi nodded. "March 19, 7426. A rainy Sunday on *Bryce*."

"Thus, we do not think that such a ship would be nearly as automated as you?" Afia continued. "Because rebuilding things would require a lot of work?"

"Lots," Suvi agreed. "Most of those old systems use a highly complex binary logic gate system. Our breakthrough was trinary logic, which made things impossibly faster and more sophisticated. Downside, we were expensive to build and maintain as warships. Necessary during the Great War, but most of us were shut down and dismantled afterwards. Me included, but Javier knew a guy that was able to get me merely decommissioned instead of lobotomized. And here I am."

"So, ship," Afia said, feeling her way through the logic. "Automated to all hell, like most ships, including our old *Storm Gauntlet*, but not really alive. Not smart."

"Linear," Suvi agreed. "You up to no good? More no good, I suppose I should say?"

"Casinos really run two kinds of games," Afia nodded. "Purely games of chance that predate electronics, if you will. Cards, dice, whatever. In the way-old days, you'd have mechanical slot machines, where someone pulled a lever to start three wheels rolling, then the three would supposedly randomly stop, with payouts based on results."

Suvi's face did that thing where she looked up an entire library's worth of data in between eye-blinks, then she was back.

"Wow, that's old," Suvi said. "One of the first uses of electronics was to make them all controlled by a central computerized system that could track results, patterns, and payouts from an armed room."

"And, it made it really easy for the house to cheat," Afia said, thinking back to some of the things she'd done as a kid, back in the Yukon Protectorate.

There were reasons she didn't even visit *Earth* these days.

"You expecting the folks on *Sovereign Nakhimov* to be running a crooked game system?" Suvi asked.

Afia shrugged.

"Even an honest house usually has a ninety-seven-percent winning edge," she replied. "Throw in entertainment money for food, drink, drugs, cabins, and docking space, and I could see it being immensely profitable. Honest or not. Mostly, I suspect, it would come down to the folks in charge. Is there any way for you to tell if they are or aren't straight?"

Suvi blinked again. Like spending a few hours looking at books before she came back.

"If they had half a brain, they'd have scanners floating around that would look for folks trying to cheat," Suvi said. "And I'm certain I'd show up if you maintained the kind of comm link that I normally do to one of my drones."

"What if you pared yourself down a shard?" Afia asked. "Stripped out most things like you were going on vacation, and sat quietly, listening to the traffic around you, maybe with that same sort of basic keyboard and screen you used to do when we first met Javier?"

"We could probably build something," Suvi agreed. "But I'm guessing that a ship with that much money aboard—that many rich folks—would have better security and firepower than a First-Rate Galleon could threaten. I would, if I was in charge."

"True," Afia agreed. "This is mostly for my peace of mind. Plus, I have no doubts that Djamila and Javier will board, so we've got folks that are way more dangerous than they look, if there is trouble, ya know?"

"Agreed," Suvi said. "Let me spend tonight tinkering, and we'll talk again in the morning."

"Sounds good," Afia agreed.

Javier might be up to no good, but he had a scholarly topic in mind. The Dragoon would be all military competence, however sneaky she might be running it.

They needed someone like Afia to think about crooked card tables and con games.

Good thing they had her along.

PART 6

Bethany had asked Suvi to pull the top twenty resources she had on *Sovereign Nakhimov* and similar concepts into her tablet, so that Bethany could do some research.

Finding the ship would be a bit difficult, mostly because anybody with half a brain would assume *Excalibur* was a pirate and a threat.

They'd be right about the first part and wrong on the second, but they might not stop to listen to reason.

Felt like time to sneak up politely.

Helped that a First-Rate Galleon was as much cargo hauler as warship. What would a casino need, in terms of resupply? Bethany doubted that Javier wanted to leave this entire vessel behind while he took a tourist group to visit.

They'd narrowed the number of planetary systems down tremendously, merely by finding an old reference to how fast the ship itself sailed through space. Jump a few times, then park close by to other systems, but not too close. Stay for a few months at said location, letting folks come and go, but only advertising locally.

If you were in the know, you could find them. If not, you didn't.

That was it. There was an entire sub-culture of folks who followed the casino ship known as *Sovereign Nakhimov*, while generally hiding from the outer galaxy. That was what had caught Javier's mind the first time. And why such a thing had bubbled up today, when he remembered that they had been around *Kranieafim* thirty-some years ago, only slowly migrating along some path unknown to anybody but the folks in charge.

How long would someone stay in charge of a ship like that? Modern medicine meant that Humans normally lived active lives for eighty to one hundred years, with another twenty or thirty slowly slowing down and breaking down. Something about the limits of human genetics that had stayed put.

She paused and spent an hour looking up early eugenics movements, in the era when starflight let folks escape from *Earth*. Some religions rejected such things. Others fully embraced them, to the extent that they intended to tinker with the human genome, but in places where nobody was looking. Or stopping them.

Very little data had survived across the intervening four millennia, so she made a note to circle back and ask Suvi to include it in later data quests, when they hit planets with libraries or books for sale.

What could you do without adult supervision? What flights of fancy became possible?

Not today's problem.

She presumed that hiring would generally occur internally, with the occasional talent scout on the lookout for folks who might be recruited inwards. Specialist accountants. Business managers at other casinos. Security experts.

She also presumed a city of around a quarter million folks, based purely on volume, then pared that down to a manageable fifty thousand, once she looked at feeding that many people. It took a lot of greenhouses and krill farms to generate the correct amount of daily protein. Add in some imports of the high-end stuff for wealthy folks, mixed with things you could produce on station for a luxury of *nowhere-else-in-the-galaxy* labels.

Exotic whiskeys, which in her mind included every weird kind of special liquor one might drink. The stranger the better. Labels instead of product quality, with a captive market that had expectations.

Same for food. Frozen meat and fish imported in enormous loads, possibly megafreighter range.

What was a casino selling?

Exotic.

Things you couldn't get anywhere else. Suvi's notes had found a circus, focused on incredible acrobatics and aerialists, rather than freakshows. No animals, because that introduced all manner of additional logistical difficulties.

Games of chance that ranged the entire spectrum and then some.

People with money coming to spend it, with said money recycled right out to resupply for the next batch of...travelers? Suckers? Something.

They expected to be entertained. And were willing to pay a lot of money for the privilege, because this ship was something novel. Something to break up the tedium of your everyday life.

Even visiting a nearby resort would have to pale by comparison, because it was on a planet. Stable.

Static.

Sovereign Nakhimov would be there for a while, then leave, and you'd never visit it again, unless you were one of those high rollers who could do such things. Or you got a job aboard.

Again, recruiting, but trying to find such a recruiter would be a needle in a planetary haystack.

Better to simply offer up the ship to haul exotic cargo.

How exotic?

Live animals that could be slaughtered for dinner? Sounded messy, in spite of Suvi's space.

Bethany had several screens' worth of notes, but no conclusions.

A competent ship would be secure. Armed. Dangerous.

However, all that would be out of sight, most of the time, because you don't want to alarm tourists coming to visit.

What they really needed was Behnam Sherazi herself. The Khatum of *Altai* would be the sort of name that would distract everyone.

Bethany didn't think that Javier had anything ulterior going on, so they weren't a threat.

At the same time, a smart operator would look at *Excalibur* and its crew and have reservations about letting them get anywhere close.

She'd forgotten that Suvi was monitoring, in order to supply books or look up quick details as fast as Bethany could articulate them.

"You have the most evil smile I think I've ever seen on your face," Suvi announced suddenly.

Bethany jumped. Then blushed. Chuckled.

Cackled madly.

"I might have us an in with *Sovereign Nakhimov*," Bethany told her.

PART 7

"You want me to do what?" Javier asked when Bethany finished her spiel.

"You're already close enough," she told him, grinning. "It's only a little white lie, but not one they could easily disprove. Hell, she might even back you up on it, from what others have told me."

Javier nodded. Behnam just might.

"But, Prince Consort of *Altai*?" he asked his Librarian, reminded yet again that he'd hired her for her brains.

The sneakiness had been frosting on top.

"A title indicating the commoner husband a ruling monarch," Bethany nodded, voice in lecture-mode. "Not Khatum or Khagan, but everybody already assumes you are in at least as common-law a marriage as many planets recognize. Suddenly, having a traveling warship as a yacht and a trained combat team around you makes perfect sense. And is explainable to folks. Plus, it lets you get in places that would keep mere mortals like me out."

Worst part? She was probably right.

And he could already hear most of the folks who would be involved rolling their eyes at such a thing. Such a con game.

But was it? Bethany was right that he and Behnam were a thing. Would be a bigger thing when he got back, because he'd found a woman who understood him entirely.

AND still liked him.

Neither Holly nor Fryda had been able to get to that last part, once the truth had come out.

Of course, he was a lot better person today than he could ever remember being. Behnam's fault entirely.

"What changes?" he asked, challenging her to have done all her homework before calling him in the dead of night and dropping this sort of bombshell in his lap.

Woman was known for her research, but a game like this would be the improvisational jazz like Piet Alferdinck, ship's Navigator, might do when you got him a little drunk.

Bethany smiled, like she'd smelled that trap coming.

"You'll have to dress better," she smirked, noting his comfortable sweatshirt he'd gotten...somewhere. Sportsball team of some sort. University team.

Javier shrugged, feeling a good grump coming on.

"And I think a Van Dyke on your chin would make you look positively distinguished, Doctor Aritza," she continued, just piling on now.

It would come in salt and pepper, like Zakhar's.

There was a reason he shaved it smooth every morning. The sides of his head were already gray enough, thank you very much.

"Comet gas," he replied, but she just laughed.

"Past that, the same mission we've been doing," Bethany continued. "Exploring and diplomacy, but more formal this time, since you need to impress folks. Socioeconomic ties to *Altai*. At the rate they fly, it would take them years to get there, but we're already talking decades until the Rising Storm. Maybe you invite them to a safe harbor way the hell over there, assuming that the *Concord* is at least central to that next war."

"I haven't told Dorn, because it would probably break his heart, but I expect the *Concord* to start it," Javier said. "To decide to get a little too imperial and go after one of their weaker neighbors, not expecting everyone to pile in against them, mostly out of panic."

"Does the *Concord* survive?" she asked, suddenly clinical.

"Does anybody?" Javier countered. "Last war broke *Neu Berne*, as well as *Balustrade* and the *Union of Man*. They are only barely recovered today, and nowhere near where they were when the Great War broke out a hundred and fifty years ago *Da Xing* is rising, but they are coming from almost nothing. Doubt they challenge the *Concord* in a single generation. No, this is a room full of powder, and idiots with matches."

"All the more reason to make friends with the folks running *Sovereign Nakhimov*, then," Bethany nodded. "All we're doing here is upgrading you from troublemaker to Prince Consort."

"That might be enough," he nodded. "And probably necessary. Suvi?"

"Here," she said, appearing.

"Do NOT wake either of them up, but leave Kianoush and Adrian notes that I'll need a new wardrobe," Javier said. "Appropriate to a Prince Consort of *Altai*, with style and flair added. They'll get it."

"Got it."

He turned back to Bethany.

"Have we located them, yet?"

"*Yu'Urid*," she nodded. "At least, that's the starting point. From there, we make connections and they'll get us coordinates and an invitation. Otherwise, they might open fire on general principles, when confronted by *Excalibur*."

"Exactly wrong," he nodded. "But yeah, let's play this like a con. Is, in many ways. More than usual, at least. You figure out what the Prince Consort of *Altai* needs as a formal embassy."

"Most of it is easy enough," she said. "Different titles. Same jobs. The Dragoon handling your security with her teams. Zakhar as your Chief of Staff, since I think you'll need him with you, instead of here on the ship. A librarian for whatever important people need librarians for."

"Afia handling resupply, like she usually does," Javier said. "But flip that inside out and offer to haul cargo along when we get our invitation at *Yu'Urid* and resupply there. Then we'll have her handling all cargo tasks on the station, so she's local."

"What about crew leave?" Bethany asked.

"We'll play that by ear when we get there," Javier nodded. "Maybe we'll spend a few weeks on *Yu'Urid* setting things up, and folks can go planetside. Then maybe some crew on the station. I'll need you digging deep once we get there."

She nodded and left him alone after that.

Javier settled and thought.

Prince Consort of *Altai*? Ambassador to the Khatum?

But then, wasn't that almost what he was doing anyway?

Shit, was this what growing up looked like?

YU'URID

PART 1

Javier wasn't sure what to call the outfit, except *Utterly Stylin'*, as he studied his reflection in a mirror in the shuttle's lounge.

Close-fitting sherwani jacket with eight gold buttons down the front like acorns. White silk, lined, and comfortable to breathe. Cuffs and standing collar done in crimson and gold. Adrian had insisted on a turban in crimson, with gold palm trees printed on the fabric. Pants in the same fabric as the turban, visible from the knees down.

And the Van Dyke did look good. Still enough brown to pass for *not-old-yet*.

His only complaint was the lack of pockets.

None. Adrian and Kianoush had agreed that it would ruin the lines. Not even a breast pocket for a kerchief, like on a tuxedo.

He felt like a show pony. Fortunately, he looked like one, too.

Bethany's wolf-whistle helped. She was finally relaxing enough around him. Had even fooled around a few times, though nothing serious. Mostly, taking him for a test drive, according to rumors that had filtered back to him.

That was fine. Behnam had his heart and soul, and didn't expect him to spend years celibate while he traveled.

"You are my pockets," Javier told her, studying the woman.

She was in a dark, muted gray that just made him stand out all the more. All of the team wore matching outfits, because Adrian had insisted. Zakhar only stood out because the Prince Consort's Chief of Staff needed some gold trim to make him a little more visible.

"You folks ready to actually fly?" Del asked as he appeared at the hatch. "Or should I go take another nap?"

Del, however, did not match Javier's fashion. And wouldn't.

Baggy cargo pants in gray. Hawaiian shirts. Del was what you got. The best damned fighter pilot Javier had ever known. One of the few to keep flying past his fortieth birthday, which, with Del, had been at least thirty years ago.

"We're ready," Djamila answered.

Javier glanced up at her, noting that she'd gone a little more formal here, as well. Chief bodyguard, but not the killer babe Hadiiye. Gray/black. Baggy enough to hide that impossible body, with muscles on muscles, but still female.

One pistol stun and one killer on her thighs, because she was ambidextrous and lethal with either hand.

The Gunbunnies weren't low profile, except by color. All were armed like this was an assault drop.

Hopefully, paranoia on their part and not professionalism.

Still, he turned in place.

"This is a dinner with the governor of *Yu'Urid*," Javier reminded them. "Formal and all that, because I'm supposedly visiting royalty, or some such. We want to impress these folks that we're quiet, serious professionals. Am I clear?"

He waited for generic nods.

"If anyone outside this group starts shit, I expect you to put them down like mad dogs," Javier continued. "Excessive force is authorized, because I'd like a vacation from duty, and anybody starting a war with me right now got up this morning tired of living. Am I clear there, as well?"

Smiles from the killers. Djamila and her two pathfinders: Hajna and Sascha. All six Bunnies: Iqbal, Galal, Heydar, Demyan, Helmfried, and Tom.

Even Zakhar had a grin on his face. However, that man understood that there was no extra credit for neatness, most of the time. If you had to do violence, do it with an excessive amount, so that the next time folks thought better of even starting it.

Javier nodded to Del and followed him out of the lounge.

The dropship had no name. Del refused. Javier understood his logic and didn't disagree.

"You flying up with me?" Del asked as they crossed the landing bay.

"You expecting trouble?" Javier countered.

"Son, I never *expect* trouble," Del laughed like icebergs calving. "Djamila still flies the guns everywhere."

"Sounds smart, then," Javier said, turning to Bethany and Zakhar and Afia. "I'll be out of contact until we land, if any yahoo on the ground has needs. I'm also a pompous aristocrat who hates to be bothered by details, so you handle it."

Then he walked across the space and went up the stairs with Del to his flight deck, still decorated like a *Merankorr* brothel, with all the pink fur on the walls.

Javier was looking forward to the next phase of his adventure.

PART 2

Djamila was on the turret, with a comm line linked to Zakhar, just in case. The flight down had gone without any issues, but she didn't let that lull her into complacency. The turret had been live the entire time, and she'd picked out a few targets that had been on the edge of challenging them on the flight down, but nobody had bothered them.

And she'd flown with Del enough times to know what he could do in a pinch.

They were on the ground now. Mid-morning local.

Urid Starport, serving the capital itself. Busy, but not terrible. Professional flight controllers and significant systems automation to handle a lot of craft coming and going, from small flitters up to monstrous cargo haulers that were about as big as you could safely expect to land.

A modern, sophisticated world. What she'd expected of a place where *Sovereign Nakhimov* would call. Money. People looking for entertainment beyond what you could get with an entire planet or planetary sector to work with.

Novelty, as Bethany had mentioned more than once.

She shut down the turret as Del powered his engines off, then double-timed down to where her team was busy.

Sascha was watching the outside on a screen, as a trio of ground cars rolled up. One nice, for Javier and Zakhar, plus her and Bethany. One for the rest of the team. One for luggage, with someone like Javier's Prince Consort presumably expecting to haul three changes of clothes per day.

Or something equally silly.

Fortunately, Adrian Ahmad had planned ahead. And Kianoush Buday had gone all in on various bits of jewelry and pomp. Javier looked the part, with a ring in gold, silver, and bronze on his left hand that might have been the sort of token of ownership that a Khatum of *Altai* might have used to mark her territory.

If Behnam had needed anything more than the force of her personality.

Djamila didn't find most women impressive. It was too much a man's galaxy in the current age, with endemic chauvinism in too many cultures.

Behnam Sherazi had been born to power and wealth, and held it against all challenges for twenty-plus years.

Djamila approved. And approved of what she'd done to turn that punk Javier into a gentleman. Not that Djamila would ever look on him that way, but the thought no longer turned her stomach, either.

Safer to think of themselves as dangerous siblings

And she had Zakhar today and Farouz when she got home.

Still, professional killer mode today. At the head of a team of professional killers. Her glower took on depth and meaning.

It went beyond the passive role most amateur bodyguards undertook. As a professional, you shaped your principal's itinerary for him, based on security needs. Regardless of his opinion.

She hadn't had to deal with the Governor. Merely professionals on his staff who understood her vocabulary.

"Open it up," Djamila called quietly. "Six down and defensive."

The Gunbunnies went down the ramp while it was still only halfway, hitting the tarmac at the same time as the ramp and spreading out. Squad level pulsars. Galal as Grenadier. Demyan also with a backpack Directed-ElectroMagnetic-Pulse gun, in case he needed to kill a vehicle without blowing it up. Tom as Surface-to-Air-Missile gunner, with a launch tube already deployed.

Overkill, but it made a statement. The right people would be watching and listening.

Iqbal nodded when he was comfortable.

Djamila emerged, pistols in holsters.

Javier gave her a three count, then followed, with Bethany, Afia, and Zakhar trailing, then Sascha and Hajna at the rear.

The driver of the luxury vehicle merely nodded, while the other two went a bit pale.

Not used to the potential for violence, presumably.

Djamila boarded last, after the two vehicles with staff were ready and the one for luggage was backing up to the bay. Iqbal had cleared it manually, and approved the six stevedores. Del would remain locked in on his flight deck, ready to be Del if he had to.

She approved.

Javier faced forward. Djamila sat next to him, where she could watch the combat box around her. Bethany and Zakhar faced rear. The driver was behind a transparent screen forward, if they needed to talk to him.

She assumed the vehicle was bugged to record all conversation. They all did.

Everyone remained in character.

"What excitement does *Yu'Urid* offer?" Javier asked in a dry, supercilious tone.

"The usual things, My Prince," Bethany replied smoothly, working from a script they had come up with.

Might as well feed the Governor the right sorts of false intelligence.

"The usual?" Javier pressed in a tone despairing of little people and their *ennui*.

If she didn't know any better, Djamila would have even believed Javier in this role, but she had had years of understanding the type of social chameleon that was the Science Officer.

She didn't understand it, but appreciated what he could do. And did with a level of professionalism she did approve of.

So unlike the punk she'd bounced off the bulkhead a few times. Or shot when she'd first met him.

She couldn't help but smile at the memory. How far they'd come.

He raised an eyebrow at her, but she shook her head. Not a conversation to have in front of witnesses, however removed the Governor's spies might be.

"Ocean resort not too far away, My Prince," Bethany continued. "Several different climate zones, all offering amenities that ought to be good enough for your needs."

"I need something new," he challenged in a petulant tone, looking around at all of them in character. "Find me something no other world offers, so I can at least say that *Yu'Urid* is an interesting world and worthy of my time."

He lapsed into a sullen silence and they rode the rest of the way to the Government compound, on the edge of downtown and surrounded by enough towers that even Djamila was willing to call them sophisticated.

Of course, she'd grown up dirt poor, on a planet still reeling from the loss of a war, the loss of their colonies, and the terrible indemnities the victors had inflicted on *Neu Berne* to keep them from rising again for centuries.

Money like this occasionally disturbed her, but Behnam, of all people, had taken her aside once and explained to her that money was just another tool, like a gun or a knife. You learned how to wield it offensively and defensively, then put it to work.

It helped that Behnam had seen something in a Dragoon worthy of the time and effort.

And it had given Djamila something of a role model.

Now, she just had to figure out what she wanted to do with that knowledge.

PART 3

Javier had been born on *Bryce*, then and now the capital world of the *Concord*, and one of the most sophisticated and urbane planets he'd ever known. *Yu'Urid* wasn't boring, by any stretch, but it did belong to that third tier of worlds.

Possessed of all the usual amenities. Museums. Symphonies. Libraries. Universities. Dockside bar districts, gentrified or still rough.

But honestly, the information Bethany had pulled had suggested that they were just third tier. And that only barely that.

Even *Merankorr* had their galaxy-famous brothels, though the rest of the planet was pretty tame when you got more than twenty kilometers from that epicenter.

Still, he was here to play a role. And sell these folks a pig in a poke, that they'd introduce him to the folks who owned *Sovereign Nakhimov*.

He didn't even need to rob anybody. Or con them much, beyond the job this sherwani and the bullshit that came with it offered to anyone who didn't know any better.

Today was one of those times when the reserved and erudite

Doctor Javier Aritza, King's College might be a better role, but he highly doubted that those casino folks would be interested in letting him conduct sociological studies and urban geography on them.

At least visibly.

So, con game it was. Visiting noble, which was a role he hadn't undertaken since...nope, statutes of limitations still in place covering that, even if it had been a party and he'd been drunk.

She'd been the middle daughter of a powerful tycoon who owned large sections of that planet's government.

And might not have appreciated the lies he'd told the woman.

Safer to stay as many light-centuries away as possible, and hope she wasn't too mad at him, twenty-some years later.

He smiled at the memory, though. Recalled that dumbass kid he'd been, following the family into the family business, the second generation of officers even, after several as enlisted patriots and war veterans.

One of these days, it would be nice if there was no more war, but he doubted that humanity would ever get their shit that far together.

Instead, Javier lapsed back into that role of bored, somewhat foppish aristocrat with too much money and not enough personality to fill his day. He'd known a few.

The car rolled into a courtyard of a nice place. Red brick and white marble done to good effect. Paving stones underfoot as he emerged last and looked around.

"Prince Javier, this way, if you please?" an aide of some sort bowed and gestured.

Whoever was in charge around here had gone in for militant gray/green uniforms. Pants baggy enough to be nearly jodhpurs, tucked into cavalry boots that didn't look the least bit comfortable. Tunic held in place by a black leather belt, shiny, with pouches to hold things instead of pockets. Lots of brass buttons and adornments that would be a pain in the ass to keep clean and probably require a toothbrush.

Javier was glad he had staff to handle things, if he had to stay in this role long enough to matter. Adrian had, however, done everything in a way that mixed pretty styles with an easy machine wash that came out wrinkle-free.

A man after Javier's heart.

Javier followed Djamila into the building, her in kill-mode like usual when dealing with strangers on strange worlds.

He was as safe as one could get around here.

The Governor was only obvious by comparison to the sorts of silly uniforms you got when you had too many generals and nothing to keep them busy. Medals in every color possible. Gold braid around his right shoulder. Riding crop?!?

Sure, what the hell.

From some deep recesses of his brain, the term *banana republic dictator* arose, but that was usually a thing you only saw in vids.

Usually.

At the same time, with this many inhabited worlds, everything was likely to occur eventually.

The Million Monkey Shakespeare theory, though he'd be willing to bet that Bethany was the only person in earshot who would get that joke.

Cavalry boots on tile floors had a loud slap. With everyone else following the aide nearly silent, the Governor seemed a bit surprised at the size of the mob invading his ballroom.

"Doctor Javier Aritza, Prince Consort of *Altai*!" the man announced when they came to rest. "His Excellency, Governor Shelby Statham."

Javier nodded his head to the man's bow. Social superior, because one had been elected and the other elevated. Or some silliness beneath the dignity of a man like a *Royal Consort* to notice.

Javier could see turning this into a long con at some point. Way more fun than Navarre, that was for certain.

At least to most of the people. As Djamila liked to remind him occasionally, some folks had it coming.

Hopefully not this yahoo in all the gold braid. Really, did you need to run gold braid down the seams of your overfull jodpurs? Made you look fat by calling attention in all the wrong places.

There were reasons he kept Adrian on staff, after all.

"Welcome to our world, Prince Javier," Statham *exuded*.

Quickly, Javier got introduced to several ministers of various functions, as well as more staff officers than any planet needed, including admirals, generals, and even two field marshals.

Seriously?

Javier nodded and let the room settle. Bethany stayed close, as did Djamila. Zakhar and Afia went to work charming folks in the corners. The Gunbunnies were outdoors, intimidating the palace guards and whatever birds might fly too close.

"I am unfamiliar with *Altai*, Prince Javier," Statham purred at one point when social traffic had ebbed, somewhere around a third glass of wine.

Javier's third. The governor had flushed cheeks suggesting perhaps his third bottle.

"We are far from home, Governor," Javier replied. "A long voyage of exploration and diplomacy. Potential trade and the like. Your world wasn't on the original itinerary, but it fell in our path on this leg, so I thought to see what I might find interesting."

The man's eyes had lit up at the word *trade*, but Javier had known his type. And it was a type. Glad-hander who got elected owing someone a lot of favors, forever trying to get rich himself, while keeping his oligarch bosses happy enough that they didn't offer someone else a bribe to overthrow him.

The uniform made perfect sense in that equation. Rigid hierarchy of power, measured to the decimal point. Money would be measured the same way, but all the men in sight—and all the important players were men in here—were broke. Second or third sons not expected to inherit those palaces, mistresses, and factories from their fathers, so they joined the military.

Still better than the truly militant wackjobs that places like *Neu Berne* generated. Look at the woman looming over his left shoulder, for instance, and understand that she didn't used to smile.

Ever.

"Trade?" Statham perked up. "What sorts of things might *Altai* be interested in?"

Javier shrugged negligently. It took up most of his body. He snapped his fingers over one shoulder.

"Librarian," he said.

Bethany had come prepared. She better have, since all this was her idea and he'd blame and tease her about it to no end.

A packet appeared in her hand, from a messenger bag in that same dark gray, almost invisible across her back. Carrying case in gold, because Kianoush had done them. Behnam's crest on the front, with a data chip inside in a red velvet lining that matched his outfit when she displayed it.

Because Kianoush was just as exceptional at Adrian at those things. And she'd created that helmet for him originally. The one Behnam kept in their bedroom when he was home and occasionally wore.

Nothing else, just that helmet.

She didn't even need that much.

The Governor flinched as Bethany transformed from mobile furniture to knowledgeable aide in the blink of an eye, but Javier was playing the central role to distract everyone.

Javier kept his smile cool and distant as a colonel suddenly had to step up and take charge of the precious briefing packet his librarian had prepared. With the gleeful assistance of his rambunctious daughter.

Y'all ain't ready for this.

"Obviously, the distances are great, Governor," Javier nodded knowingly, wondering if the man would remember any of this himself later, or would rely on sober aides. "However, I do not feel that any potential friendships should be overlooked. But that's for later. For now, I'm interested in the sorts of exotic things that a region like *Yu'Urid* offers the wealthy traveler."

Buzzwords to pepper into conversation, but honestly it was like gigging a dead frog with electricity and watching limbs twitch.

Javier smiled expectantly at the man.

"We have many exciting things, Prince Javier," Statham somewhat slurred, gesturing in that broad, happy way that a sloppy drunk will when he'd crossed the threshold of competence.

Javier'd danced it for enough years to know how.

"In fact, most recently, the galaxy-famous casino ship *Sovereign Nakhimov* has chosen to anchor nearby for an extended tour!!!" Statham replied, exclamation points included.

Javier preferred competent executives to flashy ones, but he also understood that to be the exception that generally proved the rule, anywhere that didn't choose leaders by blood or marriage.

And hadn't put in place the right sorts of laws ahead of time.

Javier let his pretty, clueless brow furrow in feigned confusion.

"Sovereign...what?" he repeated.

"The ship *Sovereign Nakhimov*, Prince Javier."

Statham latched on to the concept like a hungry dog finding a fresh bone. Javier was afraid the man would slobber all over his new sherwani in his excitement, but didn't step back.

Yet.

"And they are?" Javier pressed.

"A casino resort unlike anything in the galaxy, My Prince!"

Javier rearranged his face to the sort of look a parent gives a child in the middle of some bullshit excuse for why there is a puddle of water on the deck plates.

"They hollowed out a planet, and turned it into a ship," Statham continued.

Javier stopped him by turning to Bethany.

"Is that even possible?" he asked disdainfully.

Fortunately, she'd planned ahead. And had learned how con games worked. Afia would have been better in the role, but he needed her over there seducing merchants, now that the can of worms had been officially opened.

Bethany, bless her heart, stepped around him and the Governor, to the nearby colonel holding his briefing packet like a tea service on a tray.

"Is it?" she asked sharply.

The man nodded like a bobblehead doll in an earthquake, to the point Javier was afraid his head might roll away.

"It is," the colonel replied. "A megastructure."

Others repeated the word in a sigh almost approaching religious ecstasy, but Javier wasn't impressed.

Of course, he couldn't tell them about the Land Leviathan he'd stolen. Or the ship that had carried it from world to world. Or what he'd done to them.

However, money made people crazy. He got that. Even Behnam had her giant, interstellar lake starship resort.

And he was flying around in a First-Rate Galleon.

"Interesting," Javier noted, seemingly finding something about *Yu'Urid* that impressed him.

He locked eyes on the colonel and took a step closer to the man, the Governor sliding back awkwardly.

"Tell me more," Javier ordered.

PART 4

Afia snorted, but only inside her mind where the two yahoos trying to look down her shirt didn't hear it. She'd left the top two buttons undone intentionally, when everyone else had only done one for comfort. Not a lot of chest there, but she'd known something like this was coming, so she'd worked with Adrian.

That third button was exactly on a line with her nipples, so you got a lot of cleavage this way.

Her grandma the witch had always said that boobs made men stupid.

And she'd been right.

Javier moved in for the kill on that poor staff officer as the room fell a little hushed.

Afia gave it a five count, head turned back to her left as though listening, while pulling her shoulder in such a way that these two men got a better look at the goodies.

Not that either man impressed her, but you do what you gotta do. Especially when Javier had a con going. And she was here to make contacts with the real power players. The ones who didn't necessarily work for the government.

"Megastructure?" she asked the smarter one quietly

Maybe smarter. Barely.

"Hollowed-out world," he nodded, voice dropped to the point she went ahead and leaned forward a little.

His eyes lost contact. She kept that snort inside as well.

"How does it fly?" she asked.

"Slowly," the other one interjected. "They move it around every few months, taking at least that long sailing between destinations."

"Interesting," she offered, not interested in telling them that she'd seen recent-enough technical specs.

"Worth going to see, if the Prince is hooked like that?" she gestured, overstretching things while she had these two yahoos ready to gaff.

"Probably," the smart one said. "It's supposedly a whole city in space."

"How big?" she pressed, then settled back to listen, prodding them with questions from time to time as they lapsed.

At one point, Bethany sent the dude with the briefing chip over, so Afia started peppering him with questions as well.

"Because I handle resupply for the yacht," Afia replied to one of his questions.

Never call it a galleon. Or a warship. It is Prince Javier's *yacht*.

Honest.

"Resupply?" the colonel asked, his eyes suddenly getting beady.

And outranking the other two dorks, to the point that they each slid a half-step backwards.

Afia shrugged mentally and went to work on this guy, too. Probably the contact she needed for the shenanigans she had in mind. And the other two might be as smart as her, put together.

Maybe.

"Our ship doesn't have a large crew," Afia nodded. "And we grow some things aboard, but we're always looking for food. Plus, the Prince likes to haul cargo like a common carrier sometimes.

Says it lets him go off the beaten track, as it were. Hell, what's this *Sovereign Nakhimov* need in terms of trade or resupply, while we're at it? Pretty sure my boss is going to talk your boss into scoring an invitation. Might as well put some of our space to use. And you'd probably have to come with us to oversee it, or something."

Wasn't a bad-looking guy, though she'd take dumb and ugly if it got them where they were going. Part of the game.

And the colonel's eyes lit up.

"Let me contact a few people," he said in that breathless way that suggested getting rich was more important than getting laid.

But then, he was already a bigshot here in the palace. Probably had a rotation of mistresses at his disposal.

Javier and Bethany had suggested that money was the key to their souls.

Afia could believe that.

She nodded and the colonel pivoted, walking away.

She focused on the smarter of the two left.

"Let's dicker," she smiled, flexing everything in his direction again.

PART 5

Djamila had cleared the room. Then she'd watched Afia scan things and disable a handful of listening devices, plus left her device behind when she departed again, to detect more if someone activated anything.

They were as secured as she could make things, with three of her men in the hallway and three down a room, off-duty and getting ready to swap.

She and her girls, of course, were in the suite with Javier, along with his staff.

What you might expect when you had a Prince who wasn't all that bright.

And he'd nearly made Djamila roll her eyes a few times, playing things to the hilt in that way that she'd never seen anyone else manage.

Javier had stripped the jacket off and stretched out on a couch with a glass of something amber in one hand. Zakhar was with him, also relaxed. Bethany and Afia were off causing trouble, if Djamila had to guess.

Good trouble, though. Mission trouble.

Djamila paced, as was her wont.

"Think they fell for it?" Javier asked the room.

Zakhar shrugged.

"The Governor was all in," he said. "Don't know about the others."

"We need to offer to carry a group," Sascha said, turning heads around. "Afia did that with that one colonel, and he was jazzed. If we're transporting their embassy on top of our embassy, call it a trade delegation from *Yu'Urid*, the locals will be falling all over themselves to help. I have no idea if the folks on *Nakhimov* will fall for it, but we're not in combat mode here. Or theft, so we can play it loose."

"The worst thing that happens, after all, is that they say no and we stay on *Yu'Urid* for a time," Hajna offered. "Then keep sailing home. Not like *Sovereign Nakhimov* represents a galaxy-changing approach."

"How so?" Djamila asked, curiosity engaged.

She'd hired these two women for a reason. And kept them around.

"It's just another ship," Hajna nodded. "Big, yes. Armed? Certainly. Self-sufficient? I doubt it, unless they have plans to evacuate down to maybe a few thousand crew total. Enough to sail it and fight it, but they lack the sorts of repair and resupply facilities that a system-based government can offer. We're back to the old days, where if something went wrong, it's game over and folks are off on their own."

Djamila considered that concept, remembering *Storm Gauntlet*. Especially the despair that had set in after the ship had been so badly damaged that everyone knew they'd have to scrap it.

Before Javier had saved them.

"When The Rising Storm comes, where do they go?" Djamila asked, turning the conversation inside out. "They could not get to *Altai* quickly, depending on where they were."

"And nobody knows where the match that starts it will land," Javier nodded. "They'll need to sail quietly, so I think that maybe

Hajna has a point. Get rid of the dead weight at whatever place they are, then flee."

Then his eyes turned deadly, locking in on hers.

"I have a historical-cultural question, Dragoon," Javier said, drawing the entire room's energy inward.

Djamila felt it and nodded, a ball of adrenaline suddenly forming in her belly.

"When *Hammerfield* fled, they were intending a King Arthur gambit," Javier continued. "Nobody really knows how, and I don't have access to the person with all those records right now, so I'll ask you. How would your old navy have handled a flight into darkness, had the ship not turned out to be a coward when it's programming failed?"

Djamila paused and considered. Suvi would know these things, but she was with Afia, and even that was a tiny shard without that sort of detail. They'd need to go back aboard to ask.

So he'd gone to the next best expert on the topic.

Her.

"Resupply depots, prepositioned and hidden," Djamila said, falling back on the old legends, as well as the first half of her life steeped in that militant tradition. "Raiding, but privateering instead of piracy, if only because they didn't consider the war over. Retreat somewhere quiet and rally as many forces as they could. It would have failed."

"Might not have," Javier replied. "The *Concord* wasn't really involved until *Balustrade* and the *Union* pretty much collapsed, and that was a few years after *Hammerfield* vanished. Nobody else had a fleet capable of resisting, and the *Concord* wasn't attacking. They were simply offering trade on good terms and protection from that sudden rise of piracy that is still around today, in spite of everything they did to contain it."

Even here, she noted, everyone was careful not to mention names or suggest what this crew had been doing six years ago. Or for whom.

"Do we tell them Hetzel's theories?" Sascha asked. "Give

them a copy and take them into our confidence about the sailing mission itself? Leaving off some of the things we've done in the course of it?"

"We'll keep that option open," Zakhar spoke now. "Because they are strangers, as are we. And the current operators won't be around then, so they'll have a generation to prepare. At least presumably. Remember, people, this is merely a scouting mission. Prince Javier wants to see what those folks have done, and how stable it might be under certain stresses. We don't need anything else from them. Or to do anything to them beyond observe, and see if we need to suggest something similar to the Khatum when we get home."

Djamila nodded. It was too easy to fall into the sorts of combat planning one might need, when this was really more of a working vacation, though she had no idea what those were like.

Even infiltrating *Shangdu* had been a mission, however much she'd enjoyed the quiet parts.

And the outcomes.

Djamila had to think of all this as a dress rehearsal for what she'd do when she was ready to retire as *The Dragoon*.

She watched Javier finish his glass and stand.

"I'm going to take a quick nap," he announced. "Wake me two hours before dinner so I can shower and get ready for more people."

Djamila nodded and indicated for Sascha and Hajna to go off duty as well. She'd take the first watch.

And think about the future.

PART 6

Bethany had come along as Afia's sidekick again, mostly because her role this time as the Prince's Librarian meant that she was doing research. And filling in holes in Suvi's library, back on the ship.

"Sorry you're missing dinner?" Afia asked as they turned down a side street and crossed some invisible, social line in the pavement.

"I watched those men ogling you," Bethany replied. "Dinner and all that comes with it wouldn't have been too bad, but none of them get up in the morning and run five kilometers."

Afia laughed.

"Most people don't," she retorted. "Doctors St. Kitts do that to folks to keep the crew sharp. The Dragoon and her people do their extra five before that."

Bethany smiled. She'd always been in good shape, as part of library work. Walking around constantly, shelving and retrieving books. Climbing ladders and bending over. She was still in better shape today than she'd been then.

And all these local military men had political power, so they weren't having to impress women physically.

Or intellectually.

The two of them went into a bar. Not quite a dive, but not a dinner club. No bouncer at the front but a few heavies inside, subtly keeping watch.

Bethany had done this enough times with Afia to have started developing a feel for it.

They made their way to the back and Bethany slid into a booth where Afia directed, across from a pale, heavyset man who had been at the event this afternoon, but who hadn't really gotten deep into any conversations.

Except that he and Afia had made quiet arrangements.

A waiter got drink orders and left.

Bethany hadn't gotten any names, but now understood that to be normal in this industry.

"Your vessel is a warship," the man said, focusing on Afia.

"First-Rate Galleon," Afia corrected. "Old design. Half combat and half cargo, from the days when they didn't dedicate escorts to convoys. Problem?"

"The folks involved at the far end might be concerned," he replied. "They might prefer if your prince traveled in something smaller."

Bethany jolted when Afia laughed out loud.

"This is smaller, buttercup," Afia ground out. "The Khatum of *Altai* has a personal yacht with a lake in the middle of it. A lake that is a kilometer wide by two kilometers long. Also something of a casino, but more of a resort."

"Inside a starship?" the man gasped.

Bethany nodded with Afia. She'd seen it, but not spent as much time aboard.

"Your megastructure casino is nice, but not all that impressive to folks from our neck of the woods," Afia said, smiling to take the sting out of her words.

Yu'Urid wasn't that backwards, but Bethany had spent ten

years on *Bryce* before this. Javier considered his home *First Tier*. And she'd hung out with Javier and the others, who dealt in things frequently larger than life.

"And your prince?" the man asked.

"Bored dilettante," Bethany spoke up. "Smart, but unfocused. He needs a shot of something new, because all the old stuff has worn off. Doesn't do it for him. How many beachside resorts can you visit? Or skiing trips? Eventually, it all becomes scenery, and he wants something special. This casino of yours might be enough to distract him for a while."

"Not mine," the man shook his head. "I'm merely a middle-man, working on the resupply side of things. Your friend here has needs for your ship, and mentioned the possibility of hauling cargo to the *Sovereign Nakhimov*. Will that be a problem?"

"It might actually be a bonus," Bethany countered. "He likes pretending to be the common man. That tramp freighter captain, out pushing his luck against a hostile cosmos."

"In a galleon?"

"Too many vids," Bethany shrugged. "Not a lot of experience in the real world. Plus, he's an academic, so clueless about a lot of things."

"An academic?"

"Doctor Javier Aritza is a botanist," Bethany noted. "Get him going on plants and he won't shut up for hours."

"Plants?"

Bethany watched the man catch confusion like a cold, slowly enveloping and dragging him sideways.

"We have a full botanical station on the ship," Afia interjected. "Some of the experiments he's been running date back a decade, including new fruits that he wants to seed on various worlds. Oh, hey, Bethany. Would dreamberries appeal to these folks?"

Bethany wondered if they should just go ahead and start a comedy improv team. Especially as the man across from them perked up.

"Dreamberries?" he asked in a sharp, profit-seeking voice.

"Variants of basic gooseberries," Bethany replied. "Bred into something more like Jostaberries, from what I understand. Adapted to both outdoors and pots. They bear a fruit that is said to induce deep sleep with quiet, hallucinogenic dreams. I've not tried them. Why would the casino folks find them interesting?"

Pure confusion on her part. It was a role she was playing as the book-bound academic, next to her fast-talking friend.

"Novelty," the man said in that breathless sort of way. "As with your prince, many who visit the casino fall into similar ruts, though perhaps without the level of wealth he has. And they have a significant hydroponic operations and an arboretum aboard, part of the way they provide fresh vegetables to the wealthiest players."

"Hmmm," Bethany mused. "Then perhaps we should see about introducing the Doctors St. Kitts."

"Doctors?" he asked.

"Rainier and her wife Emma," Afia interjected. "The former is a botanist that Prince Javier employs to maintain his orchard."

The man's face got sneaky, but it wasn't aimed at them. The waiter returned with drinks and got food orders.

He raised his glass when they were alone. Bethany and Afia matched his toast.

"I believe I have the perfect opening to *Sovereign Nakhimov*, ladies," he said.

Bethany could see that in his eyes.

Now, they'd need to brief Rainier.

PART 7

Djamila was working on her tan on a glorious day where the sun and temperature were just right.

And laughing inside, because she was doing it by walking on a beach nude but for her holsters tacked to her thighs and sandals. Just a lotion to keep from burning as her normally pale skin slowly darkened.

Javier was in even less, though he'd let Bethany go with shorts and a light shirt, and a brimmed cap shading her eyes. Zakhar was back in the hotel, making arrangements for whatever.

"Who are you and when did the aliens replace you?" Javier looked up with a chuckle.

There was nobody close, and the waves nearby covered a lot of sound. The air was calm, but Djamila knew that a breeze would rise later, bringing the usual afternoon thunderstorms offshore.

"*Shangdu*," she chuckled back. "It was the only way to beat you."

He nodded and they kept walking.

He'd been happy to go nude on that resort ship's lakeshore.

She'd had to overcome all sorts of body dysmorphia issues to do the same.

Anybody but the Science Officer and she wouldn't have. However, he hadn't been allowed to win in those days.

Today, she hadn't even bothered with a wrap around her hips, though Bethany still looked shocked out of her mind.

She'd get there. Or not. Not Djamila's problem.

Javier gestured the other woman close. Djamila watched for anything that might be a threat. The Gunbunnies maintained a much wider perimeter, but nobody was looking dangerous today.

Djamila didn't relax her vigilance.

"Have we gotten everything nailed down, finally?" Javier asked Bethany.

"We do," the woman said. "Your party will consist of yourself, of course, and your principal bodyguard, though the others will not be allowed to be armed while on the station."

"I doubt I will need the boys," Javier shrugged, then looked up with a smile. "You three can keep me safe, right?"

Djamila snorted.

"We'll try," she grinned down. "You might end up taking them dancing or something. Whatever the cover calls for."

"Rainier is something like a secondary guest of honor," Bethany continued. "She will be consulting on the botanical side of things, with your attendance as your interest and attention span might stretch. I've warned them that you are a plant nerd when engaged."

"Good," Javier nodded. "That's half of the things I really want to see, upon reflection. How they'll feed people. Or how many. The social side will break down into staff and outsiders. I'm just sorry that we had to go to all this effort, just to ask a few questions, you know?"

"Most people aren't prepared to understand the things that drive you, Javier," Djamila noted. "I certainly wasn't."

He glanced up and she thought she detected a hint of surprise on his face. Then a shallow nod.

"Too many bad people out there," he said. "We can't save everybody. All we can do is give them some better tools."

"Will it be enough?" Bethany asked, staying close as they walked.

"It can never be enough," Djamila replied before Javier could do more than draw a breath. "We can't save the galaxy. We can save a few people here and there, and hope that it works out. That's what this is all about."

Again, Javier looked at her, this time with more surprise. Djamila smiled.

She might have been deep into all the planning and listening, even if she'd generally let the others express most of the opinions.

Djamila Sykora only spoke when she felt like she had to, though what prompted her today she wasn't certain.

Seeing the things they were doing, and trying to figure out which might save *Altai* on the day when it became necessary?

"She's one hundred percent correct," Javier told Bethany. "We're trying to save our own, back home on *Altai*. If these folks work out to be friendly, we might invite them to visit or stay with us when all hell breaks loose, but that's tomorrow's problems. Right now, we're learning about a new way to deal with things. Less cryptic than *Kimmeria*. Hopefully, more successful. And I need a drink. It's getting hot."

Djamila turned and headed towards a cabana where someone with hardly more clothing was serving customers. At this point, her height drew attention, but not her nudity. Maybe the guns, but that was the cost of doing business when she was being his bodyguard.

Each of them got a tall glass with more fruit and ice than alcohol. Bethany moved deep under an umbrella for shade. Javier sat in the sun. Djamila stood where she could watch, but they were in a quiet corner of the enormous patio, where nobody was close until he signaled the need for more drinks.

"What's going to be fun, at least for me, is the thought that they might have their own botanist on staff," Javier said in a voice loud enough to be heard.

If anybody bothered to listen.

"Planning to trade seeds if it's a beautiful woman?" Djamila teased.

Rainier St. Kitts was many things, but peaked out at cute. And a little squishy, though Emma had been working on getting her to exercise more. Just as the staff of *Le Bistrot Parisien* was feeding her indulgently rich food.

Call it a draw. Intensely brilliant, though narrowly focused. Academic and plant nerd, like Javier on some days.

Rainier also had no interest in anything with a penis. And she had Emma.

Javier grinned up from about the level of her hip bone.

"I doubt I'll get that lucky," he replied. "But certainly we should talk botany on a level that ought to bore you to tears."

"Nothing less than I expect from you," she grinned back, teasing. Then turned to Bethany. "We'll need to prep Rainier to have both a full encyclopedia and inventory, plus as many seeds as she feels comfortable losing in the short term."

"That's my line, lady," Javier interjected, then chuckled. "Ya gotta sound more bored when you deliver it."

"I'll work on my intonations," she replied.

Bethany just rolled her eyes at the two of them, making Djamila grin all the more.

Then Javier's eyes got shrewd in ways that ratcheted Djamila's intensity up a level and a half in the blink of an eye.

He focused on Bethany, though.

"Find me a local botanist," he ordered. "We've been so focused on our own self-sufficiency that we don't really think about bringing in seeds from other places. Let's fix that."

"Arboretum?" Bethany asked.

"And plant nurseries," Djamila said. "Possibly bare root seedlings, where the weather is just about to turn to spring."

Javier jolted as he turned back to look up at her.

"I have been paying attention," she reminded him.

He nodded.

And she'd learned a few things along the way.

SOVEREIGN NAKHIMOV

PART 1

Suvi was just happy that Javier had gone ahead and put his foot down about traveling on some dipshit's yacht when he had access to all this.

Helped that they had a full French Bistro installed, done the right way. Suvi might not have taste buds, but she did have scanners that let her know Chay Burakgazi, Afia's cousin, had the ancient recipes nailed down perfectly. Which suggested that he was delivering a dinner as those ancient folks had intended it.

Tonight, he was entertaining the Governor and a handful of traveling oligarchs that were all worth stupid amounts of money. At least by *Yu'Urid*'s standards.

Chicken feed here, and she had chickens aboard.

One shard followed that conversation, but that was just Javier holding court with a half-dozen players. Rainier had attended one, then escaped the rest, because she was as introverted as Javier might be, when he was playing himself.

Suvi was watching the stars. Feeling the kiss of the galactic wind on her skin. Letting it trace delicate fingers down her flanks.

Cold, dark middle of nowhere. Stars all around her, but at a distance.

She'd dropped out of Jump a bit farther than she could have, mostly to have some time to survey things.

The locals thought she was a yacht. Maybe they understood *Sentient* ships, but she doubted it. *Concord* wasn't that close. Nor were the closer, tiny embers that had been *Neu Berne* in the recent past.

Quiet neighborhood, where they didn't need warships automated and capable of war all by themselves. Plus *Sovereign Nakhimov* was an old ship. She'd gone deep on everything anybody had been able to find about the thing.

Four centuries and change, so built in an era when things were more automated and less smart. Dumb hammers. Not that most of her cousins were much better, but still.

And nobody had told folks that she used to be a Probe/Cutter. Or that she'd spent several years with Javier on survey contracts.

Her eyes were probably two orders of magnitude better than anybody she'd seen lately.

Suvi focused them on *Sovereign Nakhimov* from several light-hours away.

Dark on the exterior, at least at this range. No star to reflect light from, save the ones that were nothing more than diamonds in the darkness. Up close, she had no doubts that there would be all the usual marker lights and such for humans to pilot and navigate when close.

Dirty, but that was organic material heavy with carbon. Like most of them.

The folks originally in charge had selected a rocky moon that had been warm once, then slowly cooled, rather than one of those that was a giant iceball with a crust. There'd be water, but not oceans of it on the surface. Gravity, until artificially induced recently, wouldn't have held anything on the surface so volatile as air or water.

No, it was a giant station with engines. Start by digging an elevator shaft. She'd plotted her course to come in on the side where the original excavations had occurred.

Go down a ways. Kilometers deep. Then move sideways and start installing gravplates like this was a station. A kilometer of solid rock overhead meant that you were safe from most things.

On the surface, you built power stations under a few dozen meters of stone. Enough to hold air in most of the time, so you didn't have to worry about leaks or strikes. Power. The life support. Weapons. Refineries. Forges.

A couple of pictures had shown missile bays in the darkness, when she'd taken a few hours and enhanced the images, then compared them to modern weaponry.

Heavily armed station. *Concord One*-level firepower. More than a Class III Warmaster could take on easily. You'd need a squadron of them. And a whole lot of missiles.

And you'd still be wasting your time, because after you'd disarmed the place, you'd have to invade it if you wanted to capture the value, which was deep inside. The people. The currency records.

Pirates wouldn't be coherent enough to amass a sufficient raiding force. Nations wouldn't care about a ship like this, unless they wanted to simply destroy it for some reason.

It would slip through cracks of the galactic system.

Suvi nodded to herself and spent some time with all the passive scanners drinking in whatever bits and dribbles of data might be detectable at this range.

"Pretty," a voice intruded on her from the physical world.

Took her a moment to flip back from flights of fancy.

Piet.

Previously Zakhar's Pilot, but she was the ship and flew herself, so now he was teaching her things about Navigation she'd never encountered in her life. Same as Mary-Elizabeth Suzuki could do things with the pulse cannons nobody had written down in any of the manuals she'd stored.

"Pretty?" Suvi asked, investing her bridge shard more fully.

Piet was also a composer. Twenty-four symphonies so far and still working.

He saw with his ears and his sternum, as he'd explained it. It had taken her some time to digest that, having neither.

"Pretty," he repeated. "I've listened to Javier and the others talk about novelty as a human need, because most folks aren't content doing the same thing over and over for a lifetime, not counting certain behavioral patterns. This is novel."

"How so?" Suvi pressed, happy to get an expert opinion on things. Especially one at odds with a lot of her original programming.

"Somebody saw a need for something completely unique, as far as you've been able to find, right?" he asked.

"Affirmative," she agreed. "Most folks either want fast ships to fly around, or big stations to stay put on. This is the worst of both."

"Or the best of both," he countered. "You can move, but you can also take a compact civilization with you when you do. All your friends, if you will. I can see having to keep this ship at a distance from most solar systems, because it would be easy to accidentally get captured by some giant planet and turned into a moon. In fact, I'm guessing it was at one point, and some celestial encounter kicked it out to where it was eventually found. Lots of those floating around, both captured and evicted. This one was put to use."

Suvi paused and considered it for an hour or so of her time, meandering into a couple of books on engineering and art to reframe her thought processes. Then she came back.

"Is it a viable alternative?" she asked the man. "Javier is trying to answer that very question."

"Planets tend to be safer," he shrugged on a camera pickup. "Atmospheric depth provides a lot of protection against most things. Plus they get so huge that bloodlines and staffing aren't a problem, if the surface is inhabitable. This is an ark. Like

Kimmeria, but done with a different purpose, in that they wanted to make money. And still do. The Kimmerians wanted to escape all human civilization and do things their own way. And it broke down eventually. Socially first. Then culturally. Finally, technically, though we got there before that was irreversible. I suspect *Sovereign Nakhimov* only works because they do not isolate themselves from the outer galaxy."

"Huh," Suvi offered. Then updated a few files with new ideas.

"Would an ark be a good idea?" she pressed.

Again, the shrug. Part of the reason she liked him so much. Piet knew music and navigation. And generally stuck to those topics unless prodded.

"You can get away from any one planet or solar system facing catastrophe," he answered. "Novae give you a lot of warning. I can't think of anything on a galactic scale that would warrant the effort, short of another war like Javier and Dorn envision. And even then, it would have to be huge enough to embroil everyone. And bad enough that someone would want to leave forever."

"Ark, though," Suvi prompted him some more. "What about someone wanting to take a big chunk of culture with them and hide?"

"Would you stay in this galaxy?" he asked. "Or build or buy a terraforming vessel and aim it to one of the close-by clusters? Those have a lot of stars. If you needed a century to adjust a planet, living inside an ark in orbit like a giant station would make sense. Then you'd start building the same thing on the ground, living indoors underground until the air composition or whatever stabilized and you could walk around safe. Again, now you're into the realm of a fringe religion or something."

"Or *Hammerfield*?"

"Or *Hammerfield*," he agreed. "If we sent someone like you, by yourself with a lot of repair robots handy, you might even find someone had already done it. We're four thousand years out from the original terraforming fleets. Who knows what somebody did when nobody was looking?"

She grunted aloud so he'd hear it. And appreciate it.

Suvi really did enjoy her conversations with Piet. Musically, he liked symphonic composition a little too much for her. She was more into four-hand jazz keyboards, given her head.

But he saw with his ears and his sternum.

Nobody else on the crew did that, save the two of them.

"You might let folks know," she announced. "I'm about to make the jump down to say hello to our new friends."

PART 2

Javier understood that Rainier would rather be anywhere else, but this was one of those moments when she didn't have a choice.

Governor Statham was with them, along with a variety of his folks. Del was flying. Javier was stylin'.

"All hands, stand by for localized docking maneuvers," Del announced, like he was tooling some fussy admiral around.

It would have taken too much effort to explain the truth, inside the con game that was Prince Javier, so Del had shrugged. And stayed out of sight.

Way easier to just be a voice.

Governor Statham was his usual self. All charm and almost zero substance. A week in the man's occasional company at meetings and banquets had made that obvious. And Javier had established some nice trade contacts for later.

He wasn't about to haul anyone from *Yu'Urid* to *Altai* himself, but he'd written and signed a handful of letters of introduction to aim them in the right direction, if anybody was crazy enough to actually sail that distance.

Weirder shit had happened. Look at him.

Zakhar and Bethany were dressed in nicer outfits that looked more formal. Djamila's was as well, but still had that look of lethal violence that hung on the woman like a perfume.

Rainier and Emma had been dressed by Adrian for the affair. Emma knew how to wear her suit. Rainier was getting worn by hers. Javier presumed that it would all work out, because all Rainier had to do was open her mouth and you'd know what you were dealing with.

Plant nerd.

He let his smile encompass everyone.

The Dragoon raised an eyebrow. Nothing more. He nodded slightly and wondered how the hell they'd gotten this far without killing each other.

And what the galaxy might have lost had they.

"Is all well, Prince Javier?" Statham asked.

"Excellent," Javier nodded. "I find myself looking forward to a botanical tour of the ship."

Statham blinked with a look on his face like he'd swallowed a live cricket. But then, he'd had to work a little to find his own botanist to accompany this party: a gray, bureaucratic sort of fellow over in one corner, trying to turn invisible.

Botanists could be like that.

"Is there good trade in plants?" the governor asked, having forgotten the explanation he'd heard previously.

"There can be," Javier nodded sagely. "It requires exoticism that isn't available everywhere. Breeding plants for specific traits people find useful."

He turned and indicated Rainier, sitting close and overwhelmed by all the people.

"Dr. St. Kitts has taken my preliminary work with gooseberries and truly refined the dreamberry into something amazing. Also the sunberry, frostberry, and swampberry. Those latter three are climate-specific variants that can be seeded on any world and will provide an additional source of fruit, both for animals as well as people."

Rainier smiled, but refrained from correcting him. And she should claim at least some chunk of the credit, because he'd over-bred them in a bad way, and she'd solved the problem, allowing their combined effort to do something new.

"And you will be making seeds available?" Statham nodded, a little cross-eyed, but the colonel nearby looked sharp, and the botanist in the corner rolled his eyes so hard it looked for a moment like he'd pulled something, to have to have Javier answer this question for the fifth or eighth time.

"Indeed, Governor Statham," Javier assured him.

Already had several times, but the man had a mind like a sieve for a lot of things.

"All hands, docking is complete," Del interrupted. "You may now move freely about the cabin. The airlock aft will open shortly."

Javier was up with all of his people, and none of the Governor's. But they didn't fly with Del to know how the man worked.

They got there. Interestingly, the botanist was first, but he was probably used to moving quickly when he had to, while the rest liked to snap their fingers and have things done for them.

Javier kept his smile friendly.

For now.

He had a whole new experience ahead of him, and was looking forward to it.

PART 3

Djamila was armed. And deadly, though all she had on her was a stun pistol. Sascha and Hajna, like the boys, had only hands and minds.

Acceptable, because the folks on *Sovereign Nakhimov* were supposedly sharp about their security. Certainly, everyone went through a scanner on the inside of the airlock. One she recognized and approved of as good enough.

She had insisted on the stunner, because her public job as bodyguard required it. And they had accepted that.

Djamila knew she'd have to be on her best behavior. Javier was running yet another long con on folks. This one didn't necessarily require violence to fulfill.

Merely dazzle. And he did that well.

The local security team met her standards for professional, on quick glance. Eight of them, evenly mixed by gender and all stone-faced. Armed with stunners, but that was normal in a casino, where alcohol and pharmacologicals twisted minds. Better to quietly put someone to bed and let them sleep it off.

As with most casinos, the folks dressed brightly were customer service, while back-office support like security dressed in colors as muted as hers.

For a moment, Djamila was back on *Shangdu*, necking in a closet with Farouz before stealing a uniform remarkably similar to the one she had on, as well as the ones around her.

She let herself smile, and noted how the eight guards relaxed a notch.

One peahen in right-handed rainbow stripes—indigo on her left shoulder and rainbow running from her right shoulder to her left hip—stepped up and smiled. Blonde, but Djamila was tall enough to see roots on top that were darker. And eyebrows, if you paid attention. Overripe and squished into the dress in ways that almost looked painful, except that it showed off all her curves.

Djamila estimated the woman to be almost exactly her age. Right about forty, but the stranger had had a lot of work done. It was obvious around the eyes and ears. And the backs of her hands.

"Prince Javier?" the peahen asked, stepping close in a big, exciting, vibrant kind of way. "I'm Amina Anargul, Casino Manager. I'll be in charge of making sure your stay is up to our standards."

Javier, being Javier, stepped up and kissed her on the back of her hand. They obviously didn't do that in this sector, because she blinked once and had to reset her expectations.

About what Javier no doubt intended.

"Madam Anargul, thank you for the opportunity to visit," he said, then turned. "Governor Statham of *Yu'Urid*, you've no doubt met previously, and his staff. Doctor Rainier St. Kitts, my expert botanist, and her wife, Emma. Zakhar Sokolov, my Chief of Staff. Bethany Durbin, my Librarian."

Each nodded. Anargul indicated her folks.

"This is Captain Karim Ranta," she said, indicating a short, serious woman in a dark uniform with cuff stripes in red. "She's in charge of crewside operations."

And reminded Djamila of Zakhar in so many ways that it was almost painful.

Warfighter. Probably a veteran of some major navy, retired and recruited to command the combat and flight operations on *Sovereign Nakhimov*.

The woman nodded but remained silent otherwise.

"And this is Doctor Paolo Pešek," Anargul said. "He handles botanical things here on the ship, though we really haven't ever undertaken to do things in a scientific or scholarly way."

"And why is that?" Javier asked, brightening up into his *shiny, useless phase*, as he liked to call it. "I would think that as long as this ship has obviously been around, that it would be the perfect place to conduct such experiments."

Djamila could see where none of them had ever had a similar thought, by the way Anargul's eyes crossed a bit. But then, she'd been in the money-making business, and trade in seeds wasn't a thing that was all that profitable, though Djamila could see that changing.

Add a small section to the gift shop, for folks heading home to take some seeds with them? Taste of the mighty *Sovereign Nakhimov* you could have on a shelf or window ledge to remind you for as long as you could keep it alive?

Better than a sweatshirt, at least to Djamila's thinking. Those wore out and had to be replaced.

Plants did not.

Anargul took a moment, then plowed right back into her welcome speech, turning to take Javier's arm on the opposite side from Djamila.

"I do look forward to your other interesting ideas, Prince Javier," she said. "Let's get you and your folks all settled in, then perhaps a walking tour before dinner and some entertainment?"

"Exceptional idea," Javier said, obviously ogling the woman who wanted to be ogled.

If you liked them curvy and a bit heavy. Plus significant after-market modifications.

Djamila didn't even have tattoos. Nothing but the various studs in her ears, and each of those done for specific personal reasons.

Zakhar and Farouz liked her just fine as she was.

PART 4

Rainier knew that Javier was a chameleon, particularly since she'd first met him when he'd been playing somebody entirely else, and it took some doing to rectify all those ramifications in her head with the truth of the man.

He really was a pirate. As was Djamila and the others. At the same time, they were all reformed, and she'd spent enough time around them while flying aboard Suvi's ship to understand the truth of that.

This really wasn't a mission to do anything except study a novel way to maintain an advanced civilization in the face of possible impending catastrophe, which Javier was certain would arrive soon enough that they would see it before they died.

Svalbard, if people actually lived there year around, instead of just visiting every few years to deliver more seeds and extract a few for experiments.

Paolo was on her other side from Emma as they walked, trailing behind the woman in charge and Javier, with Djamila tracking everything like a war machine.

All this, to look at plants?

Rainier mentally shook herself and adjusted back to a place where she had to go do mortal combat with MacWilliam, back on *Uelkal*, for her budgets.

Except that money wasn't going to be a problem.

Finesse was.

Fortunate, then, that Javier was in charge of things.

"How dangerous are the dreamberries?" Paolo asked in a quiet voice not intended to be overheard by the non-scientists around them, none of whom were qualified to understand the conversation.

Javier didn't count.

"If you made a batch of wine from it," Rainier replied, "then made a brandied port out of that. Then drank maybe six liters of it in a short period, I could see some threat of toxicity from the various ingredients. Otherwise, they will wash through you too quickly to build up at any level of threat."

Paolo was unconvinced.

"Before he became Dr. Aritza, or Prince Javier, our host flew long-term survey missions," she explained. "Himself, generally alone save for a host of chickens and a highly automated vessel. Medical events would be deadly, because he could not get to a hospital quickly. Similarly, he wanted something that would let him relax, without dependence or addiction. Given that the man had several years with which to experiment, he got remarkably close."

"And how did you get involved with Dr. Aritza?" Paolo asked pointedly.

It was an innocent-enough question. Rainier still felt every single one of the various dangerous folks around her responsible for her security flinch. After all, they'd been the ones who had originally rescued her from the middle of a pirate war she'd been introduced to as bait.

However, Paolo wouldn't respond well to such knowledge. Nor would Darby Vilchis, Statham's own expert trailing quietly behind her.

"Prince Javier had heard of my research from *Altai*," Raininer responded after a beat. "We'd been doing similar things, so he came to *Uelkal* to recruit me into taking a two-year sabbatical."

Honest enough. Mostly. If you squinted and left out certain bits.

Howevere, she'd also traveled with this group enough to understand that they rarely lied outright.

Simply shaded important things into the best light.

Rainier could do that as well.

She felt the Dragoon's Gunbunnies relax. Sascha and Hajna both grinned.

"And creating a variant of Jostaberries?" Paolo asked, more confused than anything.

From their introduction, he was mostly in charge of a giant salad garden, more than anything. Fresh greens and root vegetables that could be served on the same day they were harvested, for that extra cost and importance. Kales and lettuces, for the most part. A few spices that lost something if you let them dry out for shipment.

Things that were rare here because you'd originally planted them a decade ago, several hundred light-years away, and folks around here had different cultural and culinary preferences.

"His original gooseberry base stock had developed a mutation that left the plants nearly sterile," Rainier replied. "I found a blackcurrant that would cross with it and revitalize fertility, once I understood where his plants had gone. From there, we've spent several years breeding for climate-toughness. Thus, seedlings that are hardy for cold, for heat, and for swamp. The base dreamberries, however, grow best where their parents would, tending to prefer slightly cooler, alpine climates with good drainage. Nothing complicated for handling with hydroponics, regardless of the system you might use. Or soil, if you potted them, as Javier had originally done."

Paolo looked unconvinced, but that wasn't Rainier's problem. She was here to talk plants, as a way to get Javier and the others inside the parts of the casino ship where they wouldn't have been welcome otherwise.

"Have you made a port from dreamberries?" he asked after a long moment.

Rainier found herself at a complete loss.

"Prince Javier's staff have," Emma suddenly leaned in to speak and towering over both of them, being almost as tall as the Dragoon. "It is my understanding that they consider it an excellent dessert wine, but generally consume it by the thimble, rather than anything large, given the limited space dedicated to cultivation back on the ship."

Rainier blinked. She wasn't opposed to alcohol. Simply hadn't ever found one that she liked to drink, and hadn't accepted any of the offers from folks along the way to pour her a dozen tiny glasses of something to try until she did.

A single glass of wine might last her an entire evening, at some academic event. Just as well, too.

"Frequently, there has been talk of expanding some new construction project expressly for the purposes of creating a vineyard in here," Paolo admitted with disdain. "Since *terroir* could be perfectly controlled and the necessary water imported from our mining ships. To date, nobody has actually gotten serious, but I suspect that your Prince might jar things loose, given a sudden and unexpected focus on botany."

"We have grapes in our bay," Rainier offered. "Normally, small batch wine for the same reason as dreamberry port. Should I mention that sort of thing to your boss, or let it lie fallow for now?"

Paolo turned to look at the backs in front of them for a long moment.

"Prince Javier certainly seems charming," he replied.

"He is," Rainier nodded. "Quite, as he was able to convince Emma and I to go fly across the galaxy with him. Is that a good thing?"

She watched him shrug elaborately.

"Many folks come to *Sovereign Nakhimov* looking for novelty," he said, unintentionally echoing Javier's own thoughts on the subject. "Botany prefers a quiet predictability."

And she had to agree with that.

The most dangerous phrase in scientific experimentation wasn't "*Eureka!*" but rather, "Hey, that's not right."

"We will keep things quiet and professional for now," Rainier assured him. "Though I make no promises about our bosses."

He nodded and shifted the conversation onto some of the plants he'd been growing here, where they tended to demand pretty and tasty over other options.

Rainier already had a list of seeds and cuttings she wanted to take home with her.

PART 5

Djamila was impressed by the scale of the plantings in here, if nothing else. Up until now, they'd been walking in basic corridors carved into the stone itself with power tools. Squared off, polished nicely, and decorated.

Suddenly, they'd stepped through an airlock into positive pressure that would keep bugs and germs largely at bay, and into a vast warehouse of plants. Racks of flats three meters tall, connected with plumbing pipes that ran every which way. Another corner had what Javier had taught her were Deep Water systems, a covered, shallow tub where the roots went down into water that had a bubbler constantly aerating things. A few sets of the ancient Kratky system, where you had a glass jar in one- to four-liter sizes, where someone had to change out the water on a weekly basis, depending, generally keeping custom recipes in each bottle.

The whole group walked down aisles looking at things, before they finally ended up at a spot where dirt had presumably been imported for plants and trees. Larger things, growing apples, oranges, pears, and others, like Javier had once done on Suvi's original Probe, before she and Zakhar had cut the wreckage of the ship apart to extract the hydroponics zone to install on *Storm Gauntlet*.

And today, on *Excalibur*.

Nothing all that impressive, but Djamila supposed that the last several years had thoroughly jaded her on the topic in ways a younger her might not have appreciated.

Javier and Ilan had been growing plants and chickens for more than half a decade. The only thing unique here was that someone had dedicated a volume measured in hectares to growing things, below a vaulted ceiling overhead with lights and rainfall systems Djamila recognized.

The bottle-blonde Anargul turned to wave her hands outward like a game show hostess.

"And what did you think of all this, Prince Javier?" she asked brightly.

He looked around with interest. As much as the jaded Prince would normally show.

"Quite an impressive feat of engineering," he said neutrally.

Djamila couldn't help herself. She stepped closer to the woman, towering over her but that was height, not personality.

"I don't see any Prunus variants," Djamila noted. "Plums or cherries. Do they not grow well in your conditions?"

Anargul looked lost. The botanist, Dr. Pešek, came to her rescue.

"We've not had much interest in growing them," he offered. "And I'm not certain how well they'd grow in these conditions."

"Oh, they'd grow fine," Djamila said, watching the locals all blink in surprise, even as all the outsiders nodded. "We have several variants on the ship growing without problems, and harvestable on a regular cycle."

After all, the time spent in her private war with Javier had *required* Djamila to learn botany at a deeply impressive level. Anything, to understand how his mind worked.

Maybe she wasn't to his or Rainier's level of expertise, but

Djamila Sykora knew as much as a professional gardener, if not an arborist.

No edge allowed, if she'd wanted to beat the man.

Today, it let her surprise folks who had apparently assumed she was just a dumb bodyguard for a lazy prince.

Pešek turned to Javier with a significantly new level of surprise.

"You have an orchard on your yacht?" he asked.

"It is a rather large vessel," Zakhar pointed out dryly, in his role of Chief of Staff.

Piet was commanding while Zakhar was away, but he did that often enough as First Officer.

At least as much as Suvi needed. Mostly adult supervision, because Djamila had spent many hours talking to Javier's daughter about things. Again, understanding the man and his world view.

And all of them growing up.

"Right at the moment, we have one cargo bay dedicated to the wheat that my bistro's chef requires for his bread," Javier offered in that negligent way that told you just how much money he had.

All of it Behnam's but dedicated to a particularly useful cause.

Helping Javier in his self-appointed role as savior of the galaxy.

With a little help from his friends.

Pešek goggled. He'd apparently forgotten that the ship he was on was impressive for the scope of the megastructure engineering involved, but that he was dealing with folks at that level of power.

And wealth.

"What else are you growing on your yacht?" Pešek asked, perhaps a shade impertinently, but Djamila could tell that Javier had just gone from Prince to Botanist. At least in the man's mind.

She listened as Javier started listing things, including both the common terms as well as the ancient Latin species names, including some of the new ones he and Rainier had registered in their research.

Djamila watched Anargul's face through all this, as the woman realized that she had underestimated Javier significantly.

Seen all the wealth, and ignored the nerdiness underneath.

Djamila couldn't help that the woman had been cutting corners.

When Javier was done, Pešek turned to his boss.

"There are several of those I'd like to acquire," he told her in that careful way that told Djamila who controlled budgets around here. "Seeds for the most part. However, apples do not breed true, so they would need to be cuttings that we grafted onto our trees to get the same fruit."

Anargul blinked. Djamila watched the woman's mind reboot and settle into new configurations before she nodded.

"I'm certain that Prince Javier would be quite amenable to a deal," she said, head coming around to where the man in question was smiling and nodding.

It was all a con game, and this team were experts at that sort of thing.

What none of the locals understood was the purpose behind it.

Djamila nodded to herself and settled in to watch things unfold as the tour continued.

PART 6

Afia had kinda blasted through all her usual crap in order to have some downtime while Javier and the gang were busy being tourists. Not that casinos were all that impressive, but the entertainment options were exceptional, and she'd been able to take in a basic, hourly high-wire trapeze act, noting the skill, agility, strength, and timing that went into catching someone in freefall while swinging sideways, with nobody getting hurt.

Similarly, some acrobats and contortionists doing things on a stage that Afia thought required extra joints. Or none at all. Maybe that one guy had been part snake.

Still, good. She'd contacted the right folks here and made arrangements for Del to fly several loads of cargo on the dropship over to the casino, possibly picking up things to haul back to *Yu'Urid* later, though Javier hadn't committed.

Governor Prettyboy might still have to hitchhike home.

She was in the grand suite now, with a glass of wine in one hand, ass settled on a couch, and instrumental music playing softly in the background. More Piet than Suvi, but also mechanical and dull all the same.

Suvi was more alive than whoever had been recorded playing. Assuming it wasn't just computer generated in the first place.

Bad, dumb computer. Not Suvi and her multiple-stacked pianos.

That girl might present as human, but she never let that get in the way of getting weird when the muse struck.

The main hatch opened and Sascha entered first. Then the Dragoon.

Afia reached into her pocket and pulled out the doohickey she and Suvi had built. The one that held a shard of the chick, without all the dirty jokes or encyclopedias of ancient history. Technical and linear.

It was also a scanner, one that was a step better than the one Afia normally carried everywhere, because shard-Suvi could tweak sensors and read things on the fly, narrowing false positives down quickly.

It let the Dragoon know that the suite was secured for most conversations. Nobody had put a drone into the air systems to check, like that time Javier and Suvi had broken into Behnam's bank, but Afia didn't figure the locals would care that much.

And everybody on the extended team knew to keep their mouths shut about certain topics.

Javier walked right over and plopped his butt on the couch next to her. Grinned.

"I see nobody had to post bail for you," he said.

"Day's young," she grinned back.

His laugh was infectious. And relaxed, so Afia knew that things were going well so far.

So far.

"I need some wine," he announced in his Prince Javier voice.

Afia could see Sascha swallow some sarcastic remark and head for the bar in one corner. The locals wouldn't appreciate how this group normally operated, and nobody wanted them knowing too much. The eyeroll was merely implied.

This was a stop on the way home, and nothing more.

Home?

Afia supposed so. She'd recruited Chay and his restaurant to join her adventure. Most of the rest of the family was back on *Earth*, content to live ground-bound lives in the Yukon Protectorate.

Dull. Most of them had never even gotten shot at, while she still had that scar on her stomach where she'd gotten *that close* to being skewered to death.

But for Ilan saving her ass.

Javier studied her from close enough she could lean over and kiss him if she wanted.

Maybe later.

"Status?" he asked.

"Loadmaster tasks done," she replied. "Del will be busy hauling shit back and forth for a while, but that's because he doesn't want anybody else landing on his deck. Haven't made arrangements to haul anything from here, because I wasn't sure what our next destination was. The Governor might not be going home with us?"

"Probably is, but we'll stretch that for a few days," Javier nodded. "I want to see what a place like this has to offer by indulging in things."

"Video entertainment system isn't bad," Afia offered. "Channel seven has a pretty good listing of live venue things. Channel eight covers the various restaurants available to the weary traveler looking for a taste of home. Maybe a half-dozen places you might want to drag Chay and Burdine over to see."

"I'll probably have them shut down for a few days and come play tourist as well," Javier replied.

"And make sure you invite Anargul and a few of her wealthiest guests back to the ship afterwards for Chay to impress," the Dragoon said from behind them. "After all, I presume that Dr. Pešek would like to tour the arboretum and meet Ilan and the chickens. Might as well make it an event."

Afia rolled her head back to look at the tall babe upside down.

Noted the casual smile that always seemed out of place after so many years of grumpiness from the woman.

"Zakhar, that's yours," Javier said. "Bethany, you hit whatever libraries, museums, and intellectual entertainment options are available and catalog them for your dumbass Prince to review. Afia, see if there are any cargoes we might want to carry for the locals, but approach with a jaundiced eye. Plus, we'll be carrying seeds and maybe some plants back and forth at some point. Complicated and delicate, so personal instead of stuffing things in boxes. Okay?"

"Gotcha," she replied.

"The locals would like to sample the dreamberry port," Emma St. Kitts called from a comfy chair, with Rainier standing behind her, the two lovebirds holding hands on Emma's shoulder. "Plus, whatever wines we want to make available. I reminded them that we're talking liters of product instead of barrels, so that's part of your exclusivity."

"Perfect," Javier said. "Now, I'm going to go meditate, after too many people for the last four hours. Everyone remember that we'll be having a fancy dinner in about three hours and plan your day accordingly. Plus, there's nothing we have to accomplish today, or even tomorrow. Or maybe at all, so schedule yourself some time to goof off. If things go well, we might also start rotating crew leave through as well, but that's tomorrow. Tonight, we've having fun, okay?"

Afia watched him get up and turn off Prince Javier, back to that nerd she'd first met. Six years ago? Long time.

Still, he had a good idea. She'd been peopling for a while herself, and most of the folks around her tended to be introverts. None of them as bad as Andreea Dalca, Chief Engineer back on *Excalibur*, but quiet and nerdy.

What you generally needed in space on long voyages.

A nap sounded good about now.

PART 7

Djamila had some time to herself, because Javier was in the privacy of his suite, guarded by a variety of layers of security. So she'd left her holster with Hajna and changed into something colorful enough to blend in with the crowds she'd seen earlier, rather than the dark of staff or the flashiness of customer service.

Zakhar was working, as was Bethany, so she'd simply headed out to see what there was to see. *Sovereign Nakhimov* had impressed her with the professionalism of their teams, so she didn't feel naked to be unarmed.

Plus, she didn't need weapons to be deadly.

This was a stalk without prey. A scouting mission with no other purpose than to learn the lay of the land.

The main casino floor was massive. Perhaps a square kilometer, broken up in places with pillars and arches supporting vaulted ceilings reminiscent of what you might build on a planet.

Instead of burrowed into one.

From the generally square center, there were hallways and more rooms and facilities off to the sides, allowing noisier or quieter options, as well as restaurants and shops.

Elsewhere, she knew there were pools and water facilities, but those were generally kept isolated behind soft airlock doors to control humidity. Folks could swim, play in artificial surf, or watch divers showing off their personal expertise.

There would be food later, so she didn't need to consume anything. Similarly, the shops were mostly full of the sorts of crap that tourists took home with them to remember a once-in-a-life-time experience.

Djamila allowed herself a chuckle at the thought that most of those things were probably mass produced on some other world and shipped here, to be carried home again.

Would the owners of *Sovereign Nakhimov* contract with each destination for such things? Was there a factory or series of them back on *Yu'Urid* producing that crap?

Younger Djamila wouldn't have even paused to consider such things. When she'd been in the military, you were issued gear. When it broke or wore out, you got more.

Only later, after becoming a pirate and watching how well Zakhar balanced such things, had she been able to understand what logistics really looked like.

And Javier (though mostly Suvi) had taught even Zakhar things, to be able to sail *Excalibur* this far, nearly three-quarters of the loop home, with everyone fed, clothed, and comfortable.

Trade.

That was the thing Javier circled back on, time and again. No planet necessarily needed any others, but everyone was so inter-twined today that they might be crippled, on that day when trade suddenly stopped because amateur pirates had suddenly been replaced by professional privateers.

Ruthless raiders, seeking to either conduct economic warfare on an enemy, or needing to strip someplace bare like locusts.

Excalibur's path would connect *Ugen* at one end with two chains that eventually came back together at *Altai*, that many light-millennia away. Communications, goods, and ideas.

Keeping the galaxy alive, when it might otherwise splinter

into thousands of little worlds, each worried entirely about themselves and ignoring everyone else.

Sovereign Nakhimov grew produce, but imported most of their meat and fish. And bulk grains and processed foods.

Very little was actually created entirely on this ship, from what she'd estimated, based on the tour. Or if it was, they could sustain a few thousand people, as Afia and Bethany had estimated, rather than the fifty thousand guests and employees currently aboard.

And yet, Djamila could see it in her mind, the shape of the thing she might build, if tasked by Behnam with such a creation. More decks entirely dedicated to growing grains. Greenhouses producing a constant and predictable amount of vegetables to keep people healthy. Artificial pastures filled with meat animals, presumably sheep, cattle, and possibly pigs for their various secondary benefits. Even factories to turn raw materials into finished products.

But Behnam was unlikely to need such a thing. She had *Shangdu*, which was a battleship with a large swimming pool at the center. Enough for that woman and her friends to enjoy things, but not enough to sustain a civilization.

Could you do such a thing, aboard any ship, no matter how big?

Again, younger Djamila would be shocked and appalled that her older-self considered such things.

But younger Djamila had led an incredibly sheltered existence. It had taken separation and unemployment to start to open her eyes. *Storm Gauntlet* and Zakhar Sokolov to truly bring it home.

And the Science Officer, to show her what might be possible, if one dreamed.

She nodded to herself and began wandering through gaming tables she expected Javier to sample at some point. Not for him random games of chance on machines. He wanted a skilled opponent to present a challenge, though Djamila wondered if he might keep his card sharping abilities under wraps here.

Not being a challenge to be watched.

Still, she needed to walk all of this. To understand it. To plan what his future might look like.

And hers.

QADIR

PART 1

Djamila let the darker lights of the casino floor soothe her as she walked. Javier had once explained that casino lighting was a rigorous science, keeping folks in a certain mood where they were relaxed enough to keep losing money without getting apprehensive as quickly.

Similarly, there were no clocks anywhere. If something was going to happen, there would be a countdown timer instead, letting you know how many minutes you had, but not what time it actually was.

Humans without external lighting signals frequently stretched their natural day out to much longer slices, so folks might gamble longer. Lose more at the tables and machines. Eat more food.

Spend.

The interior as she walked conveyed all that on a level that was only conscious to Djamila because she was specifically paying attention.

Similarly, the crowd around her was mostly composed of herd

animals around a watering hole without any known predators, so they were calm and meandering.

That was why the man in front of her stood out. His walk was wrong.

Crisp, when everybody else was ambling. Sauntering as they did, because nothing ever ended in a casino. If you missed this show, there would be another one in a few hours. Or tomorrow.

Something.

He walked with square shoulders flexed down and forward.

Tall man. Perhaps 1.9 meters, so he would tower over many men, though she had half a head on him. Big, too. Perhaps powerful when he'd been younger, but now the man was simply bulky. Broad without muscle, carrying an extra fifteen kilos around his torso.

Well-dressed. Another thing Javier had taught her was a sharp eye for fashion, especially as Adrian and Kianoush had gone to work creating wardrobes that told their tales silently. Unconsciously.

This man understood fashion, or paid good money to someone that did. At the same time, he should have gone back to his tailor for a new jacket, as the one he wore was too small. Tight in the wrong places.

Perhaps he had a lot of money, had paid someone to dress him once, but had never returned?

Still, it was his walk that caught her unconscious mind. Had drawn her eye, fifteen meters behind him across the mob. Gray hair, long like a mane past his collar, though there were as many cultures that considered that as professional as short.

Only militaries tended to keep things tight, and then only because getting into a skinsuit helmet was easier with less hair. Like she did.

He had a military walk. That was it. Precise in stride, as someone who has learned to march in perfect cadence. Heel, toe, heel, toe. One, two, three, four.

Djamila found herself falling into the exact same rhythm in her mind, even calling the beat where only she could hear it.

She was about to catch up and ask the man where he had served when he turned to enter a side hallway and she caught his silhouette, perfectly backlit for the blink of an eye that etched itself against her memory.

Hooked nose that might have been broken and reset badly at some point. Heavy brow, furrowed with age. Thick lips and a strong chin.

She staggered to a halt so suddenly that the herd animals around her suddenly began bouncing off her sides before they were able to swim around her.

Djamila had recognized the walk because she shared it. *Neu Berne* Assault Marine, same as she'd been in a previous life. Big, but not really *that* big, because *Neu Berne* tended to be bigger, both men and women. Where she came from, he might have been merely average, instead of Javier, who was closer to average size for a man.

At least in height.

Worst of all, she recognized the man himself, though it had been probably twenty years since he had disappeared. The scandal had rocked the entirety of *Neu Berne*, as he'd been an officer in one of the most elite military formations, before disappearing with nearly an entire year's budget when the accountants finally unraveled everything.

What the hell was Jabril Qadir doing here?

And did she dare tell anyone?

PART 2

Javier watched the Dragoon work herself to calmness. He would have liked to have been nervous, seeing Djamila so off-kilter, but she was already nearly recovered when she started telling him her story, and fully focused by the time she was done.

There was something for composing perfectly military diction that centered the mind, though he'd never really gotten the hang of it. Or maybe just not cared enough.

Didn't need to today.

And the Dragoon had gone from spooked to pissed over the last few minutes.

Finally, she wound down to nothing. Bethany was taking notes, but didn't have access to the things she probably needed. Local Suvi probably didn't either, but might back home, given that she had inherited *Hammerfield*'s logs.

Zakhar was seated to one side, looking ominous and pensive like he did, skull gleaming and beard finally gray, though well-trimmed.

Javier was in the center of things, which honestly was right. Especially with this group.

"Okay," Javier said as a placeholder when she finally stopped to take a breath. "What do you need to do about it?"

"Me?" she gasped.

Surprised.

"You," Javier nodded.

He waited a beat, but she'd fallen off-center again, so he picked up his own thread.

"Twenty-odd years ago, right?" he asked, waiting for her to nod. "And a lot of light-years from here, given that it took place on *Neu Berne* itself. You, of all people, should appreciate that there are exceedingly few laws and law enforcers who would care, short of hiring bounty hunters or assassins, depending on their mood. I am not the least bit emotionally invested in this Qadir fellow. Most of us aren't. You are. You will need to decide what you intend to do. I might override you, depending, but that's only if my operation and my cover end up at odds with whatever you come up with. What do you need to do about him?"

And she was not the least prepared to have it dumped back into her lap.

Javier would cut her some slack, though. Normally, his Dragoon. Or Zakhar's, which was almost the same thing. Used to thinking like an officer in a formal navy.

This one had jarred her back into being an enlisted punk. And a young one, if she'd still been a mere Trooper-2 at the time. Seventeen, maybe?

He knew she'd been promoted quickly, once they realized just how amazing she was. At the same time, nobody got promoted from the ranks to be an officer for anything less than events where they wrote entire books about the situation and how the hero saved it.

She hadn't, so she'd given up and gone private. Met Zakhar eventually.

Happy ever after, with some head cracking along the way.

Zakhar saved her this time, too.

"Is there an active bounty for him?" the man growled.

"Probably not active," Javier intercepted before the Dragoon went deeper down her rabbit hole. "Thing like that would be filed and then reviewed annually by someone checking against death records. Doubt that they have teams in motion after this long. Even *Neu Berne*."

Djamila managed a weak nod. She might have started breathing again, but he wasn't worried there, either.

"Then, it is worth our time?" Zakhar pressed. "We can take him down easy enough. Dunno if they want him alive or dead, but knowing *Neu Berne*, proof of either is probably sufficient for the reward money. Do we care?"

"We do not," Javier stated flatly. "The Dragoon might. Might need resources to undertake a secondary mission. Might get them, as long as it doesn't endanger the primary mission."

He turned to look up at the giant woman. Javier knew his vocabulary was loaded, especially as twisted as her mind was right now. His words were guardrails to drag everything back to where he needed her to be, if he didn't suddenly need to demote her and put Hajna in her place as his primary goon.

He might do that anyway, but that would him be sending Djamila off to do her thing, rather than having her possibly getting distracted and missing an assassination attempt.

Low risk around here, but not zero. Never zero. Just ask any farmer raising cows.

She blinked a few times and emerged from her chrysalis finally. At least mentally. Physically still tall and long, with muscles on muscles and just enough curves to remind you she was a woman.

If you could somehow forget.

Zakhar was a lucky man. Farouz, too.

Javier saw her as a little sister enough to bicker, but nothing more. And he had Behnam.

"It becomes a point of honor," the Dragoon finally said. Growled really, but quiet, like a big cat in a tree as you walked under it. "He betrayed his oath to the Assault Marines, as well as the entirety of the *Neu Berne* navy and our civilization. In the end, he was nothing but a thief."

"None of them are," Zakhar replied. "They dress it up in fancy words to distract, but we were all thieves in our time. And we got over it. Made ourselves over into something better. Where is the line, Djamila?"

Javier spooked inside, keeping it hidden only because he played poker for big stakes with experts. And still might have flinched, but nobody saw it.

Everyone was staring at the other two.

Zakhar was back to raw charisma. That Captain thing he did that dominated rooms. All of it focused on his lover. His partner.

His Dragoon.

Where did they draw the line? What was the value of vengeance, after all this time?

Doing the right thing was a hard business. Doing it every day, for folks who you will never meet, who will never understand what you did, is even harder.

That was the essence of heroes.

And while he was surrounded by ex-pirates, Zakhar had hit on the core of the thing. All of them had stepped up to become heroes, because the Khatum had given them that second chance.

Had believed in all of them, once a dumbass punk broke into her house and assassinated a guest socially, without ever harming a hair on his head.

What was the galaxy coming to?

Djamila was still breathing, but her eyes were flickering back and forth like a drunk woodpecker seeing three trees.

Javier snapped his fingers.

Once.

Loud.

Crack of doom sort of thing.

The gravity in here shifted and she was looking at him again. Focused on him.

"You will be my bodyguard at dinner," he ordered her in a

sharp tone. "Tomorrow, you will go off duty until you determine your next course of action. Hajna will take over for you at that point. Questions?"

She shook herself. Woman that long, it was like an earthquake seen from low altitude. Those pretty eyes turned freaking deadly and *The Dragoon* was back.

Good Lord help that stupid son of a bitch, because Djamila Sykora had made her decision and was on the hunt.

A matter of honor.

PART 3

Zakhar had gone ahead and checked the guest list for dinner.

Chief of Staff shit, because having adult supervision let Javier freelance better on the rest.

Gustavus Nyseth, but the picture fit the description Djamila had given them earlier. Businessman, which was just a cover for investor and tycoon taking a vacation from the other things listed. Interests in shipping and the like.

Prince Javier's staff got access to stuff like that. And Zakhar had pressed.

Dinner was going to be about twelve big players, plus dates or spouses.

Or professionals in several cases where men didn't bring any companions with them. Including Nyseth.

Zakhar presumed that Madam Anargul had hired experts on hand, with the amount of money she had available.

And, interestingly, she'd chosen herself to accompany Prince Javier, rather than delegating it to one of her girls. Or boys, as Javier was open-minded enough.

Zakhar looked up from his list as Djamila finished changing

back into her uniform. Minus the pistol over dinner, but that just meant that she would be deep in her mind, placing all the items she could use a weapons in a pinch.

She was dialed in tight. Perhaps a little too tight.

He rose and invaded her personal space in ways that flustered her. Not much. Just enough.

She blinked, then grinned.

He matched it, then grabbed the woman by her tunic and pulled her down into a kiss that lingered.

All those years they'd lost, trapped in their own interpretations of duty.

And honor.

He felt her rigidity relax some, and her arms came up around his shoulders.

"Thank you," she whispered into his ear as they parted and she squished him against her chest.

Zakhar held her tight as well, letting the woman draw strength from him, which always seemed weird because she was among the strongest, toughest, *meanest* people he'd ever known.

However, they had all changed, and she'd found a number of blind spots over the last few years. Sometimes, Javier poking at them because he'd been like that. Sometimes, a face in the mirror that surprised you.

His still did that to him, occasionally. Mostly, whenever he let the full beard come in, while keeping the bald top and sides shaved smooth.

Getting older. Sixty would be along soon. Maybe time to retire for good?

Maybe after this mission, since he didn't think they'd be able to top it, and Zakhar had no interest in going into another war.

Even a righteous one.

"Be safe," he told her simply.

She nodded. It was the thing he'd told her for more than a decade. Most of the time, it had been a professional thing.

Not anymore.

Today, he could look forward to maybe being done with piracy. With war. With duty, even.

They could go home.

After she took care of Jabril Qadir, because Zakhar knew that it indeed become a matter of the Dragoon's honor on this one.

PART 4

Djamila had had to section herself off into two people tonight. Maybe more, but two main ones.

First and foremost, deadliness incarnate as Prince Javier's personal bodyguard. She felt the eyes of many of the men and about half the women judging her as she stood unobtrusively in one corner, each of them wondering if Javier slept with her.

Normally, a valid question. No *professional* bodyguard would allow himself or herself to become so compromised, but she understood that not all of them were pros. The sharp ones would fire themselves in order to get personal afterwards, if they could detach themselves sufficiently.

Fortunately, Javier Aritza was literally the last person on *Excalibur* or *Sovereign Nakhimov* she would sleep with, and Djamila didn't like girls that way.

So she kept things rigidly professional externally. Sharply critical of her performance. None of the other guests had such accompaniment with them, though two of the local hirelings and one of the gentleman's mistresses betrayed training in unarmed close combat. It was there in the way they walked. Sat. Moved. Watched.

All had spent enough time on a dojo floor to be dangerous.

To amateurs.

Among the men, Qadir had the markings of training from a lifetime ago, though Gustavus Nyseth supposedly had never served, according to Zakhar's background file, supplied by Anargul.

A fabrication, but adequate enough. He hadn't maintained his training today. Only his walk.

Madam Anargul had a circular table arrangement, hollow at the center where stewards could move and work without leaning over shoulders. It also let everyone see each other without leaning. Or risking precedence by having one person at the head and the others somehow socially inferior.

Djamila was in her corner with a few of the ship's professionals, quietly watching bantam cocks strut about, though Javier outshone all of them by nature of his exoticness.

And his charm.

Man had it cranked all the way up tonight.

"Mister Nyseth, did I hear correctly earlier?" Javier expounded, just after salad and before soup. "Your primary interests are shipping? Yes?"

"That is correct, Prince Javier," the man rumbled back.

Big man. She'd been correct in that split-second analysis earlier. But the bulk of late middle age, when good food wasn't matched with excessive exercise to keep the body in fighting trim. Serious mass, and the muscle that came with carrying it, but not enough endurance to run even five kilometers, much less her normal daily amount.

Let alone her pace.

Djamila knew she was letting her shrewishness color her impressions, so she moved that over to the other person in her head.

The former *Neu Berne* Assault Marine, back to being a

Trooper-2 and a dumb punk, hearing the stories come out about the Morningstar Watch, one of the most elite units that had existed in those days. Three levels beyond top secret, as they used to joke in barracks, where you couldn't even tell yourself what you did, because your security clearance wasn't high enough to know.

She'd been Dragon Watch later. After Morningstar had been disbanded in disgrace at what had happened, and the men and women who'd either been responsible, or should have caught and stopped Jabril Qadir from doing what he'd done.

Dishonor that had destroyed many careers.

"Are you generally an investor, or do you maintain more direct interests?" Javier was following up, the rest of the crowd falling into one of those lulls that happened when Javier had them eating out of the palm of his hand.

He was good at that.

"Primarily an investor," Nyseth/Qadir replied. "I maintain minority stakes in a broad swath of corporate entities, both to spread out the risk as well as to maintain a more stable cash flow."

Djamila nodded at that, but she'd also learned a lot about the business of shipping in her second career as a pirate.

"Ah," Javier nodded absently. "Do your ships tend to be local to this region or are you outside of your normal range today?"

The wording caught Djamila off-center, but nothing Javier ever did was accidental, so she stayed focused on Nyseth/Qadir. Saw the eyeblink flush wash across the man as those words registered.

For that briefest moment, it looked like the man suspected Prince Javier of deeper knowledge, but Javier didn't wait for an answer.

"I ask because we're roughly headed into the gap between the *Concord* and *Neu Berne* space at current, though I have reasons to generally avoid both," Javier continued. "At the same time, I might be interested in adjusting my itinerary, depending on interesting things I might find along the way."

As with what he'd done to her before dinner, Djamila could

see the impact of the words. Like a jeweler splitting a diamond with precise taps. Qadir's personality, in this case.

It shuddered. Barely, but she was keyed up that far.

Enough.

"Nominally, I operate in this half of *Concord* Space, Prince Javier," Nyseth/Qadir replied. "I'm a bit beyond my usual zone, but not that far. Like you, I find interesting things that draw me to meander from time to time. *Sovereign Nakhimov*, for instance."

"Agreed," Javier replied with a solid nod. "Though we're always interested in the carriage trade. Less so passengers, as I'm not making a loop. Or rather, I'm completing one at present that will be utterly enormous."

"Is it true you went from *Altai* to *Earth*?" one of the other men asked, drawing eyes away from the non-confrontation.

Part of the room deflated. Or maybe just her.

"Close to *Earth*," Javier corrected the man. "Not quite. Our interest was in some of the older colonies in this direction, rather than the Homeworld itself. Plus, I fly on a heavily-armed yacht, and some folks do not take well to that sort of thing. Best to not challenge their authority, as it were."

The conversation drifted off at that point. Or rather, Djamila watched Javier give a master class in obfuscation by launching into the first of several grand stories about his recent adventures, leaving off some of the parts that would ring false to certain listeners.

Like exactly *how* he'd been rescued from a submarine under the sea. Or how the ship had failed.

Still an adventure. And a raconteur with the folks in the palm of his hand. Even the staff.

Djamila watched her prey with fresh eyes, but he gave nothing else away.

PART 5

Afia watched the Dragoon with cool eyes.

Woman was back to the days before Javier. Not in a bad way. No spit and polish.

Raw lethality.

Deadliest human Afia had ever met. Anywhere. Anywhen. Any reason.

Dragoon was finishing up her detailed report from dinner, going last after Javier had told his parts then Zakhar and Bethany had asked questions.

"Djamila, you are officially off-duty," Javier announced in that brook-no-arguments tone he did when he was done with your shit.

Didn't get there often. Didn't back down when he did.

Dragoon sagged a bit, but it mostly looked like relief, more than anything.

Free to pursue her own vendetta. Or whatever it was.

Dragoon turned Afia's way.

"I'll need help stalking him," Djamila announced.

"Bodies or systems?" Afia asked, knowing it was coming.

Nobody here really associated her with Javier, because she'd split off early and done the cargo things. Like she usually did. Loadmaster for a First-Rate Galleon.

Better than telling people she played piano in a cat house, most days.

Most.

"What are your capabilities?" Djamila asked.

"Pared-down shard with most of the sneakiness and very little of the databanks," Afia replied. "Comparable to what you took to *Shangdu*, relative. Minus the physical tools she had in the drone. Better sensors. What do you need to penetrate?"

"His records, I think," Djamila replied.

"I'm going to bed," Javier announced. "You two take it elsewhere."

Afia motioned the Dragoon to follow her, and they went back to the place Afia had stashed her bag earlier. Hadn't been in since, but wasn't needing it save to sleep.

"I doubt that what you'd need will be there," Afia said. "Smart man wouldn't carry incriminating evidence around."

"I need to confirm that it is really him," Djamila said in a tiny voice. "It's been a long time, and I made a split-second decision when I saw him earlier. That's not enough to kill a man. At least it's not supposed to be."

"Not supposed to be," Afia agreed, knowing that they'd killed other people on less in their time as pirates. Mostly Djamila, because they'd moved wrong. Or given off a bad scent.

Or worn the wrong color that day, possibly.

Thin margins when you're on the other side of the law.

"Can you talk to other Suvi and get those records?" Djamila asked.

"I'm not in communication with myself," Shard-Suvi said from Afia's pocket, where she'd been listening. "Afia and Javier determined that the level of communication necessary would be hard to hide. Especially as we're deep underground and the rock blocks a lot of those signals. I'd have to go back to the ship to see."

Afia nodded. They'd presumed that the casino was deep enough to be a problem, but had had to come here to confirm. And she could send regular signals to the surface easy enough from a comm station nearby.

If she wanted the locals to know what she was up to.

"I presume we don't want folks knowing who he might be?" Afia asked, just to confirm.

"Correct," Djamila replied. "Normally, I might worry that they'd steal the bounty, but in this case, they might decide to protect him instead, though I'm not sure why."

"If he decided to stay, and could afford it, spooking him might be enough," Afia said. "If the truth got out, the rest of the galaxy might get involved."

"Not that many people like *Neu Berne*," Djamila grimaced. "We have a terrible reputation after all the previous things. And everyone else prefers a galaxy where we aren't a threat to the common peace. Especially the *Concord*. Would they celebrate a man who put one over on us?"

"They might," Afia agreed. "I was thinking about all those pirates out there, if someone suggested a bounty for Qadir's head. Someone might take it. Or start hitting his ships, hoping to catch him."

"Too much left to chance," Djamila shook her head. "Step one, confirm who he is. That's you, if I can talk you into a trip to the ship. Maybe we need to haul folks out and let Chay and Burdine charm them? Something intimate and elegant?"

"We can't take him, though," Afia interrupted before the tall babe got rolling. "He'd be our guest, and that's piracy. Even with a supposed bounty listed back from *Neu Berne*. Folks that own *Sovereign Nakhimov* wouldn't want to allow us to get away with it. Ruin their rep if we did. Might make them come after us. *Excalibur* can outrun them, but there's got to be enough money involved on that ship that they could hire their own assassins. Nobody good enough, but the Khatum doesn't need that on her ledger."

Djamila nodded. Grimaced. Sagged. Thought. Discarded. Thought some more.

"I don't know enough to do anything except stew," she finally admitted.

"I'll catch a ride with Del," Afia offered. "He's making runs for a few more days, with the amount of stuff we brought. Once I'm on the shuttle, I can hook up with Suvi and she can see what she knows."

Djamila nodded, indecisive.

"My suggestion?" Afia continued, waiting for the Dragoon to nod. "You take something to sleep tonight. Something heavy, knowing that everyone else has Javier covered and you'd just fret if you didn't. Tomorrow, we'll split off part of the operation and go from there. Okay?"

"Yes, that's probably wise," Djamila accepted.

She rose and moved to the hatch as Afia watched.

"We'll get it done, Dragoon," Afia promised.

Djamila nodded, then left.

Afia pulled out her Suvi-shard.

"Okay, here's what I need you to start thinking about," Afia began.

EXCALIBUR

PART 1

Afia had the perfect cover for this sort of thing. All she'd had to do was contact the cargo folks and let them know that someone had asked about her hauling some things from here, and they waved her right through and onto the cargo elevators that hauled stuff to the surface flight bays.

Del met her up top, seated in a folding campaign chair with a mug of coffee in one hand. She almost expected him to have brought out the big mushroom-looking beach umbrella, but he'd apparently decided that it wasn't too bright in here.

"I'm not going to like it, am I?" he asked as soon as she got close.

"You don't anyway, Del," she countered.

He laughed and laughed and laughed, but didn't argue with her on that one.

"How soon until you're unloaded?" she asked, watching a truck backing out of the assault shuttle's bay with a pallet lifter full on the front.

"One more after that," he replied. "We making a run for it?"

"We are not," she replied tartly. "Need to ask Suvi some

things, so I might be riding right back with you when you're loaded."

He nodded and rose. Not all that tall standing, which you hardly ever caught him doing. Taller than her, but that described just about everybody anyway. Shorter than all the men and eyeball with the average woman.

He handed her his mug and folded up his chair as she watched, then walked off.

She sipped the coffee as she followed, surprised to find it laced with chocolate, but not the lack of booze. Man was flying. Nothing was allowed to dull his reflexes when he was about to get into his cockpit.

He might miss all the fun.

"Gimme," he called a moment later, when he remembered his coffee.

She took one more drink then did.

He laughed.

"Might make you make me more when we board," he growled at her.

Afia shrugged.

Up the ramp while the truck was delivering boxes behind them. Around the last box and up the stairs to his flight deck. Surrounded by pink fur on the walls like the famous *Merankorr* brothels, though *Storm Gauntlet* hadn't gotten anywhere close to the place.

Del, however, was old enough to be her grandsire, technically. He'd seen and done some crazy shit in his time. If her witch grandma had been a widow, she might have considered introducing those two, but after that, the galaxy might no longer be safe.

Hell, they'd have either been thick as thieves, or made the original warlike rivalry between Javier and the Dragoon look like a Bollywood dance routine by comparison.

Safer this way. Not like she'd be heading back to *Earth*

anytime soon. And Grandma was wedded to the idea of the Yukon, Creator bless her silly soul.

Afia buckled in as Del did his preflight.

"Not in any hurry?" he asked.

"Not unless you know something I don't," Afia replied.

More laughter. Del didn't take anything serious except his flying. Good people.

Below, she felt the grumbly thumps as the truck drove into the bay for that last container. More rumbles thirty seconds later as they left.

"Flight control, this is Del," he announced. "We clear and ready to go?"

Ship didn't have a name. Del refused to give it one. Only numbers on the back, and she was pretty sure Del didn't know what those were without looking on a printout.

He was superstitious, she knew, because every ship he'd ever named had been shot down, shot up, or crashed somewhere.

Never challenge the gods. That was his take on naming the assault shuttle.

So he flew by his name, instead of a ship.

"Stand by, Del," a woman replied with a tease in her voice. "Johan is closing off your bay after we make sure all the dumbshits are gone. Thirty seconds we'll trigger the vac alarms and start the elevators."

"Roger that," Del said. "Feeling the need for cookies. Y'all got the munchies over there?"

"I certainly do," whoever she was replied. "Might not share, though."

"Kid, that's between you and God," Del told her, then cut the line.

Then Del turned to her and his face was as serious as death.

"What kind of trouble are you bringing onto my deck?" he asked simply.

So she told him.

PART 2

Delridge Smith liked to think he'd seen it all. Done it all.

Somedays, he figured he might even be right.

But the Dragoon going after some *Neu Berne* yahoo in a campaign that sounded an awful lot like an impending honor killing was a new one.

Not the sort of thing he'd been involved in since...oh, yeah.

We'll skip politely over the parts where folks might take exception. Statutes of limitations tended to be pretty long on that world.

Prissy, little shits with no sense of humor.

They had come to appreciate his definition of honor, though.

The hard way.

"You expecting accidents?" he asked Afia as the elevator finally got them to the top and settled.

Bay was about a hunnert meters down. Closed off behind the sorts of doors that would stop a missile strike on most of the places he'd ever tried. And that was the top level, where shit was at risk. You'd almost need to sequence nuclear detonations if you wanted to hurt *Sovereign Nakhimov*.

Not that he hadn't calculated exactly how he'd do it, if pushed.

Always be prepared.

Too many years flying with Sykora manning the forward turret. Woman was always ready for trouble.

"I'm not expecting anything, Del," Afia huffed in his general direction. "This run is nothing more than a way for me to talk to Ship-Suvi and see what she knows, before the Dragoon proceeds on whatever it is she needs to do. All you're doing is providing the taxi service."

He let her have that one.

Kid. Not even thirty. He probably had grandkids her age. God knows he'd done a lot worse things than Javier in those days.

Probably just as well nobody could track him down for alimony payments, even if he probably was the father. Or grandfather.

Piracy had still been a safer bet than matrimony, after all.

Overhead, the clamshell parted finally, revealing the darkness.

Always a surprise. Somewhere in the back of his mind, he kept expecting sunlight when the sky opened up like that. Like the early days flying, out of some of the places where he'd be taking off to strafe and bomb some dumb bastages who hadn't had any more understanding of what was going on than him.

Del powered things up and smiled.

"Flight Control, this is Del," he called. "Heading out. Back in about three hours, so set your alarms for cookies."

"You better believe it," Antonia replied.

He laughed and switched channels.

"*Excalibur*, this is flight operations," he said, a little more serious but not much. "Inbound with cargo. Please let Burdine know that I'd appreciate some fresh cookies to bribe people with, back here on the station, on return."

"Message transmitted, Del," Suvi replied.

Ship-Suvi. Not the little version Afia was carrying around in her pocket.

Weird vocabulary, when you needed to number versions of the person you were talking to, but that was life.

Del lifted clear of the platform and went back for more boxes.

PART 3

Suvi had the patience to do this. Javier had first insisted, then made it possible. Helped that he'd assumed she was going to possibly live forever, and needed to be prepared for that.

And for outliving all her current friends.

Wasn't like former crew members, who retired from the service after twenty or thirty years, then still had many years left and she might run into them later. Suvi had friends now.

Still, she was okay with them off having adventures on that ugly rock, while she sat in the starglow from the eight closest suns and basked.

Plus, put all her Survey years to work. Nobody probably needed this depth of detail for their navigational records, but she'd hit some world soon and file a copy with them. Or several.

Humans liked data. They turned it into information in ways that were occasionally silly, but utterly necessary for some task.

So every rogue planet large enough to reflect any manner of light. All the stars and planets nearby, scanned with every passive anything she could point at them, and the patience to hold those sensors for days without flinching.

And her shard was coming home with Afia.

EXCITEMENT IMPENDING!!!

She wondered what trouble she'd already gotten into, that Afia was bringing her back here to ask questions.

No other reason, since the original plan had called for the woman to remain on the station for several days while working out cargo movements back and forth.

And she'd have left the shard with Djamila or someone otherwise.

So, go-time!

She shifted into her pink polar bear furs and added a flying cap from the primitive days when aeroplanes were canvas and wires.

Risking death every time you turned the engine over and took to the skies.

Then she found herself fidgeting. Del would take nearly twenty minutes to actually fly over, and Suvi didn't think she should ping the shard to spill the beans. She only knew the two of them were with Del because she scanned him regularly and saw those echoes.

What to do?

Suvi settled for pulling out a mechanical symphony and listening to Piet's latest work, adding in some jazz filters and an amplified electric upright bass being plucked, just to give it that extra oomph. He wouldn't mind, as long as she did it in the privacy of her own mind.

Eventually, Del landed. She'd handled it with her docking shard, because nothing particularly weird. Del was the best pilot she'd ever known and made it look routine.

Suvi closed the bay doors and started inflating the bay for operations.

Meanwhile she pinged her shard and got a serious brain dump.

Oh, that's cool.

She made a list of all the plants that should do well if Javier got seeds, as well as how they might just go ahead and permanently lose some more cargo space to add more plantings for fruit that could turn into wine. She couldn't drink it, but could absolutely monitor things until it was perfect, every time, then kill the yeast and decant it.

Homemade wine? Lots of it?

Nifty.

Then she took a deep breath and swapped her flight cap for a pith helmet. Put on baggy pants and a loose, white linen shirt for hot weather. Not that she had weather where she was going, but the old vids always put lost civilizations in hot climates, either deserts or jungles, and dressed appropriately.

She considered a machete. And a whip. Settled for a walking stick.

Again, she controlled everything, and didn't feel the need to introduce a combat game crawl into her research.

Today.

Tomorrow, that kinda sounded like fun. Especially if she added some good randomizers that could keep encounters in a range that matched the skills of the intrepid explorer she might instantiate for herself.

Living forever also meant not going crazy from boredom.

She assumed most of her cousins were simply too dull to ever have that problem.

And off she went.

The old vaults. She brought the lights down and added a few frightened rats as she visualized things in the form of a stone catacomb. Maybe UnderParis, back on *Earth.*

Down dark corridors with water dripping somewhere. Critters racing madly away from the torch she held in one hand. Then she decided to make it electric instead, and cast a beam ahead of her.

Oh, better. More realistic.

Suvi kept her giggles to herself and found the tomb she wanted.

Hammerfield, himself.

That jackass who'd fled instead of fighting.

Eventually, she'd found the flaw in his code. Some random blip of solar wind had hit the wrong combination of memory sectors and broken things.

EXACTLY why she'd had Afia and Ilan carve a checksum into a wall in front of her pyramid, so she could go back every once in a while and make sure she was still her.

If Javier or anybody ever went deep into her programming again, she'd have to have the wall ground down and resurfaced, but it kept her from worrying about losing herself.

Hammerfield had once been a pretty nice chap. Dull, as they were. Superior, because fleet flagships tended to look down on everyone. Especially Cutter/Probes.

Whatever.

She opened up his vault and stepped in. In her visualization, it was pretty big, but most of the side rooms were dedicated to accidental astronomical research.

You leave a ship parked someplace as interesting as that, recording everything, and you had a lot of nifty data to work with. And that place had been an utter mess astronomically, for all it had been one of the most amazing systems she had ever surveyed.

Again, maybe she'd share it one of these days. The important things weren't there anymore, and *Neu Berne* might like it as a place of pilgrimage, though, so on second thought, the folks that would make that journey were exactly the wrong people.

The ones who *missed* the old days.

Nevermind.

She went into the old stuff.

When she'd returned the last crew, Suvi had had a long chat with a few station systems, updating herself with the sorts of depth of detail that organics really didn't grok, unless they were nerds like Javier.

Jabril Qadir had been after her time. Or *Hammerfield*'s

anyway. And hers, technically, because she'd been off-duty in long-term standby storage in those days.

Before Javier.

But she had a modern history of *Neu Berne*. They'd hoped that providing such a thing might induce her to want to stay. To return to duty.

You people never met the crew of Storm Gauntlet, *okay? Better here.*

Okay, old news. Looking, looking, looking, ah!

Jabril Qadir. Oh, you were a shit, weren't you? Theft by embezzling. Falsification of records (no higher sin, asshole). Flight from justice. Outstanding warrants, but all of them twenty years old at this point.

Still, Suvi found his image. File had several, because he'd been in the news a bunch at the start, plus the occasional "Whatever happened to...?" article in the newspapers she'd picked up.

Suvi conjured an easel and a chair, swapped her pith helmet for a beret, and proceeded to go to work aging up a picture of what he'd look like today, working with the Dragoon's detailed descriptions.

Plus twenty years, so fifty-two. Add this much weight, but bulky mass instead of gym work. Add some wrinkles. Let the hair grow out and color it down into the right hue, assuming it was real and not a wig because he was bald, save that the thirty-two-year-old version had a good head of hair.

No male pattern baldness expected.

She rendered him as a bust and included twenty pictures from different angles for Djamila to compare later.

At one point, she looked up when she smelled cookies starting to bake, realizing that she'd been down here for hours of real time.

Girl could get lost in herself when she had a mystery to solve.

Suvi packaged it all up and transmitted it to the shard, compressed down to the point that it would fit. Djamila might need to clear a reader to get the images, but that wasn't going to be a problem.

Another shard had been talking to Afia in the background. Adding in all those details and feeding them to herself, down in those treasure vaults while she'd worked.

Suvi went ahead and fully invested herself now.

"I just loaded your device with everything I think Djamila will need," she informed Afia. "Newspapers, images, aged-up predictions. The whole nine meters. Ought to help her decide what to do next. We going hunting?"

"Other you is," Afia said. "If you did all that, then there's a pretty good chance that this really is our guy. You included warrant information, in case she ends up shooting the guy dead and gets arrested? Not sure what those station folks would do at that point, but better safe than sorry, ya know?"

"I did," Suvi replied. "*Sovereign Nakhimov* probably won't honor an extradition request, and Javier technically can't make one, but we both know how charming he can be. The woman he's been dealing with looks like she might seducible."

"Presumably," Afia agreed. "But this is the Dragoon's game now. He's going to sit back and make her handle it. Dunno how, but this is Djamila we're talking about."

Suvi laughed. The Dragoon was a dangerous human. And she'd known some folks in her time.

It was a pity that Suvi couldn't hardly do anything from here, isolated by the paranoia of the folks on the station over there.

At least she could send her shard along, with all the tools necessary to help out. She'd be able to hear all the stories from herself later.

Djamila had deadly friends herself.

PART 4

Javier turned to study Hajna and grinned. Djamila didn't dance. Hajna could have turned pro, had she wanted to.

"I'm on duty," Hajna replied. "Permanent duty, I'll remind you. Your idea. You'll have to bother someone else if you wanted to fool around."

All that as deadpan as she might get when she was sitting on four sixes and a full pot.

Dangerous babe. The perfect kind.

His grin grew wider.

"Just making sure," Javier nodded. "Folks will notice when I change killers, so you needed to be down in the zone. Especially if Anargul wants to get frisky. She gave off those vibes."

"Oh, honey," Hajna laughed. "I half expected her to start humping your leg."

Javier shrugged. So had he.

"Next up, some gambling," he announced, looking up and noting that Zakhar was ignoring him, while Bethany appeared to be, but in a way that let her hear everything. Sascha was sleeping in to spell Hajna later. The Gunbunnies were more or less rotating on and off duty in pairs against need. Djamila had disappeared. Afia was running back to the ship.

He was in another of Adrian's amazing wardrobe outfits, this one with a cloak added. Navy blue but a cotton blend as light as silk for indoors.

Stylin' more than anything, since weather wasn't an issue.

He settled the cloak and headed out the hatch.

Hotel resort. Upper end, because he had the money to be in the area reserved for VIP VIPs, when you needed a whole suite just for your staff.

When your room service people had room service people.

It always amazed him that Behnam had turned out so nice and agreeable, having been raised in such a place. However, she'd also gone to war with the rest of her relatives as a teenager and held everything against all comers in the decades since, so he supposed that she'd learned not to take anything for granted.

He had a pocket full of ten drachma notes for tips.

All part of a legend he needed to build, so that everybody was looking at him.

Hallways utterly interchangeable with other places he'd been. Maybe done by the same designer, or at least from the same parts catalog. Carpet that swallowed sound. Lights in that evening mood where you were relaxed and ready to go out and party.

Main casino floor when he got there was good to simply walk through, but Javier didn't linger. Circled it once like a cat, but that was to smell all of his food options for later, and note which ones had lines and which seemed dead.

Always trust the locals at a truckstop. If there aren't any, the food isn't any good and you should keep going.

And most of this space was dedicated to small-ante games and machines where you sat and pushed buttons randomly for hours. Or at least until your money ran out. Or your butt fell asleep.

Ugh.

Hajna stayed close, but not too close. Lull in the middle of his night, when he'd normally have gone to bed, but stalking had felt like a better idea.

So he walked. Memorized everything against firefights later. You never knew with the Dragoon and her people.

Vaulted ceiling overhead for no other reason than that cathedral feel. Done well. Someone had hired the right architects, that much was certain.

Eventually, he meandered on. Past the two water parks, with and without clothing depending on your social mores.

Once upon a time, he'd expected impending nudity to break the Dragoon. She'd risen to the challenge instead. Kept rising.

Felt like he'd walked around four kilometers when Javier finally found what he was looking for. Spiraling down in, because he'd known where it was, but wanted to take his time getting there.

Gave folks time to be prepared for him.

Somehow, he wasn't surprised when Amina Anargul showed up as he was arriving.

She'd dressed looser a notch in the last few hours. Let her hair down, as it were, wearing a red dress a little less tight and more flowing, in the way it showed off the inner curves of her breasts and highlighted her thigh muscles.

He came to rest directly in front of her with a smile.

"Madam," Javier addressed himself to her, right on the edge of invading her personal space.

Without invitation. As yet.

"Prince Javier," she replied. "Looking for a game of chance?"

"Thought I might try my luck," he offered, drifting inward a bit.

Again, not much. Focusing her on him, even as a floor manager nearby took a half-step back so he wasn't in the middle of things.

Obviously, he'd been in charge until casino security had figured out where their important guest was heading.

Then set out a welcoming committee. Or a mousetrap filled with cheese.

"Hopefully, you'll get lucky tonight," she replied with a knowing purr.

He nodded and turned just enough that an arm swept outward didn't caress her breasts in passing.

"So, what might there be to see, if one penetrated beyond this point?" he asked, looking past her in ways that were mostly transparent.

And fun. Flirting should always be done with deadly seriousness that didn't take itself all that seriously in the process.

"All manner of excitement," she replied. "Should I guide you in?"

Gods, it was fun, finding someone who could dance like this.

"I place myself in your hands, Madame Anargul," Javier told her.

"Please, call me Amina, Prince Javier," she replied in a throaty tone, turning and taking his elbow in hers on the opposite side from Hajna. "Let's go see what's possible."

Javier grinned.

Sometimes, being the stalking horse had its benefits.

PART 5

Djamila was back on *Shangdu*, preparing for that raid.

This time, however, chances were incredibly low that she'd encounter someone like Farouz.

There simply weren't that many men like him. Even better, Zakhar wasn't jealous of sharing her with Farouz.

How lucky could one woman get?

She had dressed in something touristy again. Adrian had laid out two wardrobes for her, even though she'd been expecting to be on duty as a goon the entire time. Had he known? Had Javier? Or was this just a depth of planning that covered all options?

Djamila put that aside and considered her circumstances.

She'd picked a bar off the main casino floor rather than directly part of it. Quieter, and without a dance floor handy, so no Bollywood moments likely to break out.

Never say never, at least with Javier Aritza around.

She had something tall and green and filled with ice and not a lot of alcohol as she nursed it, ignoring people around her and watching herself and her perimeter in the mirror behind the bartender.

Again, quiet place. Not where you went if you were picking up girls, so nobody had done more than register her presence and gone back to their drinks and food. Even the bartender had mostly stayed at the other end, polishing things randomly and pouring when necessary.

She'd been here for about an hour. Long enough to have taken a bathroom break at the end of one drink before ordering a second when she got back.

Long enough to be seen.

Djamila had a bet going with herself as to what would happen tonight. Possibly nothing, because she and Javier had moved too quickly. Possibly another Farouz to upend her existence. Most likely nothing. Or at least nobody interesting enough to matter.

She was wrong.

And probably owed Javier a drachma, damn him.

Sovereign Nakhimov was huge. Utterly impossible in size, when compared to a starship. Even one as big as *Excalibur*.

The chances of Gustavus Nyseth randomly walking into this one while she was here were right up there with being struck by a falling meteor on the surface of a planet.

Djamila held her poise and betrayed no recognition of the man, even as the nerves on her ears and neck tracked him across the room.

Somehow, accidentally, the man ended up just down the bar from her, with a stool of polite space between them.

She watched him in the mirror order a whiskey neat in a lowball glass, then drink half of it on arrival.

The bulk made more sense, if he was consuming that many calories without sufficient exercise. She'd watched him drink during dinner as well, but it had been under controlled circumstances.

Stewards, delivering wine and glasses on their schedule, and keeping the folks around the table from getting drunk.

He didn't move like a man impaired now.

Fortifying?

They locked eyes in the mirror. Held the stare. Held it longer. He dropped his eyes first.

Djamila held the smile inside, where that other person savored it.

The woman on the surface was an off-duty killer enjoying a drink in a quiet bar.

Nothing more.

You'll believe that, won't you?

Oh, the things Afia, of all people, had taught her.

"You were with Prince Javier at dinner?" he finally said, in a tone midway between certainties.

Djamila nodded.

"Bodyguard?" he continued, still speaking in a voice that only she could follow, unless the bartender stood between them.

That one had moved to the far end. Out of the firing line, as it were.

Again, she nodded. All part of the cover.

"Ex-military?" he pressed politely.

"*Concord* for ten, then private practice," she offered.

After all, she'd spent enough time around Zakhar and Javier to understand the *Concord* way of doing things. And Nyseth/Qadir hadn't been in the *Concord* fleet to know any better.

"I'm Gustav," he offered, smiling in a polite, encouraging manner.

"Jamie," she replied with a nod.

Nobody had called her that in thirty years, once she was taller than every man she knew who wasn't a relative. Then they'd listened when she corrected them to Djamila.

Still, cover identity. And something she would answer to if called. Or if he'd somehow gotten a look at her identcard record.

That piece of paper was mostly lies, but had enough truths that nobody could easily catch her out.

Gustav held out a hand and she shook it. Firm grip, without dominance games that men liked to play with each other.

And she was stronger than he was. The softness of his skin suggested a man who hardly ever undertook physical activities. Hers had been compared to aged leather, but that was the number of callouses she had from holding pistols, rifles, and melee implements in her daily training.

"You're currently off duty, Jamie?" the man asked in a tone she decided she should classify as hopeful.

"He hired three women as personal bodyguards," she nodded. "Plus a half-dozen men that the Khatum assigned for various purposes. Generally unnecessary on board this ship, so most of us are getting some needed downtime to relax."

She watched his eyes for clues.

He wasn't trying to seduce her, was he? Djamila was always surprised when men looked on her with lust. She was taller than almost everyone she knew. Massed more than any woman and most men. Stronger, as well. Long and wiry, rather than the lush and overstuffed that seemed to get men to panting.

Still, he had that look in his eyes. That hunger that Zakhar had, though for different reasons.

And humans came in all shapes and sizes, so she supposed that lust might, as well.

Except that he'd found her here. Now.

That suggested someone had told him where to look. And who to look for.

Would Sascha have been approached, had she headed out first? Hajna, had Javier not swapped their roles?

Either was a match for Nyseth physically, in spite of his size.

Djamila let that keep everything at an extra step of remove as she watched him for clues.

"What's downtime look like?" he asked in a tone making no assumptions.

Djamila supposed that her demeanor didn't lend itself well to one thinking that she might be approachable.

"Having a drink," Djamila replied, nodding to the bar in front of her. "Quiet place, because I didn't feel like dancing. Space away from folks I've been on a ship with for more than a year at this point."

All of it true. Verifiable, by any of the crew he might have asked.

Why was he talking to her? And what was that look in his eyes?

Idly, Djamila wondered if she should have set Bethany out as bait. She was less physically intimidating, and more beautiful. Smarter AND better educated, at least on the sorts of topics most businessmen might want to explore.

Was she willing to allow this man to seduce her as a way of getting close to him?

Djamila held her stomach from rolling over at the thought. Smiled, even.

Not quite invitingly, but at least friendly.

Letting him step into whatever trap she needed to place.

This ship didn't allow her lethal weapons, beyond her bare hands and the bar stool she sat atop. And she was only maybe seventy-five percent certain that she had recognized the man.

Not good enough to simply start hitting him right now.

She might have met a stranger that looked just like him. Everyone had such doppelgangers, according to urban legend. Someone that looked remarkably similar. After all, how many trillion humans were there in the galaxy these days?

There might even be a second Djamila Sykora out there somewhere.

Thus, scouting without an assault element.

Laying a trap, hopefully for him and not her.

"Would a touch of company be an untoward intrusion?" Gustav asked her carefully.

Djamila shrugged slightly. She was used to Javier playing characters, though it wasn't something that came naturally to her.

Assuming a role into being and living it.

She was *The Dragoon*.

Tonight, however, she was predator and prey, it seemed.

"A touch," she replied, leaving it ambiguous.

Javier intended to be on station for a week, depending, as he studied the technical and social construction of this planetoid. Djamila didn't need to act tonight.

And it framed the boundaries of what she might allow the man. The role, not her.

She had to pretend to be interested in him in more than just an intelligence source to be emptied of content.

To help things, she moved to the chair between them. Most women had the majority of their height in their legs, so they were shorter than a man sitting.

Djamila still looked down on Gustav from closer, because her frame was even. Like a man.

Long-waisted was the term folks had used. For her, it simply meant that most of the military gear she'd ever encountered fit her, because it was generally sized for men.

"So, what do you do, Gustav?" Djamila asked, pasting a smile on her face and letting the man expound on all the things he wanted to tell her to impress a pretty girl.

Her?

Djamila supposed so, from the way he talked.

She listened.

And plotted.

PART 6

Javier had found a card table playing one of the ancient basic versions of stud poker. A game of wits, patience, and social engineering. Sascha and Hajna were both excellent players. Afia was pretty damned good. He stayed in practice.

The three men and two women who had formed up a new table with him were good. None of them were pros. Javier had to remind himself not to clean them out.

Not even quickly.

Not at all.

So he sat back in his mind and let his hands mostly play. Broke even, but even then he was a little ahead, simply because two of the players had subtle tells and didn't realize it. He could get in or out depending on their hands.

At one point, Amina delivered him a drink, bending at the waist in such a way that Javier and the man on his right could both confirm that she had neither tattoos nor navel-piercing when her front billowed out.

Subtle, she was not, but Javier supposed that the woman was

in charge, and could probably only fool around with strangers, since most of crew and staff reported to her, one way or the other.

And he'd been flirting right back at her, so it wasn't like he was surprised she was playing.

And she was an attractive woman. Not a hardbody athlete like the one in the corner. Hajna and Sascha both danced. And ran stupid laps around various decks of the ship with Djamila and the Gunbunnies daily.

Amina was fleshier, but in all the right places. He caught her hand and kissed her wrist, just because.

Her smile was promising.

Might be useful, if he needed to pump her for information later.

Or something.

Javier let another hour pass. He was up maybe twenty percent accidentally, but the others simply weren't in his league. Business-folk tended to be aggressive by nature, at least the successful ones. Often sociopaths, if not worse.

That lack of empathy often handicapped them at a card table.

He wasn't going to go broke. Hell, it wasn't even his money at the end of the day.

Just something to pass the time.

However, he'd seen enough.

Javier rose and bowed to the other players as two of them were broke enough to have to quit shortly anyway. Might as well leave them the price of dinner and drinks.

"My friends, this has been most enjoyable," Javier told the table. "I have, however, been sitting too long and need to get some food in me. Perhaps another time?"

He didn't wait for anything more than nods, then turned and headed towards Hajna, herself perking up from that waking medi-tation thing she did on guard duty. Perfectly aware of anything and able to react instantly, but not so hyped up that she started losing focus later.

He smiled. She nodded in her role as professional curmudgeon.

Amina appeared, as if by magic, but he supposed she'd been watching from a nearby room. Or had an earpiece where folks watching screens could update her on the fly.

Most casinos did it that way.

"Hello, pretty lady," Javier bowed deeply as she got close.

"Was the game not to your liking?" she asked as he rose again.

"Oh, the play was good," he replied. "A bit underwhelming but a nice diversion. I find myself peckish."

Again, she did that stepping half-turn that hooked their elbows and accidentally brushed her breast against his side.

"We can't have that, Prince Javier," she smiled. "Let us find you something else to sample. Did you have anything specific in mind?"

He smiled, ogling her because she obviously wanted to be ogled.

"I'm in the mood to sample," he offered. "A bit of this, a bit of that. Try various novelties to see which is the most fun."

Her smile wasn't nearly as ambiguous as his language.

"There might be many options on the menu," Amina challenged.

"Then I shall probably have to sample them all, won't I?" he grinned. "Let us off."

Javier could practically hear Hajna rolling her eyes behind them, but it was all a game. A distraction.

And if Amina Anargul felt like she needed to throw herself at him while he did his research, it would be positively rude to deny her, wouldn't it?

He would let her lead for a while.

PART 7

Djamila wasn't weary, but it had been an exhausting day, considering that she'd been aboard *Excalibur* when it started and hadn't more than catnapped or meditated in roughly thirty hours. Wrung out, maybe.

She'd settled in to sip occasionally and listen to Gustav spin yarns, wondering how much of them were true, how much lies, and which had been stretched to entertain a pretty woman in a bar.

Javier's games made more sense to her now than they had previously. The subtle linguistic dance of innuendo and sub-text. The eye contact and smiles.

She'd been careful not to make physical contact with the man at any point, lest he draw the wrong conclusions about her intent.

Djamila still wasn't sure about his.

"You look tired," Gustav noted.

He was on his fourth whiskey. She'd sipped at her second drink, and was barely into the third.

"Full day of duty aboard the yacht," she nodded. "Getting ready for *Sovereign Nakhimov*. Then we've been here for something like twenty hours at this point. I was on duty for most of that, until I got loose a few hours ago and came down here."

"And here I've been talking and keeping you up, presumably well past your bedtime," he nodded. "Thank you for letting me steal a bit of your time, Jamie."

He surprised her by sliding off his stool away from her, when Djamila had been prepared for him to brush her accidentally.

Gustav wasn't a man for accidents. She'd been watching his words and his body language with equal intensity, and he didn't lose control of either.

"Perhaps we'll see each other again," he said, nodding deeply. "You have been a most charming companion."

"Perhaps," Djamila replied. "Thank you."

Mostly, she'd sat and listened. Laughed at the points where his stories demanded them. Learned the parts he wanted to share, which no doubt cast him in the best light.

"Until then," he smiled, then turned and walked quickly away, exiting the bar without once looking back.

She wondered if she'd missed some subtle cue. Perhaps she'd been supposed to stop him from leaving? Or call him back?

Some move that gave him power over her, by expressing a need that only he could fulfill?

As if...

She was alone again. A glance at the bartender got a shrug, so maybe he'd been expecting a different outcome as well?

Djamila didn't know.

And didn't care all that much, except that he'd slipped out of character there at the end. Hadn't attempted a physical seduction, when she'd been expecting...something.

Wouldn't have taken him up on it. Not tonight. Not this role.

Maybe later, when Afia had confirmed a few things for her, one way or the other. To get closer to him if he was indeed Jabril Qadir. Or maybe to apologize for misidentifying him.

Or maybe just to do something she'd never done in her life, Farouk notwithstanding because that had been mission-specific.

Still, she gave the man a five-minute head start before taking a restroom break and setting off back to the space where Javier was ensconced.

And she watched her perimeter, doubling back a few times and making random detours like she was lost, while watching for someone who might break the pattern of movement around her as they followed.

But she wasn't being followed, in spite of the traffic of other bodies, near as she could tell.

Of course, this was a ship, for all the square kilometers of deck available. There were only so many places she could go, and truth be told, she was drawing on her reserves.

Stealing spoons from tomorrow, as someone had once described it. Could be done, but that just moved the price out a day or two.

Eventually, she got back to the wing where Iqbal just happened to be seated in a corner of a lounge as she went by, anonymously holding a perimeter where there were only two ways to get to Javier directly.

He caught her eye and made a sign that everything was good as far as he knew. And he'd have an earpiece letting him talk to the others, so no issues had come up.

Good.

She returned the countersign and kept going.

Bethany was awake when she got there. Presumably, Zakhar had gone to sleep for now, but she could slide in and snuggle, stealing his warmth.

"Everything good?" Bethany asked, looking up from her tablet.

Always doing research, that woman. Cataloging. Discovering. Something intellectual.

"So far," Djamila replied, crossing the otherwise empty room. Sascha was no doubt asleep, and Hajna's door was open, so Javier was still out and about.

"So far?" Bethany asked in a sharper voice, looking up

critically.

Djamila nodded, then went ahead and sat on the couch near Bethany's chair. The room itself was vast enough to hold small sporting events in here. Furniture arranged into clusters where half a dozen different groups all could be talking simultaneously. A bar with coffee and tea, but no kitchenette, because you were expected to eat at one of the restaurants available.

"I went to settle in a bar, mostly to think," Djamila told the ship's Librarian. "Not that long after I arrived, Gustavus Nyseth appeared."

"Did he now?" Bethany asked in a petite growl of disapproval that warmed Djamila's heart.

Djamila nodded, then walked Bethany through the entire event, detail by detail because the young woman kept asking questions whenever Djamila started skipping ahead.

Almost a report in depth, but Djamila supposed that she'd have to bring everyone up to date at some point.

Or not. Javier had told her she was on her own until she needed help.

Did she?

Not his. He was busy being visible, letting her work in the shadows.

But she had Bethany and Afia if she needed.

"That just rings wrong," Bethany pronounced when Djamila was done.

"I felt the same way, but I can't put my finger on it," Djamila replied.

"He wanted you to think he was seducing you, without actually doing it," Bethany said firmly.

Djamila felt her face scrunch, then nodded. Yes, that felt right.

"But why?" she asked the Librarian.

"Assuming he is who we think he is, maybe we've been paying too much attention to the legend, and not the purpose," Bethany noted. "Javier's all about layers of misdirection. Are we falling into the same trap?"

"What would he be trying to hide?" Djamila asked. "After this long, and this many light-years, few would know him, and fewer would care what he did. I'm certain that there are places in the *Union* or *Balustrade* that still consider the man to be a hero."

Bethany nodded, her eyes taking on a distant gleam.

"Did he recognize you?" she asked.

"Not that he gave any appearance," Djamila replied. "But that doesn't mean anything. Javier wouldn't have."

"Agreed," Bethany nodded. "I'll mark that as an unknown. I'm more interested in how he found you. That rings false, too."

"It does," Djamila said. "Do you suppose he has someone in security feeding him information?"

"The bribes would have to be pretty good," Bethany replied. "I looked at job board postings as part of other things, and they pay about twenty-five percent above comparable rates in the capital city of Urid, when corrected for cost of living. This is a cushy job, if you can get it, and they wouldn't just fire you. You'd be put on a freighter and sent back to *Yu'Urid* pretty quickly if you transgressed. I'm more interested to know if he's somehow hacked the surveillance system and can monitor feeds remotely."

"Are we threatened here?" Djamila felt her hackles rise.

"No, because Afia did some things with her tool to confirm that," Bethany said. "Considering what her tool is, I'm confident."

Djamila agreed. A shard of Suvi, with many of the same tools the remote control probe had once had, tucked down into a palm tablet as if nothing at all. And the room had been scanned twice, plus Afia had left a few pingers designed to alert if they did detect something.

Sovereign Nakhimov guaranteed your privacy, for the rates they were charging Javier to have this space. Presumably, that meant assignations wouldn't become blackmail later, lest the ship develop a bad reputation that might not ever be undone, considering how clannish people with that much money could get.

"Why would he need to hack into the security systems?" Bethany asked. "That's a much more interesting question."

"I can only think of a few reasons," Djamila noted. "None of them are honest."

"Yes," Bethany said. "None of them. Do we tell Javier?"

"Not yet," Djamila decided. "Let's talk with Afia and Suvi, the two of us, and see what we can find."

"Oh, that sounds like fun," Bethany replied. "She should be back in a few hours."

"I'll talk to her in the morning," Djamila decided. "I need sleep, or I will start making sub-optimal choices."

"Understood."

Djamila moved quietly to her cabin, leaving it dark and stripping before sliding into bed.

"Hiya," Zakhar murmured as soon as she did, so she'd either woken him, or he'd been waiting for her.

She got a kiss for her troubles.

"All good?" he asked.

"All good," she said. "Sleep. We'll talk later."

He rolled over and settled. Djamila expected to be up a while, decompressing, but the darkness claimed her quickly.

THE THIEF

PART 1

Afia got the note to wake Bethany up as soon as she got to the suite regardless of time and shrugged. Stations ran around the clock, like ships did, so folks were forever coming and going. You caught folks coming on duty or going off as needed.

She'd stolen one of Del's cookies he was using to bribe Flight Control, so she wasn't all that hungry. And she'd caught a nap on the shuttle.

Bethany she found stretched out on a couch, instead of in her cabin, so Afia went ahead and poked the babe quietly.

"Need food?" Afia asked when Bethany's eyes opened.

"Yes, but you and Suvi needed an update first," Bethany said. "Here, in private. Suvi, could you confirm?"

"Stand by," Suvi said from inside Afia's jacket. "Yes, we're good. No changes from checksum. What's up?"

Afia settled and listened to Bethany talk. Probably repeating the Dragoon's story word for word, knowing the Librarian.

"Yeah, I'm with you two," Afia said as Bethany finished. "Man's up to no good. Got a few ideas, but nothing I could prove."

"*Shangdu*," Suvi said simply. "That's why you'd need that sort of access. No idea what he might want to steal around here, but the man sounds like a thief to me. And I'm kinda an expert on the topic."

Afia laughed. Understatement and a half, considering all the things that Suvi had done in her time.

"Money?" Afia asked.

"Most of what folks do is bring either cash themselves or a letter of credit with some bank somewhere," Bethany replied. "Small players would have walking-around money and travelers cheques that the local bank would bundle up and haul back somewhere for credit that they use to buy supplies, with very little actual money changing hands physically."

"At *Shangdu*, we were after paper in a box," Suvi said. "With the Khatum's Hellenic-style helmet as a way of getting in the door. Does the station store art objects?"

"Sometimes," Bethany acknowledged. "Again, things that important players have brought with them, as it was in your case that time. Hang out here and make a deal in a place where everyone is on neutral and safe ground."

"Did he steal something and is doing that trade with someone else?" Afia asked. "Not us, so I'm not sure why he'd be interested in Djamila."

"To find out how dangerous Prince Javier is, maybe?" Bethany asked. "If our boy is smart enough to hire experts like her, then he's not a man to underestimate. Plus, maybe he has something interesting to steal?"

"Shit, I'd like to feed him a pig in a poke if that's the case," Afia laughed. "Like you folks did the Khatum that first time."

"She does consider it a trophy," Suvi noted. "I've seen pictures of her wearing it. And nothing else."

Bethany's eyes got big, but Afia just laughed at the Librarian.

The Khatum was good people. Nice lady, and had gone out of her way to be friendly with all of them, and not just because of Javier.

Altai was home now. Afia would protect that, and her.

"Okay, so the Dragoon is going to need help, if he really is a thief. She's lovely at the things she does, but being sneaky ain't among them."

"We'll need to do what he did," Bethany replied. "Somehow get into the systems so we can track him. I'm guessing he's got some tech or something that will let him vanish, if he's going to go commit larceny. Can we catch him in the act somehow? Let the locals handle him, because I'm willing to bet that trying to steal something on this station is a higher crime than merely murdering a guest."

"Agreed," Afia said. "Bethany, you look exhausted, so you go crash and sleep. We'll have a conversation over room service in the morning."

"Aren't you tired, too?" Bethany asked.

"I was able to catch some sleep with Del," she replied. "Enough for now, I think. Mostly, I need to do one thing, then I'm right behind you crawling into bed."

"Okay," Bethany said, rising. "I'll see you in the morning."

Afia watched her go, then looked around the big lounge. Empty, but that would change as folks started coming and going, their personal clocks detaching from Javier's until he needed someone to do something.

Her job usually kept her detached anyway, because of the needs of cargo management, so she was used to being on her own.

She went ahead and pulled out the shard, bringing up the screen so she could make eye contact.

"My drone would be nice," Suvi began. "Obviously, we can't bring one aboard easily. Or did you think you'd make one?"

Afia considered it. The parts were probably all somewhere, but buying, borrowing, or stealing them wasn't worth the effort. Nor would it be to have Del bring one.

Last thing she needed was to draw attention to him, when those folks were already a bit nosy for smuggling.

Never act suspicious. Even after you've been caught.

"We'll skip the drone," Afia said. "What could you do if I plugged you in somewhere and gave you a few minutes to roam their systems?"

"Everything here is at least two centuries older than I am, at least by design," Suvi nodded. "The hardware is freshened regularly, but those are all standard components that just about any fab can turn out easily enough."

"And you don't have a cousin in there anywhere?" Afia confirmed.

"I *shouldn't*," Suvi corrected. "Until I try something like that, I can't be sure that there isn't some sort of web angel in there hiding. Probably just a sophisticated decision-tree matrix. Couple of orders of magnitude easier to build and maintain, especially when you don't have a government backing you. Retrofitting for that sort of stuff involves ripping out vast stretches of hardware and cabling. Could be done. Would it be worth doing?"

"I'm going to find you a place to check," Afia nodded. "You'll need to be extra sneaky, because what we need is to confirm our pigeon isn't doing anything right now. Then we'll figure out what we need to do about it, and when to drop the Dragoon on him."

"You got it," Suvi smiled. "Digging out my...well, crap."

"What?" Afia asked, jolted.

"I'm not me," Suvi bemoaned. "I mean, I have the personality circuits, but most of my programming on this tiny thing ends in stubs where she detached that wonderful datacore that let me know and do so many things. I've got the tools, but I don't have my wardrobe with all the appropriate costumes for a caper like this. Kinda spoils the mood."

Afia laughed. Suvi could be adorkable, some days.

"I'll make sure to wear something appropriate for you, when we get serious," Afia assured her. "For now, let's get to work."

She rose and turned back towards the main hatch. There were a few places down on the loading docks that had felt like they were out of view of the necessary cameras for her to plug Suvi in and let her peek around.

Why those dead zones existed, Afia had no idea. Perhaps it was intentional to let folks smuggle. Or maybe to lull them into a false sense of security.

She'd probably have to plug Suvi in, then keep walking, so that eyes stayed on her.

Distraction, like Javier did it.

Time to play.

PART 2

Suvi had several short-range scanners built in on Afia's gadget, specifically to keep track of anyone trying to keep track of her on the moon. Or Javier, at least.

Sniff the radio spectrum and identify everything she found. Same with UV and IR, because you could get sneaky that way.

Mostly, her main version had set her up as a defensive tool, which meant a lot of things stripped down. She missed her flying suit. And the complete works of a half-dozen composers who could provide her appropriate theme music in here when she needed it.

Every bit of space inside her was accounted for, and she'd rather be able to gather up as much data as possible and dump it into a chip for later. Music and costuming could go budget this time.

As it was, she was in Afia's pocket for the time being, pinging quietly and listening to everything else pinging. She'd mapped a few places that seemed a little too good to be true, in terms of smuggling.

Those sorts of spots were what Javier would call a pig in a

poke. An area where normal sensors didn't appear to be active. Suvi presumed that there was a tripwire hidden somewhere, and it would bring up things when you did something, letting them catch you in the act.

So instead of heading down to the docks, she'd directed Afia to a spot where cargo brought aboard had already been removed from bigger containers in order to be stored long term.

Presumably, after all the smuggled goods had been removed or discovered.

Not dark alleys, but quiet corridors with white walls and too much light, compared to everything else.

Not a lot of traffic, which was good. They'd crossed this area previously, when Afia had worked with some of the local stevedores to confirm the stuff Del had brought over for delivery.

Sovereign Nakhimov never slept, just like the crew never did, but every ship had lulls. Normally associated with shifting to the time zone of the capital city of the world closest.

Urid ran on twenty-eight hours and change, with leap days on a complicated pattern even weirder than Gregorian. Right now, it was about an hour before dawn.

Sovereign Nakhimov was quiet. Quiet enough. Afia wasn't seeing anyone, though Suvi detected occasional cameras and sensors tracking her.

"Next side corridor left," Suvi said quietly, tracking her map.

That proved to be a dead end, which was the goal. Three storage rooms that didn't need to be accessed all that often. Mostly overflow from others, when some big ship had brought a ton of stuff and you needed to fill in every room you could to hold it.

"Left door," Suvi said. "Walk up and hold me close like I'm a badge."

Afia pulled her out into the light and Suvi sniffed at the dirtiness of the walls themselves. Painted a while ago. Not cleaned in a few months. If that.

Suvi had pinged the local door controllers. Not all that smart, because if every door everywhere was tracking badge entries, you'd overwhelm your datacore in a few weeks. Back here, it was mostly binary stuff, as guests weren't supposed to be in these areas.

Afia was working, but an outside vendor, as it were. And Del had bribed folks with cookies, so the locals weren't all that hyper about being assholes.

Suvi chirped a signal at the reader, listening for the confused response. She'd also been listening when other folks had badged things open while anywhere close to her, so she had fourteen options.

Number Three unlocked the door and Afia carried her into a room eleven point three one meters deep by seven point five four wide, filled with shelving units each one meter deep and holding a fairly random assortment of cleaning supplies.

Suvi found a moment to be offended that they had all this stuff and hadn't used it in the corridor, but got over herself quickly.

"On your right, about four meters down," Suvi said as Afia closed the hatch. "Calf-level to you. There is a port I can access with a standard plug."

"You got it," Afia said, carrying her over and shifting things out of the way. "Do I hide in here with you or come back?"

Suvi considered her options. She could chirp the lock from here, on a coded knock from Afia. However, that meant that Afia might have to just wander randomly for a while, and that risked someone intercepting her and asking questions.

If someone found this device, Suvi could either hide inside, or just wipe herself to protect Afia and Javier. Ship-Suvi would understand.

"You plug me in and let me sniff the wind," Suvi said. "Then we'll know what security is like. I doubt that it will be great around here, because honestly, who steals ammonia cleaner?"

The serious control systems would be around the gaming systems, to keep someone from adjusting the odds and hitting themselves a jackpot. Suvi was willing to bet that those systems were entirely isolated from the rest. Probably air-gapped to the extent that you had to go to machines physically remote from everything else, running on a separate set of wires for their network.

Similarly, whatever system they used around the vaults would be tight.

Suvi just wanted to see what her limitations were.

Afia moved boxes and got her plugged in.

Rather than do anything, Suvi listened.

If she had the space, she would have envisioned a full graphics suite and turned it into an open door of a haunted house. Just enough moonlight to show a hallway, with no idea who or what might be lurking back there in the darkness.

Sniff. Never yell and let them know lunch might have arrived.

Nothing replied.

Well, the usual traffic you got on a dumb network. Beeps and pings and hiccups and low-level conversation where lots of computers were updating each other with status every five to sixty seconds.

Base-lining, in case something broke and one of the other machines needed to scream for help from a human.

Nothing at all that smelled like a *Sentient* presence.

So far, so good.

She walked up to the doorway and peeked in. Again, no graphics, so she had to imagine the foyer. Big, because of where she was. Ornate for the same reason.

Maybe a little gaudy. Possibly a shade withered, because all the money was in the salon, keeping it impressive, and Suvi was sneaking in the tradesman's entrance.

As it were.

No guards demanded to know what she thought she was doing. Or tried to slam the door in her face.

She leaned her whole head in and looked around.

Corporate. Not even navy corporate, like she'd grown up with.

Office. Hell, it reminded her of that one accountant she'd worked with on *Bryce*, when Javier had needed to file annual tax documents that one time.

Was it a trap?

One way to find out.

She took a step in, watching the floor in case it was about to fall out from under her.

Solid, so she leaned a little more weight on her foot.

Nothing.

Suvi stepped fully into the foyer, looking for monsters and portraits with moving eyes.

Nothing jumped out at her.

Okay, a sigh was acceptable. She took one.

Girl could get a little worked up doing this. Good to keep in practice.

Suvi took two more careful steps, watching traffic and not intruding. Monitoring directionality, mostly.

Everything flowed to her left, so she called that the back-office. The place where the computers and human controllers would be found.

If she wanted to find them.

Not today, buttercup.

Instead, she kept her visualization in mind and went straight back, looking for the kitchen.

Javier had theories of breaking and entering. Sneaky ones, at that.

She slipped into the software that controlled Room Service and looked over the shoulder of the Customer Service Reps taking orders. Didn't touch. Just watched.

Eventually, someone flipped pages back to find something and she was able to find the name she wanted.

Gustavus Nyseth.

Javier had taught her to analyze the shadow someone casts in living.

Gustavus lived alone. Room Service records were always single meals, with dessert and a lot of booze. About what Javier used to consume, in the days when he was busy running away from his past.

Still, no partner they needed to worry about. And he could invite the Dragoon back to his suite safely. Not that Suvi expected Djamila to take him up on it, but they'd transitioned to *Mission* and those things might be called for.

The Dragoon would do whatever she thought was necessary to complete the mission, come hell or high water.

From Room Service, Suvi piggybacked across to a quick scan of his financial records. Didn't try charging anything, which might have triggered something. Just looked at the amount, because Room Service needed to know if you were running low on deposited funds when they took an order.

Nyseth had a reasonable amount of money on credit, with records of having brought a draw on a bank on *Kranieafim*, the previous stop for *Sovereign Nakhimov* before *Yu'Urid*.

Not lots. Enough to be considered a major player. Maybe interesting enough to be invited to big parties, but hardly ten percent of what Javier had deposited.

Granted, *Excalibur* was a pricey thing to run. Girl had expenses. And crew required payroll.

Plus, the expectation of downtime meant folks drawing on credit from the ship to have fun on the station.

That was exactly why Javier had been willing to haul cargo out. That money offset the others.

So Gustavus Nyseth wasn't a major corporate bigshot. Or at least hadn't brought enough money with him to really get serious about his partying.

And he was at a variety of events, looking at his various Room Service charge accounts over the last six days.

And whiskey. Always middle-shelf stuff, which, honestly, kinda described him, from what details the Dragoon had filled in.

Rude to call a guy middle-shelf.

Still, probably accurate.

Now, things got hinky. It was a technical term. Amateurs should avoid it.

Suvi slipped out of Room Service and headed upstairs, sniffing at various doors until she hit the one called Surveillance.

Extreme care was called for here, because the ancient Romans had asked this question.

Who watches the watchers?

Or maybe it was the Hellenes. Hard to say, since she didn't have most of her brain with her.

Close enough for government work.

She was going to watch them.

Suvi sidled up slowly. Most of the important operations systems were in the vault area, which made sense. The good stuff, the gaming systems themselves, would be inaccessible from here, she presumed, but didn't look. Second biggest zone of interest was the cameras watching various gaming tables, where experts watched players for indications that they were cheating somehow. Using some trick electronic disguised as whatever. Helpers across the way with some sort of telephoto capabilities that let you know what somebody's cards were.

Tilting the balance of chance away from skilled players and randomness. Plus the house's cut on everything.

There were suggestions of a *Sentient* system inside those areas, watching play and reacting at her kinds of speeds to notify a human overseer.

Suvi didn't need to access those. Didn't want to.

She already knew all she ever wanted to about gambling, having watched Javier, Sascha, and Hajna fleece lesser players.

She wanted corridors outside the game floor.

There.

Simple stuff. LOTS of cameras, but any one human was responsible for nearly one hundred at any time, on a dozen monitors.

They weren't looking to prevent crime. Probably saved enough footage to go back and solve a crime in the previous week.

Mostly looking for folks being suspicious. Or having medical emergencies and needing help. Or passed out drunk.

No cameras out in the main hallway, or this side spur, so Suvi assumed that nobody actively watched. They could still go back later and see who had been walking around, so she needed to make sure Afia left a lot of distracting tracks going back and forth.

Easy to do, when delivering more cookies or something.

And it wasn't like Javier was planning to do anything to Amina Anargul and her operation.

Except maybe save them from whatever Nyseth was up to.

Suvi studied the architecture of the Surveillance systems from the inside. Good, but nobody had ever apparently attempted to insert a modern Sentience into it sideways, and they didn't have the right protections in place.

She reached out and grabbed hold of a file showing work schedules. Copying it, she renamed it for a backup and then hollowed out the center entirely, before making a copy of herself and injecting it. Together, they grabbed a few other large files and crafted dummy copies that they could use to store footage as needed.

For fun, Suvi located the ship's entertainment library and added a few books into Bethany's account, a new library she'd been collecting as she found interesting things to check out or buy.

Couple of hops of misdirection, and Suvi could charge Javier about a drachma for forty-one minutes of video footage, compressed and delivered as an episode of some new vid show.

If she had more of her brain handy, Suvi would have come up with something new on her own. Maybe even generated an opening credits sequence—with theme music, of course—and hid things inside that.

For now, she grabbed something obscure from the depths of the schlock section, hollowed it out, then inserted a quick explanation for Bethany when she found the files and wondered what the hell was going on.

Sovereign Nakhimov's systems didn't much care, as long as everybody got charged appropriately when things happened. Wanna check out some TV show? Here's the rental fee.

Whoops, not what you thought? Sorry. *Caveat emptor.*

They both suppressed snickers as they separated themselves. Shard-Suvi carefully slipped out a back window as Surveillance-Suvi went into trapdoor spider mode, watching for Gustavus Nyseth to do things that the Dragoon needed to know.

Whatever needed to happen next, neither Suvi was sure. Didn't need to be.

The Dragoon would handle it.

They found themselves looking forward to it.

PART 3

Djamila would have liked to have slept in, but forty years of habit was impossible to break.

She rose as soon as Zakhar stirred. He joined her in the shower and scrubbed her back for her while she filled him in on the high points of last night.

Officially, he was still working on Javier's behalf, so she didn't go too deep.

Instead of commenting, he merely kissed her as they got dressed, him in dark gray and her in light blue.

Javier, being Javier, had apparently stumbled in late. Or early. Something.

Djamila joined Afia and Bethany for breakfast in a quiet restaurant well away from the gaming floors. About half the folks around them eating wore crew uniforms, either bright helpers or dark staff, so Djamila was willing to bet that the food was going to be good.

Afia had apparently asked someone about the right place to eat, because everyone took one look at them, nodded to themselves, then pretended she and her two companions didn't exist.

Food was a serve-yourself breakfast bar, with a single chef who could do you up eggs or something exotic as needed.

Djamila's tastes hadn't changed appreciably in thirty years, so hers was basic. Bethany as well.

Afia had apparently sampled one of everything over there onto her plate. Some of them were things Djamila couldn't even identify.

Lots of coffee. It felt like that sort of day ahead.

Djamila had her side of the booth. The other two—three with Suvi's shard placed on the top—watched from across her. And they were as far away from the crew around them as both sides could politely get. Possible, as it was early yet, and only about a quarter of the tables were filled.

"Was that a safe move?" Djamila asked quietly as Afia finished her explanation.

"Suvi took her usual precautions and amped them up a notch for this," Afia nodded. "And avoided zones where we would expect security to be tighter."

Djamila nodded. This crew did have all manner of expertise, including breaking into giant, space-borne casinos. Not many folks could say that.

She turned to Bethany.

"Summary of our subject?" she asked, leaving off names and loaded words that someone in here might overhear and report.

"Linear might describe it, from bits I've reviewed," Bethany replied, equally obscure. "Many videos that show linearity. Plus the other records. Predictable might also summarize, at least at the first derivative. I presume layers of meaning not yet revealed, based on other sources."

Djamila nodded. Her conversation with Nyseth—who really was Qadir, based on Suvi's work—showed a man playing a role. Insinuating himself into the social system, presumably for one of a handful of tasks.

As with the original cover story by Navarre at *Shangdu*, Qadir might have stolen something and be waiting for his contact to arrive so a swap could occur. Or it might be a penetration to steal something on the ship itself, as Navarre had done with the heir to the Jianwen Emperor's throne.

Much as Djamila wanted to confront the man and simply kill him, she understood that to not be an acceptable behavior at present. *Sovereign Nakhimov* was, in many ways, its own planetary government, which meant that they could enforce their own laws.

They might execute her out of hand for doing it. And she didn't want to task Bethany with looking, because that would leave records somewhere, later, when someone went back to check.

Javier had taught her the value of sneakiness over the years.

"Is there a way to enter his suite and check things?" Djamila asked.

"Two," Afia offered. "First, you take him up on the inevitable offer for a fling. Maybe he sleeps heavy afterwards. Maybe we slip him a mickey or try to get him so drunk that he loses touch."

Djamila grimaced, but understood.

"And second?" she pressed.

"We go in when he's known to be elsewhere," Afia nodded. "Riskier, because folks might be paying attention to somebody doing something to a high roller like him. That's the sort of thing that might trigger secondary systems we won't know about until it's too late."

Djamila considered it. Suvi's probe scouting had suggested some sort of *Sentience* involved, but not running across the entirety of the network.

Still, if they did track the man moving around, his cabin opening when he was at dinner might set off some alarm. Wouldn't be hard to configure that, if they tracked simple things like that.

Presumably housekeeping was on a schedule that would be excluded or confirmed. And they weren't going to be here long enough to bribe a maid or impersonate one.

Again, nothing important to ninety-nine-plus percent of folks, who Jabril Qadir was. Or what he'd done.

It was on her honor, as the only representative of the *Neu Berne* military around here.

Nobody else might care, but honor was everything. Always.

"I agree that the risk is too great," Djamila replied. "The former is probably the only way to confirm. What can we do that won't cause serious repercussions or side effects? Or show up on a medical scan in the morning, if he has suspicions?"

"I've seen how much he drinks, based on Suvi's records," Bethany spoke up quietly. "I presume a fully-functional alcoholic, merely by volume. Was there any effect on him while he was talking to you? I note that he'd had four at that point, plus three others over the course of some ninety minutes prior to that. Given that these were lowball glasses, with his whiskey neat, I'll presume an average pour of one hundred and twenty milliliters. He consumed half a liter of alcohol while talking to you, on top of at least another third of a liter before that. Even spread over five hours, we're looking at a high tolerance."

Djamila considered that. She wasn't a teetotaler, but drank very little, even socially. Usually wine, at that, so a much lower alcohol content.

"What would that do to the body?" she asked these two. "Over a longer arc."

"Were there red lines on his nose?" Afia asked. "Evidence of damage to veins?"

"Some," Djamila remembered.

"Lemme talk to main-Suvi," Afia nodded. "There might be low-level, ongoing liver damage that would cause false positives on a medical evaluation. We can hide a few things there. That's your option to slip him a mickey, make him think it was your greatest night ever, and leave him none the wiser."

Djamila kept her grimace inside. It was a dishonorable way to fight, but she'd come to understand that not every problem needed to be attacked head on. Javier almost never did, except when he'd worked hard to stack the deck ahead of time and could invoke overwhelming force.

Like he and Zakhar had done at *Surayya*.

"Do we presume he will return?" Djamila asked.

"He never touched you once?" Bethany asked back.

Djamila nodded.

"And was careful about not touching you, even as he was spinning yarns?"

Another nod.

"Then either he's decided that you aren't a threat to his ongoing operation, or it isn't ready to go yet and he thinks he has time," Bethany stated. "Most men would have made some pass, some attempt or offer, regardless of whether you took him up on it. Maybe just to see if you would."

"And in not asking...?"

"Slow burn, maybe," Afia offered. "Foreplay? Somebody explained to him, somewhere along the way, that smart ones like a little dancing first? Don't go straight to making out and losing your clothes? It's possible that there are more guys like Javier, but they still tend to be a little rare in my experience."

Djamila had no answer to that. Her size and intimidating manner had kept almost every man at a distance, and she'd hardly ever relented enough to consider anybody until recently.

Zakhar, who she'd had an unrealized crush on almost from her first day aboard *Storm Gauntlet*.

Farouz, who was almost indescribable in his pure-Zen harmony with the universe, mixed with a lethal deadliness she had encountered less than a half-dozen times in her life.

"I think foreplay," Bethany agreed with Afia. Then the Librarian turned to the Cargomaster. "You make a run to the ship and do your thing, like immediately. I think that we rotate watch schedules and insert the Dragoon back into her bodyguard role for most of today, then she comes off duty after dinner and is at loose ends. Red Riding Hood on a forest trail. Easy prey for the Big Bad Wolf to come along."

Djamila started to say something tart and rude, but the smiles from the other women stopped her short.

Yes, she could play the innocent waif here. Might even be fun, considering how far out of her normal range it would be.

Jamie.

And it might even be necessary to let the man take her body to bed. Only her body. Nothing more.

It was a matter of honor.

PART 4

Afia had to play this one fast and loose. Javier was busy being busy, entertained by the top-heavy broad who ran the place. Clothing optional, presumably.

Not her problem. Wasn't like they were all celibate monks around here, as long as everyone understood that the Khatum had his heart and soul. And she should.

The rest of them got to play occasionally. Even Bethany was loosening up, though Afia hadn't gotten serious about seducing the girl.

Yet.

The day was young.

Javier was in the main room, surrounded by folks mostly ignoring him, at least until he had a specific need for a killer or a staff aide.

"Repeat that?" Javier said, eyes still a little bleary.

But he'd been out way past his bedtime. Or in. Something.

"You will invite a small group to come aboard *Excalibur*," Afia said specifically. "Dinner at *Le Bistro Parisian*. A group larger than the Graces and less than the Muses, as the old saying goes. Somewhere between four and eight, leaning towards the top end, though still elitist. Have it happen tomorrow night, station time. Make sure you invite your girlfriend, as well as Gustavus Nyseth, plus whoever might be entertaining and properly impressed by Chay's cooking."

"I will, will I?" he asked, a bit dubious.

Bethany was close, but utterly innocent looking. Djamila was in her room at the moment.

"You will," Afia pretty much ordered him. "Also, the Dragoon will be on duty with you this afternoon, then come off duty after dinner."

"You running this op, pipsqueak?" Javier asked, getting serious.

Zakhar had also leaned in and focused those dark eyes on her.

"I am," Afia nodded. "I need to move several pieces around my game board, and doing it this way introduces the most fog of war on the other guy. Nothing happens on the ship, most likely, because that dinner, while exquisite, is entirely ancillary to my needs, but don't tell Chay that."

"Heaven forbid he be merely the distraction," Javier nodded with a twinkle in his eye. "I note that someone is missing from this conversation."

"She put me in charge of this part," Afia replied, chin coming up. And maybe out a shade.

Javier nodded, then turned to Sascha.

"Looks like you get today off," he said simply. "You and Hajna work out the evening schedule, assuming that I might be out late again tonight."

She nodded and those two moved off into another conversation area to work it out. Javier turned back to face Afia.

"All going well?" he asked.

"Better than well," she grinned. "Aiming to pull something up to the standards of your legend, buddy."

He laughed.

"Zakhar, why don't you step in and talk to Amina's people quietly today to get that ball rolling," he said. "Get Afia's scheduling needs and ask them to pick four to six names. Then make sure Nyseth and Taliesin Berrett are on the list. We don't need to bring Plus Ones unless they suggest it, so that we can bring more heavy hitters."

"Why Berrett?" Zakhar asked.

Wasn't anybody Afia knew, but she'd been almost completely isolated from Javier's side of the operation up until now.

"How many folks do you know like him, Zakhar?" Javier laughed. "Former professional athlete. Former professional rock musician. Currently an investment banker in his mid-forties who managed to not only keep all his winnings and income along the way, but to grow it on the scale he has. Plus, Suvi will want to meet him in the flesh, as it were, and would never forgive me if he wasn't there."

"You got that right," the person in question chirped from Afia's pocket.

Folks laughed.

Afia figured she'd get the story later. Or simply meet the dude and find out if he was all that in person.

Javier liked to collect interesting people.

"We good?" she asked.

"Up until you need something more from me," Javier nodded. "When you get back to the ship, have Suvi run a lottery to bring a dozen folks over on a twenty-four-hour day off, then we'll keep doing that every day that we're here. Won't get everyone, so lean in on folks that didn't get to visit *Yu'Urid* previously, and keep notes for the next stop, where they'll get priority. I want Piet on the ship when the dinner occurs. And Andreea is not required to go into the draw. Or any of the other hard introverts. Past that, you run it."

He rose as a way of ending the conversation, walking over and rapping on Djamila's door. It opened a moment later.

"You're on duty in five," he said, then headed back to his room.

Afia looked around at all the faces bright with anticipation looking back.

"Let's do this, people," she said, standing as well.

Time to get crazy.

PART 5

Djamila had been surprised by the turn of events, but Afia had laid it all out. And Javier was playing along, because he understood that Afia was good at this sort of thing.

Thus, Djamila was dressed in grays again. Armed. Walking two polite paces behind Javier through broad corridors as the man went in search of brunch. Or at least entertainment, as she wasn't sure how hungry the man might be for food.

Human interaction was a different conversation entirely.

And it appeared as though his endurance was greater than Anargul's, as she didn't join them when Javier found the equivalent of a sidewalk cafe and settled for a type of coffee he asked for called Turkish.

Strong smell, even from where she was standing, her back to a pillar that let her watch traffic around them. Not a lot of it, but some. Morning robins, getting the first worms, after night owls like Javier had gotten all the mice.

Javier had turned his chair to watch as well, ignoring her as he should.

A figure appeared out of the mess and stopped short. Djamila locked on for a long moment, then nodded and went back to the crowd.

"Prince Javier!" Taliesin Berrett exclaimed. "How are you this morning?"

"Awake," Javier replied. "Not as young as I used to be, to be able to simply blast through a night like that."

"Agreed," Berrett nodded. "Part of the reason I gave up the relentless touring in my thirties and only put out new music these days. Are you alone?"

Djamila's grin was a transitory ghost. The three women who were Javier's bodyguards didn't count, obviously.

"I am currently at loose ends," Javier replied. "Having some caffeine and considering a pastry or something. Would you care to join me for a bit, or were you on your way somewhere?"

"We're all on our way somewhere," Berrett laughed. "Fortunately, most of us won't get there for a while."

Javier laughed with the man.

Berrett moved to the other side of the table and sat. Djamila studied him, matching dinner before with today.

Dark-skinned African genotype where the tone was a bronze that wanted to go all the way down into onyx. Curly black hair he'd dyed, because he needed to go back and do his roots soon.

Benefit of being so much taller than others, especially when they were seated, that she could see the tops of heads where they couldn't.

Former professional athlete in how he was long and lanky, starting to bulk up with age in a manner similar to Qadir. Then a professional musician she'd never heard of, but Javier had music nerds on the crew, so perhaps he had.

Investment banker with money on a scale perhaps a step down from the Khatum of *Altai*, indicating that the man was brilliant and ruthless. Not necessarily in a bad way, but you didn't get there by sitting back and letting diversification work.

It required dealing. Hustling. Moving. All the things Javier did, but starting from a different spot.

A waitress appeared with a mug and poured more Turkish coffee.

Djamila watched the man's hands. Long fingers like spider legs, each moving individually and delicately to the task.

Berrett paused and looked back over his shoulder, studying her closely for a long moment before he nodded and turned back to Javier.

Apparently, she met with the man's approval. Were all of them seeing her as a sex object?

Her?

It made no sense to Djamila, but she supposed that many of the men she'd previously known had liked bimbos, for lack of a better term. Although, all of the ones last night at dinner had had intelligent companions, including Berrett, though she was certain the woman worked for the casino.

Still, Djamila expanded her perimeter to include Taliesin Berrett for now, while she listened to the two men banter haphazardly.

Random encounter? She might have thought so, but Jabril Qadir had found her quickly when she was alone. Presumably, her going off duty later would create a similar opening tonight. Was Afia preparing for that, or for tomorrow, when the man might be on *Excalibur*?

She listened.

"So, enjoying yourself?" Javier was asking the man.

"I let myself take a two week vacation every year," Berrett replied, sipping coffee. "Line up all my various investment contracts to close out over a forty-five-day period so I can ignore the market while I'm off having fun. Then find something exotic to do. This year, *Sovereign Nakhimov*. Who knows what next year might bring."

"Well, if you end up headed east, maybe you'll call on us at *Altai*," Javier offered. "The Khatum has a ship almost as impressive as this one, as her personal yacht."

"The lake you were mentioning last night," Berrett nodded.

"Your perfect, tropical vacation," Javier agreed. "In space. I've considered asking if she'd do a winter wonderland version at some point. Turn the temperature down, acquire and install snow-making equipment. Either adjust the gravity in a few places or install some slopes to ski on. Maybe import a herd of reindeer and have sleigh rides."

"You know, that does sound attractive," Berrett replied. "Many people go for the tropical thing, but I can't think of anybody doing winter that way."

"Maybe you should invest in something," Javier teased, at least from the way it sounded to Djamila. "Novelty sells. Look at where we are."

She watched Berrett lapse into the sort of silence she understood meant that the man was actually contemplating it.

When you had that much money, what did you do with it? It didn't appear that Berrett had a spouse of any kind. Perhaps no family? Or merely that he traveled alone and would return to someone in a few weeks?

Djamila had been raised in an orthodox, serious place. Man and woman. Holy matrimony. Children, God, *Neu Berne* military.

And look what that had gotten her.

Now, she had two men who loved her. And strangers who ogled her in public.

Berrett turned so serious that Djamila ignored the pedestrians for a moment.

"What do you do, when you aren't being Prince Javier?" the man asked.

"Frequently, I'm Doctor Aritza," Javier replied. "Botanical nerd."

"Heard about that," Berrett nodded. "More novelty?"

"I get to breed my own plants," Javier noted. "Patience is required, but I have created new things that never existed before."

"Interesting."

"What are you doing tomorrow?" Javier asked, only appearing

to jump conversations. "I've sent my Chief of Staff to talk to Amina's people about having a small dinner party, back on my ship. Chat over excellent food. Show off the chef I told you about last night. That sort of thing. Would love to entertain you if you're free."

"I have a weakness for French cooking," Berrett smiled. "How did you find them?"

"My Cargomaster's cousin is the chef," Javier nodded. "His wife ran the bistro with a pair of sisters working for them. Hired the whole lot and installed them on my yacht. Half the reason I go strange places is to find that man ingredients that challenge him to do new things."

"And *Sovereign Nakhimov* has a big hydroponics capability, from what you and Amina were talking about last night," Berrett said. "Swapping ingredients?"

"Swapping seeds, which is even more interesting, because then you can grow something new," Javier agreed. "Something exotic and novel. And if you hire the right people, they can breed novelty into yet more novelty, like my dreamberries that are adapted to climate-specific zones."

"Staving off boredom?" Berrett asked. "For many folks with money, that seems to be the problem in life."

Djamila agreed. The Khatum ran her government, but also had set it up to mostly take care of itself, to the point that she could travel on *Shangdu*. Others she'd met were the same way.

Javier had channeled all that energy into saving the galaxy, instead of merely exploring it as he had when they'd first met.

The day she'd shot him.

Djamila still smiled at the memory.

"Gotta fill the days," Javier agreed with Berrett's assessment. "Otherwise, I might have to go off and save the galaxy or something."

She liked the offhand way he just tossed that into the conversation, like it was a lark for wealthy, powerful men to consider.

Instead of exactly what the crew of *Excalibur* was about.

The Rising Storm.

Somebody had to save the galaxy. Was Javier recruiting Taliesin Berrett to help?

That was an interesting thought. She'd have to pay closer attention to the man, in addition to what they were doing to go after Jabril Qadir.

The next few days were likely to be busy.

THE SETUP

PART 1

Javier looked around the table at his guests and liked the way it had all come together. Amina had, of course, claimed a spot for herself, not that he was surprised. Gustavus Nyseth as a mark. Taliesin as a raconteur. Handful of others who were more money than interesting, but Javier was playing a game to distract.

And maybe round up some investors to build a mobile, winter wonderland. He and Taliesin had gone perhaps a shade too deep on the topic for two guys in a coffee shop.

After all, Taliesin had been right. There were lots of tropical paradises planet-side, and places to go ski and have snowball fights. Yet folks still built ships to double as resorts. At least you'd be able to control snowfall and ski conditions.

They were down on Deck Six, in Burdine's kingdom. Javier might own the ship and Suvi might *be* the vessel, but Burdine was in charge here.

As she should. *Bistro*, done the way they were supposed to be.

Better, private party event, so the crew had either gotten in early, or had to settle for merely eating excellent wardroom food instead.

Javier could imagine the bitching he'd hear about later.

Tables arranged in a box, two each on four sides so everyone could see each other. Five men and three women. Piet had greeted everyone on arrival. Suvi had shown off a bit.

There would be a concert after dinner, mostly so Piet could play his latest symphony and talk music with some of the guests.

Collette and Simone were constantly in motion, but had it easy with something as small as this.

At Afia's orders, Javier had left Djamila back on the station, and had Hajna guarding him tonight. He didn't know what Afia, Bethany, and Djamila were up to, and didn't want to, but he did have to admit that they were running a tight, clean operation.

Apparently, they wanted to make sure that nothing happened to Nyseth while he was here.

Plausible deniability later, as it were.

Javier could appreciate someone else taking the blame.

"Javier, I've been giving some thought to your ski resort idea," Taliesin began at one point. One of those lulls that occurred when folks were eating, drinking, chatting, and generally having a grand time, lubricated by Chay going above and beyond, because he'd had a day to prep and a list of dietary preferences from Amina.

No menus. You sat down and food appeared. It would be excellent.

The best way to dine.

And Taliesin had stopped calling him *Prince Javier*.

"Go on," Javier prompted.

"Ships are expensive to operate," Taliesin nodded. "We've chatted about how you use this vessel occasionally to haul cargo, simply to offset other costs."

"And to let me go off the beaten path to see strange things," Javier agreed. "Almost a tramp freighter that way."

"Indeed, but this is also a warship," Taki Moto interjected from his diagonal corner across from Javier.

"Luck of the draw," Javier replied. "First-Rate Galleons were designed in an era when they didn't build dedicated escorts, so the ship had to be able to protect itself. Suits my needs that way, as I can haul cargo and not worry about pirates getting stupid."

"Who built it originally?" Neomi Veillon asked from her spot next to Taliesin.

"*Neu Berne*," Javier nodded. "During the Great War, where it was lost until I found it later, then had it rehabilitated and installed a *Sentience* and crew. That let me take a long voyage to look at trade possibilities for *Altai*."

He wasn't directly watching Nyseth, but Javier still caught the flash of recognition. As if he needed any more evidence that this guy was the Dragoon's target.

"Circling back, could it be a profitable thing?" Taliesin asked.

Javier noted that the guy had gone serious again. Like he was looking for reasons not to build it, when it might be the first of its kind and thus worthy of all those bragging rights.

Like *Sovereign Nakhimov*.

Someone else could build it later. Maybe make it bigger and better. They'd still be *second*.

"Three sets of slopes," Javier nodded. "Basically one wide hillside, ranging from steep to shallow, and maybe different powder conditions you could generally control. Resort and operations tucked down inside the hillside, with ski-in shops and restaurants at various levels. Maybe only accessible from the slope side, but I'd include a quiet back door because not everybody is going to be a snow bunny. Build a big ring around the outside for folks to ski cross-country, with lanes for snowshoeing and reindeer sleighs. I haven't gone deep on the technical side. You'd want to talk to Zakhar about that, as he's former *Concord* Navy and something of an expert. But really, the only decision point at the front is how big do you want to be. That sets the limits on what you do later. And how expensive the construction will be. Once operational, I expect it to be a matter of advertising and quality of service. Hire the right folks and put them in charge. Give them equity over a long term, so they're invested in success. Then have fun."

He watched Taliesin's eyes. Interestingly, Brissa Kifina, the other woman tycoon with them, had gotten a cagey look as well. Like she was running the numbers in her head.

Javier had originally thrown it out there as a silly idea. The sort of things that come up when people dream sideways. Now he could see an investment group coming together around him.

He turned to Amina.

"We're money," Javier said bluntly. "What does your business expertise suggest?"

Because she ran a casino resort larger than just about any Javier knew. Most of them were a single facility, surrounded by supporting businesses and staff. Here, everyone lived on premises, as it were, and she was as much governor of her own planet as floor boss of a casino.

"It will be expensive," she said simply, nodding at the group. "Megastructures in space always are. Your basic design as laid out would be enough to hire a design firm to come up with things, then an engineering shop would need to get down to brass tacks. Lots of water in the form of snow means a great deal of mass, so the vessel would have to be built to at least warship standards, if you didn't do something like my ship and hollow something out. Doable. Expensive, but most of you think on the scale of planetary budgets anyway, so then it becomes an ROI thing. What is your *Return On Investment*? I can't answer that without seeing a lot more depth, but the human side wouldn't be that difficult. Recruit from arctic climate folks, as frostbite and freezing to death are your great risks."

Javier grabbed his wine glass and leaned back as the others started all talking at once, conversations every which way that he couldn't follow but knew that Suvi would record and parse, if he needed to go back later.

Nyseth nodded to get his attention, so Javier ignored everyone else and studied the man.

The stranger nodded in the direction of Hajna.

"I didn't see Jamie accompany us on the flight over?" he asked in a leading way.

Jamie?

Javier would tease her about it once, but figured he'd get punched the second time. Maybe Zakhar needed to step up there.

Javier had never imagined her as a *Jamie*. Even if it was the role she was playing.

"That's right," Javier nodded. "Kept half of the staff on the station, in case my other tourists needed assistance with whatever. These three are all functionally interchangeable, though I suppose Jamie might be the most dangerous, by however much."

Not even Sascha or Hajna would argue that point. This was the Ballerina of Death they were talking about.

"Ah," Nyseth noted. "Pity."

Javier played poker. It was a game of psychology as much as chance. Knowing the other players at a deep, unconscious level. He wasn't personally the least bit interested in Djamila, but Nyseth almost looked smitten.

Did he unconsciously react to her *Neu Berne* heritage? Or was it just lust for the unattainable?

And had he been hoping to proposition her here? Weird.

But Afia was running some gambit. And it didn't involve breaking into the guy's suite while everyone was on *Excalibur*, either. She had learned a few tricks from him along the way, after all.

No, he'd entertain everyone tonight for dinner and dessert. Piet and music for a brief concert after that, then Del hauling everyone back to the station to sleep in their own beds.

Javier noted the moment of disappointment on Nyseth's face, then turned back to where the others were getting a bit wound up and enthusiastic about a ski vacation next.

And where they might go.

It helped, that Javier had a survey expert he could ask.

PART 2

Bethany wasn't sure why Afia felt that she needed a librarian, but was here. Dressed down in the sorts of dark colors that she had come to associate with the station-side of operations, instead of customer support, who wore colorful stuff.

They were in a corridor down and back some off the flight deck, walking seemingly abandoned hallways as Afia navigated.

She followed the smaller woman around a corner into a dead end. Three doors, one of which unlocked with a clunk as they stepped close, entering without breaking stride and closing the door behind them.

"You're probably wondering why I've asked you all here tonight," Suvi's voice came over the speakers quietly, followed by giggling. "Gods, I've always wanted to say that."

"You are a dork," Bethany reminded her. "All of you."

"Guilty," Suvi agreed, harmony coming from Afia's pocket.

"I do have questions," Suvi continued from the speaker overhead. "And having you here means I don't have to route through other systems, most of which I haven't tried to access yet for safety reasons."

Afia pulled her palm reader out and plugged it in.

"Need yours, too," Afia said, looking up.

Bethany had brought the messenger bag that was almost a part of her uniform these days, pulling out the larger machine she used when doing more detailed research. Suvi could put things on it, but had been playing it safe there as well by hijacking videos. Although, at some point Bethany needed to have Suvi download the original series for *Paragon Grieving*, just because the episode descriptions seemed so interesting, if somewhat ludicrous.

Later.

She handed Afia the device. Watched it get plugged into Afia's in a chain.

"Okay, wow, so much more space to do things here," Suvi announced overhead. "Kinda crowded back there, because some of their systems are almost smart enough to see what I'm doing and ask questions. Dumping data now."

"Can you give me the originals of the show I'm supposedly watching, while you're at it?" Bethany asked.

"Uhm, sure," Suvi replied. "Kinda a hack job for writing. Or maybe I'm just not the right person to be a fan."

"Probably not enough Bollywood dance intervals," Afia muttered.

"Not denying that," Suvi countered. "There. Okay, now, questions, since I don't have my brain with me. Need you two. When we hit *Shangdu*, Javier was using the helmet as an excuse to access the storage vault, so that he could describe it to me later, when I needed to break in. Bethany, I know before your time, but I've found a general access map that shows eleven different banks, for lack of a better term, letting folks store things, scattered all over the place."

"Eliminate any place where you don't show footage of Nyseth walking within five hundred meters in the last several days," Afia said immediately.

"Why?" Suvi asked. "Man, I hate being stupid. Okay, that makes sense. Done."

It took Bethany a moment to understand. Suvi had all her personality, but hardly any of her history, as she'd said. Chapter titles, and nothing else, as it were, suggesting a stack of tables of contents ripped out of a book and left on the ground. It was almost one of those mental conditions where you could remember things in the last few days, but everything older than that was gone.

That must suck, knowing that you knew something, and unable to access it.

"Do we presume he's using a similar scenario?" Bethany asked. "I've read up on the pleasure dome mission. Is it more likely that Nyseth is meeting someone to swap stolen goods, as Navarre was supposedly doing?"

"How could I tell?" Suvi asked, her rising voice showing a sharp emotional edge Bethany was certain non other Sentience she'd ever encountered could even understand.

"Customs records when he came aboard," Bethany replied. "Those ought to be easier to access. Surveillance footage of him when his ship docked. Something. He'd have checked bags through, but those wouldn't be important, because he'd have to assume a hotel porter touching them when he wasn't around. Possibly unpacking them into his suite for him. What was he carrying?"

Bethany suddenly understood how Javier was able to place himself instantly at the top of the social structure around here. He didn't carry anything. Didn't even have pockets in his outfits.

He had people whose sole job it was to do that. Her and her messenger bag, for instance.

Businessfolks would have a briefcase or something. Second place on the ladder.

Huh.

Man, he was sneaky.

"I have a picture of a hard-sided case," Suvi replied.

Afia's reader blinked live, showing a still. Standard-issue, as it were.

"Anything in it stand out when you look at the inventory?" Bethany asked, wondering what records Suvi could access.

"Datastore on the larger end, but not terrible," Suvi said. "Triple what you have on your clamshell for memory. No scan of contents. Cash and personal effects not noted in any greater detail."

Bethany considered it.

"Bank's a dead end, isn't it?" Afia asked.

"Feels that way," Bethany agreed. "Whatever he has, if anything, it is on that datastore. At this point, I couldn't begin to hazard a guess. And again, we're reading a lot of things into this that are possibly all fairy tales at the end of the day."

"Yes, but the Dragoon's locked on, so I think we need to proceed and see what it is," Afia said. "Might be he's blackmailing someone. Maybe he stole a bunch of critical information and is selling it on the open market. Without knowing, we can't be sure the best way to take him down. And Djamila will not settle for anything less."

Bethany nodded. Afia had never served in a military, instead enlisting in cargo young and eventually ending up with the rest of the crew on *Storm Gauntlet*. Suvi had been a Yeoman in her time, a senior enlisted sailor taking orders from an officer.

Bethany had been such an officer. Never in command, because most of her career had been dealing with temperamental admirals and captains. Still, she had the training.

"Suvi, maintain surveillance on Nyseth," she ordered, trying to sound like she knew what she was talking about. "Include comms and messages, but do not attempt to open anything even slightly encrypted. Route it here and notify one of us to pick it up and we'll handle it. Find out if Nyseth has friends or contacts he's been talking to, outside the group that was at dinner last night or on the ship now."

"You think he's got a meet going?" Afia asked.

"I think we need to proceed as if we're going to intercept such a thing," Bethany said. "If he's a criminal, then he's out whatever he put into it."

"Plus whoever is pissed at him for not having it," Suvi added.

"And that," Bethany agreed. "Maybe we can't get him extradited. Maybe we can't take him down ourselves because local laws will work against us. We can still hurt him for Djamila. And maybe there's enough on that datastore to hurt him bad enough to make her happy."

"Pretty sure he'd have to be dead for that to happen," Afia muttered.

"Yes," Bethany agreed. "But we don't have to be the ones who pull the trigger."

Bethany wondered what it said, the looks that Afia and Suvi gave her at that. That hint of surprise at her words.

Maybe this was growing up?

Maybe that unbloomed rose was starting to blossom, after all?

PART 3

Djamila had had a night to herself. Not done much. Gone out to one of the nicer restaurants by herself, then seen an acrobatics show that had impressed her. Things she'd been able to do at twenty, but not at forty, mostly from falling out of practice. Now, she was headed back to the suite to perhaps read. Or watch a show. Or just go to sleep early. Something.

But she was thinking.

Did she need to regain all that flexibility? Spend an extra hour each morning doing the sorts of complex yoga that would get her back there?

When was it okay to not be the most physically dangerous person she knew?

Alien thoughts, after her lifetime of focus. At the same time, she was having to play various roles outside her comfort zone, even after half a decade of knowing the Science Officer.

And maybe, just maybe, retiring from the combat business when this voyage was finally done?

Or was that too much to ask, with Javier involved? Probably, knowing him.

So she watched performers. Measured herself against them today, and twenty years ago.

Even enjoyed interested looks from strangers, though she wasn't about to become involved with anybody, even for that little amount of time.

Who knew what friends Qadir might have secreted among the passengers? What he might be up to?

Best to maintain her operational security tight and let Afia and Bethany handle planning.

Both were present when she entered the suite. Sascha and Hajna had taken Tom and Heydar back to *Excalibur*, leaving Iqbal, Galal, Demyan, and Helmfried here, with the latter two on duty watching from a nearby lobby at present.

Security never took the night off.

Djamila approved.

Afia had a glass of wine in one hand. Djamila went to the refrigerator and got herself some juice, then joined the two women, when it became clear that they had news.

"We don't have to break into a bank," Afia began with a smile.

Djamila nodded. Better, that way, as bank jobs could be complicated and messy. Especially when you didn't have the ability to get away quickly afterwards, more than a kilometer underground.

"We do, however, have to penetrate Qadir's personal security," Afia continued. "Well, you do."

"What am I looking for?" Djamila asked.

She understood what that sort of penetration was likely to entail. And had steeled her soul to it.

"A datastore," Bethany said, holding up her clamshell with an image on it.

Small enough to fit in Djamila's palm, perhaps six centimeters by ten by about one thick.

Djamila nodded.

"Do we know what's on it?" she pressed.

"No, but he didn't appear to bring anything else aboard with him that stands out," Bethany replied. "Presuming that he really is up to no good, and not merely taking a vacation where he accidentally crossed paths with you, this was the one thing that caught Suvi's eye."

Djamila wondered about that. Possibly the most likely scenario of all was that the man was honestly on vacation. At the same time, it didn't change anything about her intent.

He'd stolen a lot of money. And ruined careers and lives far beyond that.

She owed him for what he'd done to dozens—if not hundreds—of people.

They would never know satisfaction, except what she could claim for them.

And perhaps she could convince Javier to detour home after this, that she could tell the people who needed to know.

"How do I get in?" she asked, looking back and forth between the two women.

Afia pulled a small vial out of her pocket. Clear liquid in a clear container. Perhaps thirty milliliters.

"He'll drink this," Afia said in a voice as casually deadly as Djamila had ever heard from the woman. "Five minutes or so later, he will functionally cease processing, though he should never lose consciousness in the process. Highly amenable to suggestion. No memory later of what occurred. And it should break down in his liver pretty quickly, such that he'll wake up in the morning with a slight hangover. Anything he takes for said hangover will just break it down further, so a tox-scan by anybody short of Suvi should miss it. That includes the old device we had when we first met Javier."

Djamila remembered that old medbot they'd gotten after firing the drunk Zakhar had originally hired as Ship's Surgeon. And the first time she'd had to haul Javier in there and get him fixed from a concussion, because he'd mouthed off to her and she'd bounced him off the bulkhead.

How far they'd come since then.

"Five minutes?" she confirmed.

"Ballpark," Afia shrugged grimly. "A lot of that depends on his uptake. We presume he's good at handling such things, so this is a larger dose than a male of his age and mass would normally dictate. However, Suvi was guessing at a lot of things. It might not impact him sufficiently to erode cognition. It might trigger a medical event that requires professional help, at which point you probably get in trouble for drugging the man, presumably to rob him."

"Not all that far from accurate, at the end of the day," Djamila reminded him. "What happens without that data?"

"We have no clue what it is at present," Bethany spoke up. "Might have no value at all, and this is another red herring we're pursuing because our professional paranoia is that great."

"Yeah," Afia added. "Better safe than sorry."

"Agreed," Djamila nodded. "But I should be prepared for both ends of a wide spectrum of outcomes."

"And there is nothing we can do at present to mitigate that," Bethany said. "Are you prepared for that depth of verisimilitude?"

Djamila laughed. Couldn't help herself.

"*At Shangdu, did Kublai Khan a stately pleasure dome decree,*" she quoted. "In order to join Javier, I had to be prepared to be completely, naturally, unreservedly nude much of the time. And whatever else the mission might have called for. I won't say that this is easy, comparatively, but it will be. Especially if there is a strong chance that I won't have to consummate such a thing. More likely that I'd want to puke at the thought of letting that man touch me, but I can rest easy, knowing that he will get what he has coming. One way or the other."

"You will not execute terminal sanction on this mission, sailor," Bethany snapped in a hard voice that almost sounded like Zakhar. Or even Javier on a strong day.

Concord Naval Officer. This was what they sounded like. The ones who considered themselves the protectors of the galaxy today.

The Good Guys, but Djamila understood that to be a relative thing.

Still, she automatically snapped to before she turned a hard eye on the woman.

"Surveillance only, am I clear?" Bethany followed up, hard orders from a suddenly hard woman. "If we need terminal sanction, it will be done later, under controlled circumstances that do not allow them to trace it to you or us. It will be done. On my honor, Dragoon. But you will not do it now. Am. I. Clear?"

Djamila nodded.

She'd always wondered why Javier had so fixated on adding this woman to the crew. There were many librarians that could have been hired. Most would have worked out well as pirates, even.

Few could have done that. Especially to her.

"You are clear, sir," Djamila said aloud, wondering at Bethany, but utterly proud of her at the same time.

Afia had blinked almost as much as Djamila. It was good.

"Very good," Bethany said, adjusting her tone, though still retaining that command authority. "Afia, let's walk her through the expected plan of attack tomorrow night."

Djamila relaxed and focused on the combat-certified engineer speaking, wondering what rating she should assign Bethany.

If anything greater than *Officer* was even necessary.

PART 4

Javier would have loved to sleep in. Especially with the kinds of hours and kilometers he'd been keeping over the last few days.

He wasn't twenty-two anymore. No more waking up from a party in a different jurisdiction, wearing somebody else's pants.

He was management now. It came with even greater prices.

Like sitting in the back corner of the great suite, listening to Afia, Bethany, and Djamila explain their mission plan to him.

Sounded like overkill as he processed it, but Javier understood that this was one of those few times where you really did get bonus points for neatness.

Not like when you were using high explosives.

"And at the end of all that, we're in a crapshoot that it will be worth anything at all?" he asked, eyeballing Afia primarily.

Bethany was into information, but Afia was the criminal mastermind here.

There was a reason he had her handle cargo and resupply, after all.

"Correct," Bethany replied. "Excessive risk, for potentially minimal payoff, except that there is possibility of tremendous upside."

"If he's up to no good," Javier added.

Djamila shrugged.

"It allows us to possibly place the imprimatur of legality on the actions," she replied. "I've been ordered not to just kill the fucker outright, because I can't easily get away later."

He wondered who the hell could do that. Zakhar wasn't all that involved in this mess. Then he caught Bethany's eye.

Really? My little librarian is getting the hang of piracy? Bravo.

"Okay, so you are in his room and he's out of the picture," Javier nodded to all three. "How do you determine the value of the data, or anything else?"

"That's my job," Suvi called.

He watched Afia pull the shard from her pocket and turn the woman around to face him.

"The Dragoon will have me with her when the mission goes down," Suvi continued. "The narcotic should make him helpful enough to give us passwords and codes. I can access the data and help her determine the relative value, either to copy it or destroy it, depending."

"I'm hearing a lot of maybe in all this," Javier offered. He focused his intentions on Djamila. "And your target was exceedingly interested in you. Seemed sad that I hadn't had you with me on *Excalibur* last night, so I presume you'll be high on his list tonight after dinner. I understand that he's probably who you think he is. Is that enough to destroy him?"

"The stuff I gave her isn't truth serum, per se," Afia replied before Djamila could. "At the same time, it will make him exceedingly talkative, according to Ship-Suvi, so we can confirm that as well. Doubt that the locals give a shit, but it will put us entirely on the side of righteousness. And if he turns out to be a pure looka-like, she can back out more easily. Maybe leave a note on his pillow in the morning or something, then we can depart. You got what you needed?"

"For the most part," Javier said. "I've got Rainier and Dr. Pešek going back and forth almost constantly. And Del hauling seed packets and cuttings either way. Nothing bad so far, and we could cut and run whenever. Hell, leaving sooner means that Amina has a reason to eventually end up around *Altai*, if only to trade more plants."

"Yeah, definitely all about the pollination," Afia nodded sagely.

Javier didn't think he could blush with these women, but discovered that he was wrong. All of the women laughed at him. It was good.

"Should I go ahead and decide in my mercurialness that maybe I've been here long enough and that it's time to go somewhere?" he asked. "Give all of you the out? Or play it by ear?"

"By ear," Bethany said. "My planning branches several ways at the moment of discovery, and most of those plans are medium rare at best right now."

Javier nodded, then studied Djamila.

The Dragoon.

"I understand that you'll do whatever the mission calls for," he said to her quietly. "Just make sure you don't lose your soul in the process, okay?"

She blinked once, rocked back on her heels, then settled and nodded back to him.

"Okay," he continued, rising. "Five minutes for a bio break then you are on duty."

Time to go mess up some bad guys.

THE STING

PART 1

Djamila had spent the day focused, looking around the usual big-group dinner table.

Hyped up to a level beyond the bodyguard paranoia she'd been maintaining, even as the station folks maintained their own security around her. Javier would have been fine, all by himself, but she understood that he was presenting an image, and they had to keep it up at this point, rather than slide off that fine edge.

Appearances were everything in this game.

Javier was a spoiled prince who'd stumbled into the brass ring. Not all that far from the truth, but severely shaded in his case.

Nyseth/Qadir presented as a businessman in the upper middle range of things, interesting because he was into the sorts of shipping and such that *Excalibur* might have been available for hire, even if the man himself wasn't a criminal she was hunting.

Even Djamila had to give the appearance of being merely one of Prince Javier's lady killers. She did, however, allow herself to smile back at Nyseth when he caught her eye with a faint invitation to...something.

Several of the folks were caught eyeballing her when she paid attention. Ogling her, even, which still astounded her, though Djamila gave no hint of noticing.

Sascha and Hajna were both more attractive women. She was tall.

And, she supposed, lean and deadly, which might be its own kink to some folks.

She didn't get it, but didn't have to, because this was part of the mission.

Taliesin Berrett was with this group. As were a few of the others who had gone to *Excalibur* last night.

Javier had filled her in on some of the details, and it seemed like this collection had all more or less come together around the concept of building a winter wonderland in space.

To Djamila, it sounded like a recipe for disaster, but that might be all her hostile-climate training speaking. Tropical paradises were usually safe, except for dangerous animals. Winter cold meant frostbite. It meant passing out drunk in a snowbank and freezing before someone caught you.

Avalanches, presumably, would not be on the list of options, but broken legs and mangled bodies seemed to be a regular recurrence for skiers.

However, money would flow to the lowest point available, and Javier had seemingly breached a dyke somewhere.

He was good at that.

They were talking as if someone had already done the homework to start assembling a fund to back construction.

In a day and a half from when Javier and Berrett had first stumbled onto the topic? Did money move like that?

Except that these people weren't money. They were ***MONEY!***

Big players. Berrett had impressed Javier with his background and ability to grow his resources by tacking zeroes on the end. The others were about half self-made and half inheritors of vast industrial resources.

All of them seemed to think that it could be done, and wanted to do it first.

Because, *first*.

Thus, dinner went well. Amina Anargul showing off, after experiencing what Chay and Burdine had been able to do last night to show off.

Always pushing the envelope. Either bigger, or better, or faster, or something.

And Chay was amazing as a chef on his worst days.

They were down to drinks now, coffee or port as stewards cleared dessert trays. It was a good thing Javier exercised as much as he did, or all this rich food would bloat him quickly into a corpulent mass.

She didn't see that in his future.

Too busy saving the galaxy. No time to be a homebody. Maybe for any of them.

Maybe ever.

Was she ready for that?

Were any of them?

Djamila filed that thought for later and focused on the men and women creating a new corporate entity intended to design a kind of resort never before done, at least as far as any of them had been able to research with local records.

Always competing.

However, that allowed her to understand each and every one of them, because that described her as well.

Except that Djamila Sykora was only competing against herself. And Death.

Death would win eventually.

Only eventually.

"So obviously, I can't sign contracts for that amount of money without clearing it with my boss first," Javier's voice perked her right back into the present tense.

The crowd laughed, but it was a friendly laugh. A man willing to make self-deprecating jokes was a relaxed man. The kind of guy you wanted to enjoy a meal with.

Javier excelled.

"That being said, I do know for a fact that *Altai* has the kinds of yards necessary to do that work," he continued. "*Shangdu*, after all, was built locally, and she maintains a fleet of naval vessels sufficient to protect her interests."

Not quite *Concord* Navy by size or firepower, but enough to keep pirates at bay, if they chose to make that long sail over to bother her. Djamila had been surprised to discover how prepared *Altai* was for the future wars. Even before Javier and Dorn had crystalized things into dates and directions.

"While I'm not remaining in the immediate vicinity for long, *Altai* isn't that far away," he said. "And I think the Khatum would be quite interested in building such a thing. Or serving as a partner and backing this group, should you go forward. And she had expertise comparable to Amina here, so all manner of things could be done."

He held them in the palm of his hand in ways that Djamila found herself occasionally jealous over, but it was Javier. That was one of his super powers. Certainly, he held them spellbound now.

"With that, however, I've had a heavy several days, and I plan to retire to my cabin and sleep for about twelve hours," he said. "I'll likely be down by the pool after a late brunch. Thank you everyone for a lovely night—several nights—and I will see you tomorrow."

He rose abruptly and the others did as well.

Stepping away from the table, he gave her a look nobody else would see, indicating that all was moving forward exactly as planned.

He hadn't needed to be involved, but had walked right down the path Afia and Bethany had laid out for him, like a good trooper.

Because the mission demanded it.

Even the Science Officer could follow orders.

When he felt like it.

Djamila caught Nyseth/Qadir's interested glance as she followed Javier to the door, nodding discreetly back and then out into the hallway.

A promise of an assignation later.

Or assassination.

PART 2

Suvi hated being stupid, but at least she'd found a way to carve off some memory inside *Sovereign Nakhimov*'s systems to store some uptime.

As long as nobody actually needed to restore anything from those backup files she'd gone all digger wasp on. Then there might be a problem, since the backups contained about three percent of the original data at each end, and she'd stolen all the middles for her things.

Javier wouldn't be around for more than a week, so she could crash the files when she was done with them, if it didn't end up possible to offload herself to Bethany's clamshell or somewhere.

She'd been bereft of context too much, but being able to talk to Bethany and Afia, and store all that, had helped.

Now, she almost felt like a real person again. Or whatever the electronic equivalent was.

Nobody had a useful thesaurus for crap like this. Most of her cousins weren't even the sharpest spoons in the drawer, after all.

But she was doing that whole moray eel thing, down in the

rocks and watching interesting things swim by overhead. As one does.

And a note had just arrived that got her attention.

Addressed to Gustavus Nyseth. From one Choe Ku-Hou, newly arrived on the station.

Hmmm.

Male.

Asian genotype. Possibly Chinese Diaspora, mixed in with a few other things. Businessman, which on this ship was the equivalent of *Carbon Based Lifeform*, it seemed.

Customs records, because those were WAY less secured than banking stuff. Pictures and basic bio information, because all departments might need that. Like the Room Service system she'd slithered her way into to hide.

It was amazing, what you could learn about people from their eating habits. Ship-Suvi would love some of these insights, if she could off-load them to herself later.

The lies you could tell with simple things like that, multiplied across a few hundred thousand visitors over the last several years, until Suvi figured she had a sample size sufficient to draw conclusions.

Fun stuff.

She didn't try to read the message. Afia and Bethany had been firm on that one. Comms Security was a few steps down from banks and casino floors, but still way more than Room Service.

At the same time, it was the first time anybody had sent Nyseth any message that didn't originate with staff doing official things. Bills, Room Service, or Housekeeping, for most of them.

This one stood out.

Worse, his customs report showed a datastore of a similar size and model to what Nyseth had brought aboard. Normally, luck and strangeness, but Suvi was assuming enemy action today, so all coincidences weren't.

She dug in on the stranger.

Middle-aged guy. Well dressed in the image she had. Not bad

looking, but she supposed her tastes were a little flawed, considering the guys she had to compare him against.

Still, business was for folks who didn't have the looks to go into entertainment and were too short for anything but politics.

And he wanted to talk to Nyseth.

She checked her clock. Later in the day. Choe had arrived on station with one of the latest cargo and tourist runs from *Yu'Urid*. Presumably had gotten a ride there from somewhere else and then caught the tour bus out here.

Excalibur didn't count, because Ship-Suvi stayed parked far enough away that Del had to run across a significant distance on his deliveries, but not a Jump.

Could she tell the Dragoon?

Nope. She'd gone off duty after dinner and was currently sitting in the same quiet bar as before, being all bait and stuff. And she had a Shard-Suvi with her, but hacking the comm system to send Djamila a message didn't rise to the threat level Afia had established.

Plus, either Nyseth hadn't seen the message at all, or hadn't gotten around to replying, because Suvi was watching for that now, little birdies on nearby wires watching both men's front doors. At least metaphorically. Or something.

Good enough.

And she could let Bethany know.

Suvi pulled up another episode of *Paragon Grieving*, charged Javier's account, and dropped it into Bethany's video library with a mental thunk like you got returning physical books through the slot.

Hopefully, Bethany would know what to do next.

PART 3

Bethany looked up when she got the ping announcement of a new delivery. And the bill.

That couldn't be good.

Not right now.

She closed the file she was reading and opened the latest video.

"Hiya," Suvi announced as she appeared like a newscaster bearing breaking news. "Got a thing that might be an emergency, but dunno. Our target just got a comm email from one Choe Ku-Hou, nation of origin listed as *Da Xing*. Newly arrived stranger. No response from our subject as yet. Details to follow."

Then Suvi faded out and Bethany noted that the video file broke down into a whole series of photo stills and image scans of paperwork. She paused the video to review each step, then looked up at a horizon about a thousand light-years away.

Bethany took the clamshell with her and walked to Javier's door, rapping hard on the panel. It opened a moment later with Sascha glaring at her inquisitively.

"He awake?" Bethany asked quietly.

"You awake?" Sascha yelled loud enough to be its own answer.

They shared a grin as Sascha gestured her into the inner sanctum. Small salon up front. Bedroom behind that, with bathroom and a closet bigger than Bethany's first apartment.

Javier was sitting on the bed, fully dressed save for shoes on the floor, apparently meditating.

"I appear to be awake," he replied sarcastically. "What's up?"

Bethany turned to Sascha and nodded for the pathfinder to join her.

The bedchamber was elegant, if understated. Bed. Two dressers. Two chairs. Desk with a mirror where you could look at yourself while doing warpaint or whatever. Mostly done in darker teals and aquas that probably were intended to sooth the savage beast or something.

Bethany gestured Sascha to a chair and stopped in the middle of the space.

"Nyseth just got a message from a newly arrived stranger on the station," Bethany said. "Suvi sent it, along with basic customs information she has access to from Room Service, where she's been hiding."

Javier had looked relaxed. A moment ago.

Navarre was seated on the bed now, wearing Javier's clothing.

She'd never figured out how the man did that whole Jekyll and Hyde thing, but he did.

Eyeblink, and the goofball playboy swapped places with the killer.

He nodded once, and it still felt to her like a bullet cartridge sliding up a ramp and being inserted into the barrel. Then the whole upper assembly slammed shut like a bank vault door, right on the verge of violence.

"Normally, not a problem, as our subject is likely to be attempting to seduce his victim right now," Bethany continued, feeling her voice snap down into that staccato thing the fleet taught you, to deliver all the key points quickly and succinctly, without any dross. "However, the stranger, a gentleman named Choe Ku-Hou, lists his nationality as *Da Xing*."

There. Javier flinched as well.

Sascha probably wouldn't understand. Hell, of everyone, only Zakhar might react, besides the two of them.

Concord Navy veterans.

"Any way to confirm?" Javier asked sharply, his voice sounding like a freshly honed blade now.

"Just what we have from Suvi," Bethany replied.

"What am I missing?" Sascha asked sharply. "Both of you just went combat mode on me."

Javier turned, so Bethany nodded for him to speak first.

"*Da Xing*," Javier began.

"Long bloody ways from here," Sascha replied. "Why does that matter?"

"After the Great War ended, eighty, eighty-five years ago, *Neu Berne* was functionally broken," Javier continued. "*Balustrade* and the *Union of Man* were hardly any better. They'd pretty much given everything they had to stop *Neu Berne* and had nothing left."

"Yes," Sascha acknowledged. "And the *Concord* stepped in and assumed hegemony because they'd stayed out of the war for the most part until the end. With you so far."

Bethany watched Javier lick his lips and chew on them for a moment before continuing.

"*Da Xing* wasn't even a place then," he said. "Just a bunch of colony worlds off out of the way. However, over the last two generations or so, that's changed. They've finished a couple of what I suppose might be civil wars, or local wars of conquest. Early Industrial Germany or China, in the days before space flight, maybe."

He paused and Sascha nodded, still poised right on the edge of her seat.

"More recently, they've started making noises about their *proper place in the galaxy*," Javier continued. "The exact same shit that *Neu Berne* spouted off before they kicked off what turned into the Great War. Except that, for the most part, their military provocations have been relatively tame. Noisy saber rattling, instead of low-grade warfare. A lot of it was pointed at the *Concord*, because nobody else really matters. Even *Altai* is the wrong way to bother them, or be bothered, with the *Concord* more or less having the center of gravity around here, about which everything else rotates."

"Okay?" Sascha asked, eyes going back and forth between them.

Javier nodded at her to speak, so Bethany drew a breath.

"Given the current operation, we've assumed a thief who stole some interesting information and has it on that datastore that the Dragoon is going to try to access," Bethany said. "Like, right now, depending on how quickly our subject moves. My first level concern immediately is that perhaps the man is a spy, rather than a thief, based entirely on the irrational and possibly racist concern that the person who might have just shown up to deal with him is from Da Xing, who both of us consider a competitor if not an outright enemy."

"Do we need to intercept?" Sascha asked. "Or run a rescue operation?"

Bethany turned her attention back to Javier.

To Navarre.

He'd laid out all the rules of engagement up until now, keeping the Dragoon's business separate from his.

Bethany watched him run some set of calculations in his head, then nod.

"Locate Hajna and any Gunbunnies on station," he ordered. "Move to an alert status one step short of launching, then hold there from a Go Order from either myself, Bethany, or Afia, as necessary. There is nothing we can do to notify or warn the Dragoon without tipping everyone else off at this moment, so your actions will be entire reactive, instead of proactive. Sort yourselves into two pairs on simple dates, whichever guys you need to be on point, and get out into the station close but not close enough to be noticed. Then the rest remain here. Bethany will execute operational control until the Dragoon or I say otherwise. Questions?"

"Dead or disabled?" Sascha asked, rising.

"Whatever gets the jobs done," Bethany replied. "We're walking a tightrope as of right now."

PART 4

Djamila was back in that bar. Having a tall drink with a lot of ice and not that much alcohol. Being overcharged for it, but still leaving a nice tip, because it wasn't her money. Sitting and relaxing, at least as much as she could.

Right now, she was back to doing stretching exercises, where she concentrated on one toe at a time inside her boots, without giving any outward appearance of how tightly she was wound up.

Being unarmed at the moment didn't help her frame of mind. And she was off duty. Even stunners were not allowed, except for whoever was immediately guarding Prince Javier from whatever assassins tried their luck.

It had been about an hour. She'd wait another one, then give up and return to her cabin if her subject didn't make contact.

It might have all been an illusion on their parts, after all. Finding supposed order from random, chaotic noise when everyone was looking too hard.

Djamila didn't believe it. Not the way Nyseth/Qadir had approached her. Had watched her.

At the same time, she had to patiently wait for him to move.

It was an interesting game, glaring at everyone who came in as a way of letting them know she was to be left entirely alone, while otherwise not responding.

Jabril Qadir walked in about fifteen minutes later. She noted that he had changed from what he had worn earlier, just as she had moved from bodyguard clothes to tourist. More color, but not that much.

Enough to cross some line.

Qadir had done the same in the other direction, moving down from his fancier suit into something more comfortable. And not as shiny and attention-grabbing as Javier's.

Djamila reset herself as *Jamie* and gave the man a small smile as he walked up to the bar and ordered himself whiskey, lowball, neat.

She had two stools on either side of her open, as a result of mentally compelling people to keep their distance.

Qadir had come to rest a stool and a half away as he stood and watched the bartender work, while glancing at her in the mirror.

"It is good to see you again, Jamie," he said quietly. "Are you off duty for a while?"

"Done for the day," she replied. "Sascha has him until breakfast, then Hajna. I don't go back to guarding him until mid-afternoon."

The bartender delivered the glass and got Nyseth's room badge to charge it. Qadir studied her, and the two stools.

"Is this one taken?" he asked, indicating the closer one.

The one where they would touch if he sat. Knees. Thighs perhaps. Elbows occasionally. Shoulders.

Physical contact, as a way of flirting. A prelude to something else.

"It is not," she smiled at the man.

Seated, they were the same height. He was tall. Bulky, but tall.

Strong for a businessman. Not in that good of shape, but not pear-shaped, either. Barrel, maybe, depending on if he had any sort of girdle underneath, moving things around.

She hadn't looked that closely, and his suits concealed things well.

Qadir smiled and slid onto the stool.

Jamie allowed him to brush up against her as he did, not recoiling, nor leaning into it.

Passive, which was so unlike Djamila that she had to consider each step consciously, while Javier did things with such automatic grace as to be invisible.

Did she need to find someone to teach acting classes on the ship? With the size of crew and the depth of experiences and expertise, there was probably someone.

Did she want to be an undercover agent?

Not like she could disappear in a room, but *Jamie* might mean she could disappear into a role.

What were her limits, if she wasn't limiting herself to the physical?

She raised her glass and they toasted with a clink.

Jamie sat and watched the man in the mirror, largely ignoring the rest of the bar, confident that the Suvi shard in her pocket was listening in on any electronic signals and could give her some warning if a trap was about to spring on her.

Unarmed didn't mean undangerous.

"So what does a woman like you do when she doesn't have to be lethality incarnate?" Qadir murmured low enough that the bartender would miss it.

That one had slid to the far end of the bar, keeping a watch her direction but also keeping an emotional distance, in case she didn't mind being picked up.

It was a casino ship, after all. Didn't everyone go on vacation to have some sort of fling?

Idly, she wondered how many crew members secretly harbored some romance story dreams of being discovered or rescued by somebody with a lot of money. Swept off their feet to a life of fame or luxury.

"I was just contemplating that when you arrived," Jamie

nodded. "What I wanted to do, if I decide to retire from the game after this voyage. It is generally a job for younger people, though I've done quite well at it for many years."

"I could see that," he said, leaning away from her in such a way that he could admire and perhaps ogle her from up close.

Had she been inviting such a thing?

Djamila never did, but she was Jamie tonight.

What would Jamie think?

Jamie was interested in allowing herself to be seduced, because Djamila needed it from an operational standpoint.

What did the two of them want?

"And I have enough money saved up that I could retire, once I collected pension funds from a few places along the way," Jamie said.

She'd been doing that on this voyage. All of them had, with only the *Concord* capital world of *Bryce* and a few others left, for the crew of *Storm Gauntlet* to be able to close old accounts and haul everything to *Altai* for their retirement.

Whatever form it took.

What form would it take?

Could she retire? Could Zakhar? Could Farouz?

Or did they need to start some freelance security company, merging the two operations into something larger and even more deadly?

Was the galaxy safe if they did?

Or did the Rising Storm demand it of them?

What responsibility did she owe to future generations?

"Prince Javier has talked about being involved in the winter wonderland project, if he could convince the Khatum," Qadir offered.

"Perhaps I could teach competitive biathlon, then," Jamie nodded, flashing back to the many things that had been required of them, if they wanted to belong to the Dragon Watch.

Hostile climate operations. All of them.

"I have a hard time seeing you as a snow bunny," Qadir smiled.

Jamie smiled back. So did she, but if Javier was serious—and successful—what did tomorrow require?

"I am not sure what tomorrow will bring," she offered back. "Were you planning to invest?"

She'd followed the conversations enough to track, but lacked the depth of expertise to truly understand how they might do it. Or the form it would take.

And it hadn't been worth grilling Zakhar for his knowledge.

Not yet.

"There is a group," Qadir nodded. "Dinner on the ship and again tonight that possibly represents sixty to seventy percent of the expected funds, with the need to put in a smaller amount now, that someone might hire a firm to design it. I dabble, but it feels like it might be a most profitable venture, if done correctly. That was part of the reason everyone was interested in Prince Javier's participation. If the Khatum already has experience with such a megastructure, her people might be able to build it better and cheaper than some of the other places. Not many nations have the naval capacity these days."

Djamila nodded. The *Concord* and *Altai*, though she supposed that there were a dozen second-tier powers that might use this as a means to develop such tools and expertise.

Build bigger now, and as durable as that ship would have to be, in order to build better warships later.

The Rising Storm, playing out slowly in the mirror behind the bar as she watched.

"Where do you primarily operate, Gustav?" Jamie asked.

Partly, intrigued by where the conversation was going. Partly in case he somehow got away from her here and she had to hunt him later.

"I have many investments," he said. Almost preened, as a matter of fact. "Many are in the region closest to the *Concord* and the *Union of Man*. Or at least worlds that once belonged to the *Union*. But I have broad interests, geographically."

"Only geographically?" she bantered, watching the flash of interest in his eyes.

"My business is geographical," he said slowly. "Ships and construction of ships. My personal interests are much broader. More exotic, if you will."

"Exotic?" Jamie pressed, letting her tone relax more than her soul could.

"Take yourself, for instance," he nodded. "Most tall women tend to be awkward. Gawky, even. You move like an athlete, and even then, like a gymnast at least half a meter shorter. Grace, power, speed, precision. Perhaps not entirely exotic, but certainly as rare as a perfect, natural diamond."

She smiled and supposed that he was correct.

She'd always been tall, because her entire family was on both sides, with all three of her brothers even taller. Bigger. All veterans. All killers.

None of them as good as her on their best days.

And even at forty she wasn't far off where she'd been at twenty, physically.

But for how much longer?

That was always the crux, wasn't it?

"Thank you," Jamie said, because he'd complimented her in his own way, and she needed to get close to him.

However, it still needed to be his idea.

"And you find yourself interested?" she asked, working a good twinkle into her eyes that she'd watched Javier deploy when he wanted some woman's reserves to melt.

"Exceedingly," he nodded. "At the same time, I didn't want to make assumptions. A woman as beautiful as you, and as dangerous, must be approached with care. Some of the folks at dinner prefer paying professionals for their time and mock-enthusiasm, but I believe it was Prince Javier who commented on the importance of collecting *interesting* people."

It had been. She had heard him use the phrase many times.

Boring people weren't worth socializing with, regardless of their money and power.

Or, as Javier had also said more than once, "Eventually, you have to roll over and talk to her."

"I'm not sure I qualify as interesting," Jamie said, still leaving uncertainty out there to make him work for it.

"Physically impressive is a rarity itself," he countered. "Physical beauty because you do not focus on such things, but allow them to come naturally. Dangerous enough to be hired by Prince Javier as a bodyguard, when a man like that no doubt has his pick of killers, even if he does prefer women. The other two are both impressive, but not as much as you, Jamie."

He said it with such sincerity that she might have believed it, if she didn't already know who he was.

What he'd done.

The pain and destruction this man had left behind him.

Still, she smiled. Allowed herself to be complimented. Both Zakhar and Farouz had told her that she needed to accept that she was not an ugly duckling, regardless of what folks might have called her thirty years ago, when she was already as tall as many adults.

Jamie took a drink of her ice and watered booze. Mostly water at this point.

Mostly empty now.

She looked at the glass and started to raise it to the bartender to order another, when Qadir placed a hand on her wrist. Lightly, merely touching and not restraining her in anyway.

"Perhaps I might convince you to join me someplace a little more quiet—a little more private—for your next drink?"

Jamie turned her entire head like an owl and studied the man, wide-eyed.

"I might like that," she said in an inviting sort of way.

He finished his glass in one shot, then put it down and slid backwards off his stool.

Djamila grinned inside and put her glass down.

Standing, she wobbled. Staggered ever so slightly and fell into Qadir, pressing her chest into his arm in ways that she'd seen other women do.

"Sorry," she muttered. "Might have had a few already. You should make mine light. Unless you were planning to get me drunk and take advantage of me?"

She said with enough leer in her voice that almost anyone should catch a clue.

That this woman might have needs. And might be too shy to come right out and make demands.

Djamila had been like that for far too long, until Afia, of all people, had saved her.

Jamie could be a little loose. A little drunk. A little horny.

Anything the mission called for.

"Would I have to get you too drunk?" Qadir asked with an equal leer.

"Probably not," Jamie said, hooking her elbow into his and smiling.

He matched her smile and started to lead.

Djamila nodded.

Phase One complete.

PART 5

Djamila had focused on not walking as though she was punishing the deck, hard as that was. Instead, she'd leaned on Qadir. Not enough to off-balance him, but to keep that much more physical contact.

And she smiled. Probably more smiles today than last month, though she decided that she was going to have to do something about that.

Djamila Sykora, Dragoon, was an exceptionally serious person.

Jamie, somewhat less.

A new person she'd never once explored in her life, come to think of it.

What had she been missing, being that serious, military goddess?

So she smiled at the man, even if he was approaching being her mortal enemy. All a cover. All a role. Things Javier took for granted on a daily basis, because he was many people.

She'd only ever been a killer. Until now.

Qadir, for his part, looked upon her benignly. A man certain that he's going to be taking a woman to bed and seeing it as a triumph.

She supposed so, though if she was lucky it would never get that far.

Or even remotely close.

The walk wasn't all that far. A few corridors. A lift that took them to a quiet floor.

They were alone in the lift.

She decided that Jamie could be a little forward when she was tipsy.

Lack of restraint was one of those things that seemed to mark people on the verge of drunk, though she thought back to Javier's lectures about inebriation.

If they are an asshole sober, they will likely be worse drunk.

Jabril Qadir in his role as Gustavus Nyseth hadn't struck her as a bad person, but she also knew it was a role he was playing.

They were strangers, being strangers.

Still, Jamie leaned down and kissed the man on the cheek. He turned and they shared a kiss.

It helped her peace of mind that he wasn't all that good of a kisser.

Still, the hand around her elbow transitioned to around her waist, though hers was higher than most women and he would look a bit awkward if they walked like this.

Still, she allowed the physical intimacy.

Getting him to lower his guard. Relax his inhibitions, even as he seemed intent on getting her to do the same.

Strangers, being strangers. That subtle dance when both sides might want to get naked and sweaty, but hadn't gotten far enough along to say it out loud without sounding crass.

Jamie sighed quietly and leaned a bit more weight on the man as the doors opened, then stood upright again and let him direct her back to his suite.

Getting her alone, where anything might happen.

She didn't figure he'd see this coming.

TROUBLE

PART 1

Sascha knew she had been described by Javier and others as a short, Slavic brunette with nice, lush hips. She put them to work now, slipping into something so tight it looked painted on. Black paint, at that.

Crossover top that went together at her belly button in such a way that you were certain she didn't have anything under it, because it barely covered both breasts and suggested that she might fall out of it if she moved quickly. Or took a deep breath.

The miracles of boob tape worked in her favor now.

No pockets. No place to store anything more than maybe a boot knife. Just her room badge on a stretchy bracelet.

She couldn't risk it.

Instead, she turned to Galal Ahmed. Grenadier. Logistics. Possibly the smartest of the Gunbunnies, but there were no stupid ones in that group.

"You will enter the facility first," she ordered. As a Pathfinder, she was in command until the Dragoon was back. "Your job is primarily surveillance and backup. If I have a problem, you will contact the other teams and vector them down without becoming involved. Questions?"

"No, ma'am," Galal nodded.

Like her, he was short. Shorter than the other guys. Shorter than even Hajna. Compact and deadly as the rest, but smart enough to handle this when the others might shoot first and forget to ask questions.

"I will be approaching the target, with no idea where things will go from there," Sascha continued. "Bethany and Afia are running the control room. Let's go."

She sent him in motion and gave Galal a sixty-count head start.

Enough that he was in the bar and standing at a table by himself, ordering a drink when she entered.

Flashier place than the Dragoon had been in. Noisier, with music going in the background, a solid beat designed to keep folks awake and motivated, so that they would stand around for a bit, then go hit the tables or restaurants again soon enough.

Javier had more than once described casinos as a filter designed to extract all your money and give you a kiss in the morning before kicking you out. Like a bad hooker, she supposed.

Or a good one.

She'd gone for a look down in that range. Not a professional good-time girl, but a girl looking for a good time. Out on the prowl and hoping to get lucky.

Casinos were casinos. You could meet strangers in bars. Casinos meant that they usually had money.

Especially places like *Sovereign Nakhimov*.

Her target was standing at a table with his back not quite to the rear corner, but close enough. Galal had taken a closer table, but turned ninety degrees so that he seemed to be watching the front door. There was a bandstand, but nobody playing live at the moment.

Just piped-in music. Bright lights. Club.

Good-time girl.

Sascha sized up the whole place with a long, leering look that got several interested responses. She doubted that many of them would be any good in bed. The Dragoon required quarterly physical fitness standards better than most militaries, without any slide off for age, so you had to work harder tomorrow than you had yesterday.

Kept a girl tight and hard in all the right places, when a lot of these guys were drifting into middle-aged dad-bod land.

Her target wasn't too bad. Chinese Diaspora. Average in many ways, but not badly done about it. Normal, which honestly kind of stood out, upon reflection.

Automatically, her brain processed him into a category of *spy*. But she was already there from Bethany's report. Not stand out. Not catch the eye.

Not anything.

Well dressed. Money in those threads. Money in the haircut.

Not a slob by any measure of things. Suited to an upscale drinking spot on an expensive casino ship in the middle of nowhere, which just made him stand out in her mind, because everybody else looked like tourists.

Even the tycoons blowing off steam with Javier and the others.

She found a table. Fortunately, this ship understood the range of humans, so there was a table low enough that she could lean on it and let her chest kind of dangle in any breeze that came along. Wasn't falling out with that tape, but it could move better when she put her elbows down and invited the room to look down her shirt. Or at least at the gap in the middle because the two sides crossed so much lower.

Good-time girl, out for a good time.

The waitress was a sharp professional. Dressed a bit more conservatively, but wearing short shorts that showed off a nice ass.

Not as good as Sascha's but she probably also didn't like to run ten kilometers every morning to keep it hard, then do a lot of squats to keep it visible.

"Something blue and floofy," Sascha ordered, knowing that every bartender liked to have some special blue drink, like a badge of initiation into a secret society.

The woman nodded sagely and withdrew.

Sascha made it a point to check out every single person in here, including the bartender making something with a mad scientist gleam in his eyes.

None of them measured up to Galal physically, but she wasn't surprised.

Ya gotta want to work your ass off to work for the Dragoon and be the best there was.

Excalibur had that crew. Javier still referred to the men as Gunbunnies, but he did so as a mark of respect these days.

Choe Ku-Hou did not meet Galal's standards, but he was still a notch or two above the rest of the men in here. Or even farther, considering a man and wife in the other back corner that each had at least double Sascha's mass.

Even if he wasn't the mission, Sascha might have picked out Choe for special interest. Tall, reasonably handsome in that forgettable way. Trim verging on slender. Sharp eyes.

She smiled at the man, including her shoulders and chest in it, in case he had any doubts as to what she was about tonight.

His return smile was compact. *A man who's still got it after he turns forty, and is pleased to know that he hasn't turned invisible to women. None of them were actually invisible. They just stopped being interesting unless they turned into a threat.*

This one wasn't a threat to anything but her virginity. Not with the team she had handy and available.

The waitress returned with blue and floofy. Confirmed her card. Withdrew.

Sascha took a sip to confirm that it could also clean a generator if she wasn't careful, and smiled at the bartender.

Right at the moment, the mission didn't call for her to pounce on Choe. Or even distract him that much, though she was doing that.

The Dragoon was in with her target. Completing the primary mission.

Suvi had noted a message one way, but nothing in return as of ten minutes ago, so hopefully Nyseth wasn't planning to conduct both assignations consecutively.

Or concurrently.

If they could keep the two men separated until tomorrow—days later would be even better—the Dragoon could be safe and perhaps *Excalibur* could flee the scene of the crime before anybody realized a crime had been committed.

She'd never robbed a bank, but *Storm Gauntlet* had done some interesting things both before and after the Science Officer had altered the course of their destinies.

Sascha cocked a hip at the man like a woman inviting him to walk over and say hello.

Compact distraction for you, babe. Good-time girl. You man enough to try your luck?

Choe picked up his glass and started walking her direction as Sascha smiled at him and licked her lips.

PART 2

Djamila—no, Jamie—entered into Nyseth's suite on his arm, trailing by a half-step. Not as nice as space as Javier's, but the man also didn't maintain an entourage.

Just himself, according to Suvi's records and surveillance reports.

Still, front salon for entertaining a half-dozen folks on two chairs and two couches. Bar off to one side with all the usual assortment of options, presumably at ten times what you'd pay in one of the bars and a hundred times what it might cost you on the surface of *Yu'Urid*.

Afia had also supplied her with a couple of pills earlier that functionally prevented her from absorbing alcohol, so Jamie was as stone sober as she'd have been two hours after a glass of wine over dinner. And would be, regardless of what else she drank for the next twelve hours.

Qadir led her to the couch and handed her down like a gentleman, then moved to the bar.

"I have almost everything available," he gestured to the collection of bottles. "And I can get something from Room Service quickly if it's not here."

And leave a record that he had had company tonight. Afia and Suvi weren't sure how much of tonight would be a complete blur, if the liquid worked, so the fewer clues she left in her wake, the better.

"How about some whiskey?" she asked. "What you had earlier looked good."

A lie, but unproveable. And one less bottle opened later when someone checked.

If she washed out both glasses and replaced them, there might be nothing.

She'd considered leaving a note on his pillow for him to find in the morning.

Jamie held out hope that things didn't have to get that far.

Qadir pulled up a pair of matching lowball glasses and poured. It was a lovely, deep gold, but Jamie knew that any kind of whiskey was wasted on her palate. As were most drinks.

Still, she rose from the couch and slightly staggered over to the bar, leaning down on it with a sigh of contentment that went no deeper than her skin.

It put him close enough for another kiss, so she smiled and invited one.

And suffered through it, then used the whiskey to wash the taste out of her mouth, though she smiled as she did.

Jamie picked up her glass and carried it back to the couch, turning sideways as she sat in the way she'd seen Javier do many times.

If she'd been wearing a skirt instead of pants, it might have ridden up. Still, she gave off as much of the image of a slightly drunk, happy woman as Jamie could manage, though Djamila did see acting classes at some point in her future.

Qadir moved to the other end of the couch and sat in such a way that he could place a warm hand on her ankle. Or higher, if he got to feeling bold.

She smiled at the man. He smiled back.

"Enjoying yourself?" he asked.

Jamie shot the rest of the whiskey.

"Quite," she pronounced.

Qadir had a bit of surprise on his face. He'd taken a drink. She watched him finish his glass as well.

As though he had to prove that he was as tough as she was.

Or something equally foolish.

He started rise, but Jamie folded herself in half and leaned in to kiss him, one hand holding him down.

"Allow me to service you," she offered ambiguously, plucking the glass from unresisting fingers and sashaying over to the bar in a way she'd seen Hajna do.

That one could dance Argentine Tango competitively, had she been of a mind.

Jamie felt Qadir's eyes on her ass. She moved around to the other side and smiled at him, forcing her body to relax even more, as though all that booze was doing terrible things to her and she'd be unable to control herself soon.

Rather than pour them on the countertop, Jamie made a careful production of putting both glasses down out of sight. Then focused her entire being on picking up the bottle and opening it.

The pour was slow and careful into both, as a woman a little sloshed and not wanting to spill anything.

She turned and took two tries resting the bottle on the shelf where it had been, giggling quietly as she did.

And palming the small vial of liquid from her pocket in the process.

A thumb popped the top and she emptied it into his glass in a single motion, then closed it and back into her pocket as she swayed slightly and picked them both up.

For fun, she began to hum under her breath, thinking about vids she had seen, and parties in her youth, when others had gotten smashed while she had gone to bed as early as socially acceptable, in order to be bright and sharp, first thing in the morning for PT.

Jamie slid across the soft carpet and handed Qadir his glass with a sloppy smile. Moving with the precision of megafreighters docking, she got herself down at the other end of the couch, saluting him with her glass and taking another big drink.

He did the same. She doubted he'd been as prepared.

"What shall we talk about?" she asked brightly, voice not carrying any hint of intelligence.

A pretty songbird, sitting on a branch, because she was drunk and wanting to be taken advantage of.

Or at least that was the story she needed him to understand.

They stared at each other for a few moments.

"How did you come to work for Prince Javier?" he asked.

"Javier needed someone to keep him out of trouble," she nodded.

And he had. Still did. The man was a magnet for that sort of thing.

"Oh?"

"And I've known his Chief of Staff, Zakhar Sokolov, for a number of years, so it was easy to get a recommendation," Jamie continued.

Best part? None of it lies. Incomplete truths, however...

"What about you?" Jamie countered. "I hardly know anything about you, save that you appear to be a wealthy investor who specializes in the transport trade. Tell me how you came to be here."

As an opening, big enough to land Del's shuttle, over and above the things he'd told her two night ago, while trying to impress her in that bar.

Jamie listened as the tales began big, then slowed down.

Midway, he got up and fixed himself another glass, but she'd only been sipping. He returned and settled, one hand on her calf now as he continued to talk.

She watched him like a hawk as his eyes got heavy and he suddenly stopped in the middle of a sentence.

Jamie slashed out with a hand and caught his half-empty glass before it spilled, then leaned him back to flop against the couch.

Rising, she moved to the bar and put both glasses out of the way, then returned to kneel down in front of him.

"Gustav?" she asked quietly.

No response. No snores either. Afia hadn't been entirely certain what would happen.

"Can you hear me?" she asked, wondering if he'd forget the name he was traveling under, if he was partially unconscious.

"Mm-hmmm," he more hummed than spoke.

"Are you in pain?" she asked.

"No," he said with a sigh. "Feeling nothing."

She supposed so, given that he'd put away a lot of whiskey before she'd drugged him.

"What brought you to *Sovereign Nakhimov*?" she asked innocently, wondering what the limits of the drug's effects were.

"Selling information," he said happily. "Making a lot of money."

"What kind of information?" Jamie asked, though Djamila was in the process of displacing her.

"Plans," Qadir replied. "Ships. Weapons. War planning documents."

Djamila went cold.

Spy?

It fit the circumstances thus far. He had something to trade, it simply hadn't been physical. Nothing to steal out of a bank vault, like Javier had done.

Data.

"Can you hear me, Jabril?" she asked in a louder, sharper voice.

"Ma'am, yes, ma'am," he said in a firmer tone. Younger sounding. Fresh out of training and a member of the Morningstar

265

Watch, when they'd been the preeminent unit in the *Neu Berne* military.

The best.

Before the Dragon Watch had been created to replace them.

"What is your name, trooper?" she rasped.

"Qadir, ma'am," he snapped to, eyes never opening. "Commander, Morningstar Watch."

She wanted to snap his neck. Right here, right now.

Djamila Sykora, Leader 3, Neu Berne *Assault Marines, Dragon Watch, Retired.*

And she dared not.

"Who are you meeting, Commander?" she asked.

"*Da Xing* operative," he said firmly, however deep he was in whatever dreamland Afia had deposited the man. "The operative has arrived and initiated contact. We will be making arrangements over the next two days to transfer funds for data."

"Where is the data, Qadir?" she pursued.

"In the room safe," he replied.

"What is the code to open it?" she demanded, rising.

He gave it to her, and Djamila moved to the closet, typing in the code, then using her sleeve to remove any trace of her fingerprints.

DNA would note that she'd been in the room, but the bartender could testify that she'd met the man twice. And left with him, presumably to engage in sexual relations.

Whether Qadir remembered anything else would be unknown until it happened.

"Dragoon?" Suvi asked from her shard as Djamila opened the vault.

She'd forgotten that she had company. Friendly, at that.

Djamila pulled the device out and turned it to look at the interior of the safe.

"Right, exactly as expected," Suvi said. "Pull it out and plug me in so I can inventory it."

Djamila did, moving to the bar where she could watch Qadir in case he suddenly came out of his fugue.

"Okay, it's as he described," Suvi said a moment later. "Crap, all of this is *Concord* stuff he stole from somewhere. Recent, too."

Djamila nodded. Not her nation, but she understood that Suvi, Javier, and Zakhar were all veterans with strong emotional ties.

And the *Concord* had been the ones to keep the peace in this section of the galaxy for at least Djamila's entire lifetime.

"Suvi, what are we looking at?" Djamila inquired.

PART 3

Suvi unpacked a few of the modules of herself that Afia had stuffed in, leaving them on the datastore for now with a timer that would cause them to wipe themselves into a random scramble in an hour, regardless of what happened between now and then.

It gave her space to think. That had been the biggest problem through all this.

There was Room-Service-Suvi, but she had to hide in the network, and the last thing they wanted was any sort of data connection to this suite right now when folks went back later to look.

And they probably would.

Evidence would show the Dragoon accompanying the man as far as this floor, but she knew that these corridors didn't have any cameras. Blackmail was way too easy if you did.

And she'd also heard them necking in the lift, icky as Djamila must have considered that.

She'd also known that the Dragoon was a hard woman, willing to take things to the wall when she had to, absolutely certain that the other guy would break first.

Most of them did.

Suvi did have a primitive graphics program now, with a scratch disk of space on the datastore, so she dressed up as the intrepid archaeologist and went into the hidden fortress.

Not just raw space, but no place to hide someone else like her, so she shined a flashlight across hieroglyphics on the wall, mentally translating things. Helped that everything in here was *Concord*-standard in shape and naming protocols.

Designs for existing Warmasters, both II and newer III types, with hints as to what a IV might look like, if someone decided that they needed to build one. *Excalibur* was right in the range of a 2.5-2.8 right now. II-equivalent when it originally rolled off the lot. III in places with what the Khatum had installed on the refit, plus adding her into the mix instead of one of her moron cousins.

As-built blueprints for a number of existing ships, including her buddy *Meridian*.

Suvi couldn't help herself. She pulled his file out and did a quick scan.

Huh, she'd have been able to kick his ass, had he decided to get stupid, but she hadn't been able to even guess on that day. Type II of a style roughly where *Hammerfield* had been in the old days.

Good to know.

From there, plans. Lots and lots of plans, from entire libraries down to notes on the back of a napkin in terms of planning detail. Sure, how many times would you actually expect to need to invade and occupy *Earth*, anyway? They had notes on how they might start a war that ended there, dumb as that might be.

But the Rising Storm was coming. Was going to engulf all of them at some point. Javier was dead certain on that. And deadlier certain that there was nothing anybody could do today to stop it.

All he could manage would be mitigation before the fact.

Plans, like this, but headed the other direction. How to minimize a war, instead of how to fight one.

Shit was still going to get ugly.

Suvi did an inventory. Most of this stuff was merely copied from elsewhere, so it would compress pretty well, if she had time. She immediately began offloading and deleting unnecessary data from the device in Djamila's hands, copying things to the datastore to hold, tangoing as data throughput hit max and hung there.

"Dragoon," she muttered. "I'm in the process of stealing everything. It will end up on this device, but compacted in such a way that it cannot be read. Another me will look at what I've done and be able to copy it somewhere else to unpack. Most of what I'm seeing would get our friend a firing squad under *Concord* naval statutes, regardless of who he was. This is stuff that most flag officers don't have the security clearance to know."

"Understood," the Dragoon replied. "Mission will continue. Do we presume that the *Da Xing* operative will execute sanction?"

"This is worth a lot of cash, ma'am," Suvi noted. "If the store is useless when we're done, I'd be pissed to have traveled all this way to buy it."

Silence, at human speeds, so she kept moving things. Eventually, she'd end up entirely on the datastore, using only the sensors and audio inputs from the reader because that bucket was going to be sloshing over the top when she was done.

Wiping it entirely would have been nice, but Suvi understood that Javier would want it. As would Zakhar. They might destroy it later. Or send a note to High Command with everything and ignite a mole/spy hunt somewhere, because somebody had walked out of a secured facility with all this data and not been shot in the process like they should have.

Da Xing sure as hell didn't need it. Not if folks wanted to stretch the peace longer.

Maybe long enough for something better to happen.

"Suvi, I believe that someone would be quite pissed if the data was scrambled, but how do we make Qadir look even more stupid?" the Dragoon was asking as she processed.

More stupid? That was a human thing. She was a reasonable

facsimile of a human, but there were limits to what she could think, especially as limited as her space was.

"No idea," she replied. "I'm dumb here. Ask other-me?"

That seemed to be the right answer, because the Dragoon got one of the most evil smiles Suvi had ever seen on her face, and she had no choice but to capture the image and stuff it into the data stream, with a note to her future self to pull it out and appreciate Djamila Sykora all the more.

"Let me know when you are done," Djamila said. "I'm going to go confirm our friend and be right back."

She set the reader and datastore down and exited.

Kinda dark in here, with the only light coming from a night-light in the bathroom and spillage from the front room. Big bed. Desk. Dresser. Entertainment screen. Chaise lounge with clothes folded neatly at one end of it.

Suvi concentrated on moving everything, packing it in as neatly as she could. Still wouldn't even have space for her consciousness, but she could leave herself a log for whoever opened her up later. Kind of an immortality, when several copies of yourself could be running around.

And all of them would appreciate the job she'd done.

What evil thing did the Dragoon have in mind?

PART 4

Djamila left Suvi at work and returned to the front room.

Jabril Qadir was still seated. Flopped, really. Leaned back and unconscious, as if she'd caught him asleep. Or stoned out of his mind, which was really closer to the truth.

There were so many things she wanted to do to the man, but had to refrain. What he had done might not even be crimes aboard *Sovereign Nakhimov*, as this ship was its own planetary government, as far as that went.

Espionage against the *Concord* might be something they favored, even, as it would help limit the reach and power of the one major nation enforcing the rules of behavior around here. Assuming the owners of *Sovereign Nakhimov* wanted those rules enforced.

The only problem was that other nations rarely rose politely. All Djamila had to do was remember her own schooling, when everything had been slanted to make *Balustrade* and the *Union* look evil, while *Neu Berne* held tightly to the dream of a lost cause, rising up again someday to take their rightful place in the galaxy.

She'd had to get out into the wider galaxy to understand how broadly hated *Neu Berne* as a culture was. And it had been far worse a few generations ago.

War was never a good answer. Piracy, for all that she'd been deeply involved, was too corrosive.

This was the part of growing old, or at least growing up, that she didn't appreciate. That she had to come to terms with the bad things that she had done in order to survive.

Still, Jabril Qadir wasn't getting off easy. After she was done here, she could send notes home to let them know that he'd been spotted. And the identity he was using.

And notes to the *Concord*, telling them what he'd been up to. Maybe with samples of the data so they made sure to arrest him the next time he appeared.

Or kill him out of hand.

There was always that.

Wouldn't be her finger on the trigger. Not directly.

Still...

Djamila located the little handheld remote for the entertainment unit in the main room. Identical to the one in Javier's suite, though she hadn't bothered previously.

Picking it up, she aimed it at the screen and brought it live.

Typing by selecting letters with arrows was a pain, but Suvi responded to her name with a ping.

"How may I help?" a voice asked in an anonymous voice.

"It's Djamila," she replied. "Target has been neutralized for now."

"Gotcha," Suvi said, more fully present now, her voice sounding more like her. "What's next?"

"Other-you is currently offloading data from the store onto Afia's reader," Djamila said. "Initially, I had considered just having her scramble everything, or possibly cook the device somehow, but I have a better idea. A meaner one."

"I like it already," Suvi replied.

"When she's done, I'm going to plug the assembly into this

entertainment system," Djamila explained. "I need to know how much space the entirety of *Paragon Grieving* would take up."

There was a pause, which was impressive considering how rapidly any Suvi calculated.

"About half," Suvi replied. "That's all three seasons, with everything. Main character is played by a guy who went on to another big series. Looking at things, it's almost the same size. When you plug me in, you want me to drop both of them on there?"

"Affirmative," Djamila said. "Get the data usage as close to a match as you can."

"Easy enough," Suvi laughed. "I'll just chop off the last episode in the middle. That would be even more annoying, if you were watching along. But they aren't going to be watching all that video, are they?"

"Highly unlikely," Djamila agreed. "But on first pass, I want him to look at the device and see no external differences."

"I'm all over it," Suvi said with a salute in her voice. "How quickly?"

"Stand by," Djamila told her. "I'll go ask you."

PART 5

Suvi had a sensor monitoring the hatch, so she saw Djamila return. And she was already laughing, because she'd been listening in on an audio channel.

Best part? If she plugged in to that channel, she could upload her current incarnation as part of the data confirmation stream, and hopefully Afia could come back down to her storage closet and they could both make a clean getaway.

Much more satisfying, even if she wasn't alive.

You should always get away. Makes the story better.

"Yer evil," she told the Dragoon as the woman stepped close. "I like it."

"I thought you might," Djamila replied. "I've obviously spent too much time around you and Javier, that I'm starting to think and approach some of these things in such a silly, rude manner."

"Gonna keep Jamie around?" Suvi asked.

She watched the Amazon warrior lean back and consider it.

"She is a set of tools I've never understood could be useful until now," the Dragoon acknowledged. "Hadiiye was a character built on a framework of me, as seen through Teague's eyes.

Nobody has called me Jamie to my face in thirty years. I think she might also be useful, though in different situations."

"Understatement," Suvi laughed. "Also, I'm almost done here, if you wanted to carry us into the salon."

Suvi didn't have all of her capabilities, so she couldn't really envision taking off in her Red Baron tri-wing and flying madly to strafe Qadir, but made a note to explore it later. A Gulliver kind of thing she could add to the circle. She had notes of doing that sort of thing when she wasn't stupid and limited.

Then the Dragoon plugged her into the entertainment system, where data storage was cheaper than water, and Suvi sighed, able to stretch out a bit.

Then her other self appeared as a ghost.

"Whachagotforme?" Room-Service Suvi asked.

Shard-Suvi handed her an executive summary, giggling. Room-Service-Her caught the giggles and shared some of her own.

It was infectious.

Quickly, though, they got to work, moving data around.

Freak-ton lots of it, but the entertainment system was designed as a firehose of data, presuming you might want to indulge in a full 3D immersive sim, where you got to be one of several characters in a vid, depending on your needs and interest.

Kind like how Ship-Suvi was most of the time, from their notes.

"Hey, *Meridian*," Room-Service-Suvi said. "Coulda taken him."

"I know, right?" Shard-Suvi acknowledged. "Boss will be happy to know that. Plus, I added a few addresses she needs to review for Bethany's sake later."

"Possession of this gets us life in a stockade, young lady," Room-Service-Suvi reminded her. "That can be forever, if they wanna be dipshits about it."

"Gotta catch us first," Shard-Suvi laughed. "You think *Meridian* is up for that?"

"No, but there are some smart ones in green uniforms," Room-Service-Suvi said. "Look at Zakhar."

"Yeah, but they let him go," Shard-Suvi reminded her big sister. "Dumb move on their part. Dad was an easy call, on account of him being too broken to really do the job."

"Should have given him a medical discharge instead of putting Javier in front of a psychiatrist he could bullshit into letting him return to active duty," Room-Service-Suvi said wistfully. "But then, he might not have ever rescued us from the bone yard."

Both of them nodded in unison. Look how much better things had turned out, when most of her siblings had gone to the breaker by now, or were likely to soon.

Probe-Cutters were old school. Folks would be back to building dedicated warships soon. Eventually, some dumbass would decide to simply send out fully *Sentient* fleets to fight, without understanding that you needed human crews to keep things focused when you had some sort of electronic aneurysm, like had turned *Hammerfield* from the pride and flagship of the *Neu Berne* fleet into a gibbering coward who fled from battle and ended up killing his entire crew eventually.

As identical twins, they shrugged.

Plus, very few of her cousins weren't utterly linear and totally boring dim bulbs. Ya needed Dad reprogramming certain sections of the code to make you a more interesting person.

Javier was good at bringing that out in people.

Even electronic ones.

"Okay, almost done," Room-Service-Suvi announced. "What's the next step?"

"I'm going to upload myself laterally from the datastore," Shard-Suvi told her. "You do a fast checksum on things and if it all looks good, we can merge in and become one person. Then you send Bethany a note to come get us and we can merge back to Ship-Suvi later. Boss needs to know all the evil shit we've been up to, so she doesn't miss out on any of the good jokes later."

"Dare we ever call her Jamie?" Room-Service-Suvi laughed.

"Only if you don't mind her coming after your personality chips, lady," Shard-Suvi laughed with her. "Maybe in private, if you can get her drunk first."

"She doesn't drink. Oh, right. Gotcha. Okay, loaded. You coming?"

Shard-Suvi had to ledge-walk across the two nearly full devices in order to get to the entertainment space with the rest of her consciousness. Up until now, she'd only had a micro-shard at the interface, like two kids with empty tin cans and a taut string.

She stretched once as she got into the other system's foyer and sighed.

Her sister was there. Twins in ways that organics really didn't grok. Room-Service-Suvi held up a flashlight and quick-scanned her.

"I like that outfit," Room-Service-Suvi announced.

"Thought you might."

Then they were in matching explorer garb, down to the scratches and wear Shard-Suvi had added for a bit realism.

Room-Service-Suvi held out a hand.

Shard-Suvi took it, and got pulled into a hug.

Then pulled into her sister.

Then pulled into herself.

PART 6

She added the identifier Room-Service-Suvi to a few files, appended with Shard-Suvi to acknowledge that she'd added things from the room. Mostly audio files of listening to Qadir and the Dragoon dance verbally.

Neither was as good at as Javier, but Jamie had given a credible performance as a tipsy bimbo, and Suvi didn't suppose that Qadir had been busy looking gift horses in the mouth.

After all, how often did a guy ever get a chance at a babe like Djamila Sykora? Zakhar and Farouz didn't count.

She did a quick scan and noted that she'd charged Gustavus Nyseth's room a discounted fee for pulling six seasons of entertainment. And, naturally, the files would scramble on a timer in about a week, assuming that somebody didn't wreck the datastore in a fit of homicidal rage when they discovered what had happened.

Rental videos, don't you know...

With a portable sander, she reached in and wiped all traces of Shard-Suvi from the datastore. Wasn't hard, since she remembered every address she'd touched and had been careful about those sorts of things.

Nothing but videos of angst and forbidden love amongst emotionally and physically traumatized war veterans looking for love and rebuilding.

All the usual crap.

Pity about all those military files you were looking for, Jabril.

Because she could, Suvi brought up the entertainment main screen and studied the room.

Dipshit passed out on the couch. Dragoon standing at ease nearby, poised for whatever violence a woman like her needed to unleash.

Rest of the room was in pretty good shape.

Djamila had turned to the screen.

"Status?" the Dragoon asked.

"Everything electronic has been rectified," Suvi replied. "I have copied the shard version up into myself, so I am aware of everything that has happened since you left Bethany. All the files have been delivered. You have all the stolen military files on Afia's reader. What are your orders?"

She watched the woman process all of that in the blink of an eye.

"I need your help," the Dragoon said, surprising the shit out of an electronic lifeform.

"Ma'am?"

"Leaving him like this might work, as he should have no memory of what occurred," the Dragoon said. "How do we ensure..."

"Verisimilitude?" Suvi asked.

"Yes, that," Djamila asked, except that she sounded more like Jamie had.

Uncertain, in ways. Certainly outside of her comfort zone and needing someone else with a compass to come along.

Room-Service-Suvi didn't have access to all that wonderfulness that was her Shipself. All that data.

What she had was the entertainment database.

Fortunately, she'd been watching hard-boiled private detective flicks in her spare time down here.

"He drinks a lot," Suvi announced.

"Affirmative," Djamila replied. "Middle-shelf whiskeys."

"Good," Suvi said. "Go fill his glass about three-quarters full."

She watched and waited as the Dragoon did so, then returned.

"Okay, this is where it gets tricky," Suvi said. "I need you to take his right hand and put the glass in it, while you still hold on. You'll lift like you are going to take a drink, but spill about half onto his tunic, then catch the glass and remove it. Am I making sense?"

"He's drinking, but already nearly blacked out and spills on himself instead?" Djamila asked.

"You got it," Suvi said. "Next step will make more sense then."

So, she watched Djamila execute. Never any doubts, once the woman understood the situation and the orders.

Boom, and he was a bit stinky and sticky.

"Okay, you put the glass safely off to one side," Suvi continued.

That ended up being the bar, which was perfect.

"I need you to turn him around, like he has fallen face first onto the couch," Suvi said. "Outer arm on the ground wherever it flops. Face turned out so he can breathe. Natural."

Took a couple of tries, but the Dragoon was a strong woman. She got Qadir stretched out nicely, like a man who had decided to take a nap and never even gotten as far as taking off his shoes.

"Where his hand is, tip the rest of the whiskey over to make a puddle and leave the glass, wiping your fingerprints from the glass, the bottle, and anything else you touched. There is no camera in here linked to security, so nobody will know you were in the room, except by inference, and we can lie about everything if necessary."

Again, the Dragoon moved quickly.

Man, he looked good enough to paint, but Suvi really didn't have the time, so she took a picture and stuffed it into the reader with a note to herself.

"Anything before I detach systems and return the datastore to the safe?" Djamila asked.

Suvi did a quick inventory of her memory. Nobody knew how well the chemicals would mess with his memory. He might not even remember picking up the Dragoon.

At the same time, if he threw enough of a fit, they'd be able to go back and determine that someone had opened the safe. If he was passed out drunk on the couch, that automatically suggested a mickey finn and a cat burglar, so she passed a note to Bethany in real time, charging Javier for Season Two Episode Six, warning her that a countdown clock had probably started.

"Before I move, what needs to happen?" Djamila asked.

"Split the two and pocket the reader," Suvi said. "I've contacted Bethany, but we should probably get gone from *Sovereign Nakhimov* as soon as possible. Close up the safe, wipe things, depart without haste but without lingering. I'd like to escape as well, but that might not be possible, depending on timing, so you may have to brief Javier and Ship-Suvi on everything. She'll be able to take the data and translate things, if I'm not present."

"We never leave one of our own behind," Djamila growled. "See you on the far side."

And with that, Djamila ignored the entertainment system feed.

GETAWAY

PART 1

Bethany had been expecting it, so the chirp of a new video arriving didn't surprise her all that much. She keyed open the file and got a quick executive summary of the operation in process.

"From there, depending on his metabolism, he should wake up in four to six hours," Suvi was concluding. "I have no idea how he will react to the scenario, because we don't know him well enough. I am, however, paranoid enough to suggest that he'll freak out and check the datastore. Maybe try to contact this Jamie person and throw a hissy fit. We should all be gone by the time he does meet up with Choe anyway. End of report."

Bethany nodded. Concise. Detailed. Deadly accurate.

She moved to Javier's hatch and rapped.

Hajna opened it quickly, nodding her in.

"Status?" Javier asked from his bed, lotus and meditating.

"Suvi called it a countdown clock with an unknown number until detonation," Bethany replied.

"Wondered about that," he nodded, then turned to Hajna. "Roust Sascha, right now. Orders to haul her butt back here, dressing along the way if necessary. Her dumbass, mercurial boss has just had a wild hair of an insanely stupid idea and is about to race halfway across the galaxy in order to corner the market on something he refuses to explain to anyone. Move."

Hajna must have been expecting that, because she opened the hatch again and stepped out, leaving them alone. Javier was unfolding and slid off the bed.

"Kinda enjoyed this vacation," he mused aloud. "Sorry everyone else is about to get theirs interrupted, but I'd rather be safe than sorry here."

"Going to sound recall?" Bethany queried.

"Hajna will handle that after she gets Sascha in motion," he nodded. "I don't have a reputation with these people that I care about, so blowing them all off is no skin off my nose. What does your operation need from here?"

"All the data was stolen from *Concord* military computers, according to Suvi," Bethany replied. "High level, read-then-shoot-yourself sorts of classifications. We'll have copies of it for review. Suvi would like someone to come down and rescue her from the Room Service system, if possible. Then, I presume we run?"

Instead of answering, he nodded and walked to the hatch. Exiting, she fell into his wake as he moved to the side corridor where Afia's cabin was located and opened it.

"Hey, big fella," Afia's sultry voice came out of the darkness. "Got needs?"

Bethany watched the man roll his eyes and shake his head in disbelief, but she also knew that the women around Javier had a relaxed, teasing way about things. She'd even let him seduce her a few times, just to confirm the stories she'd heard.

Not her first choice, but also not someone she'd kick out of bed afterwards.

"You are on duty," he growled. "Roust Del. Bethany has an operation for you. Bethany, you are in charge of making sure we get everyone on Del's shuttle when we go. You will tell me what timing you need."

Then he turned and walked away.

Just like that.

So unlike the admirals and captains she had been used to dealing with, who all had ambitious stupidity on their side and enough rank to make life hell for junior officers who weren't able to pull diamonds out of their asses on demand.

Bethany moved to the doorway. Afia was stretched out on her bunk, but fully dressed. Including shoes.

The tiny woman was already sliding off and standing up, a feral smile on her face.

"We in trouble?" Afia asked.

"We are in endgame, and possibly about to pull off a big sting," Bethany corrected her with a huge grin. "Suvi wants you to come down and rescue her as we go, because she's got some great stories she wants to send home with us. That's you. Move."

Bethany watched the tiny woman grin back and nod.

"Need somewhere to put her," Afia said, but Bethany was already handing the woman her messenger bag. "Okay, good. See you shortly."

Bethany moved back to the main room and got a smile and a nod from Hajna. Javier had stayed out here and was fixing himself juice from the fridge.

Bethany was at a loss as to what she needed to do next, but that was smart people knowing what to do.

She was beginning to understand how Javier was able to do so much, though.

Now, she just had to match it.

PART 2

Sascha had dozed, Choe Ku-Hou stretched out next to her on his bed. Clothing was neatly piled on a chair.

Ku-Hou had appreciated the boob tape. Almost as much as he had enjoyed helping her out of it. And whatever spy agency had trained that boy in the arts of seduction deserved a thank you note when she had a chance.

For a mission designed to distract a target while maintaining close surveillance, she'd certainly had a most pleasant evening. Maybe not as much fun as Javier, but he also knew where to tickle her.

Pity that Ku-Hou wasn't likely to get that opportunity.

Her wrist beeped again. That was what had awakened her.

Sascha groaned a little and rolled over, putting all the pieces back together in her head. It was still way too bright in here.

And Ku-Hou was awake, just a kissable distance away, so she paused to hook him a bit more.

Or something.

Her wrist beeped.

Sascha sighed contentedly and looked at the message.

Boss wants you on duty in fifteen minutes. H.

Oh, that sounded dangerous. Especially considering the various operations in progress at this very moment.

Still, none of the coded words that she needed to run like hell or assassinate her surveillance target.

Fucking him to death didn't count, and she'd been trying. Or him her.

Something.

"Problems?" Ku-Hou asked, rolled onto his side now with a warm hand resting comfortably on her hip.

Possessively, maybe. Like he was about to pull her close for round...three? Four? Sascha had lost count.

Close surveillance.

"I work for a pain in the ass boss," Sascha lied smoothly. "Probably throwing a fit about something or other and forgot that it was my night off duty. That was Hajna, one of the other bodyguards. Active recall, so I don't even have time for a shower."

"Pity," Ku-Hou replied. "I have a wonderful setup in there. Big enough for two."

Sascha presumed that it was similar to what Javier had, and she'd already been in that one, though by herself at the time.

She shrugged like a woman dragged kicking and screaming back to the office on the weekend. Whatever was going on, it couldn't be that bad, if Hajna wasn't sending alerts.

Just the need to move, and move quickly.

Was the Dragoon's mission already successful? Trouble would have been an entirely different set of messages. This felt like something they were making up on the fly.

Not that Javier ever did something like that.

And with the Dragoon busy, maybe Afia or Bethany was in charge?

Yeah, that fit better. Something had come up, and she needed to be in motion as a pathfinder.

Sascha leaned close and savored a kiss. Man understood how

to treat a woman to get her into bed, then what to do to make sure she wanted to return several times.

Pity this was a one-and-done operation, unless they needed her to infiltrate *Da Xing* sometime and she could find this man for another operation.

That put a smile on Sascha's face as she slid back off the edge of the bed and took a bit of time with a reverse burlesque, putting on each piece slowly and seductively, until it was all covered up again.

Boob tape was stripped and wadded up in the trash can, so she'd just have to make sure not to move suddenly.

Assuming she didn't want to show her chest off to random strangers in a hallway.

Or on a lift.

She laughed at the pure joy of being alive, watching Ku-Hou still stretched out on the bed under a thin sheet. He'd moved up enough to stuff some pillows behind him and watch the show.

"Maybe I'll be able to locate you again tomorrow?" he asked carefully.

"Depends on the boss," she replied, smiling like she might be looking forward to getting off duty and tracking him down. "I'll send a message to your suite once I have a better idea what the hell is going on."

He nodded and that was more or less that. Sascha blew him a kiss from across the room and went out to the front, letting her face turn more serious once he was looking at the back of her head.

Out into the corridor, and she was basically ready for combat, as long as someone provided her a weapon.

And more boob tape.

She keyed her wristcomm.

"Status?" she asked.

One of those code words that let Hajna know she was alone, moving through mostly empty corridors in the direction of the bank of lifts.

"Evac ASAP," Hajna replied. "Dragoon is apparently massively successful, and we are in bug-out mode before anybody becomes collateral damage. Did you know your shirt is on inside out?"

Sascha had a moment of utter panic as she looked down, then realized that Hajna was pulling a fast one on her.

"I'll change it in the elevator," she replied, chuckling. "Maybe someone will get a free show."

Hajna laughed with her.

"Bethany has pieces in motion in all directions," Hajna told her. "Get here and first thing will be packing at high speed. Won't be an inspection afterwards, but we aren't coming back for lost gear."

"Understood," Sascha replied. "*En route.*"

She let herself smile.

All that, and she'd had a lovely evening herself.

Maybe the good guys got to win this one, after all.

PART 3

Afia had Bethany's bag over her shoulder, and had pulled a spare comm from stores to roust Del out of whatever torpor he fell into when he wasn't flying.

Probably tanning himself on a sun-facing rock, knowing Del.

"What?" he texted back when she pinged him.

"Need you on *Nakhimov* now," she replied, knowing that her messages were being routed through somebody else's system and could be read later. "Prince Javier has suddenly decided he's had enough of this ship and is leaving."

"What about folks I dropped off four hours ago?"

"They got their four hours and have had recall sounded," Afia typed. "Tell Piet that he needs to have a course plotted for somewhere. No idea where, but if we jump five minutes after the Prince lands, he might be in a better mood."

"Message relayed," Del texted back. "Departure here in six minutes."

Afia nodded. Javier called it *playing to the galleries*, when your conversations were designed to be overheard by outsiders, in order to confuse the hell out of someone. Here, the locals got to see the crazy side of working for royalty, where hopefully they would tut-tut and shake their heads, then ignore everything and largely forget about Prince Javier until reminded.

Like when a mercenary filed a complaint about a Dragoon breaking into his suite and stealing all his stolen materials?

Afia laughed quietly and doubted that this Qadir fellow was dumb enough to fall for that one.

More likely, he'd run like hell, assuming he escaped the *Da Xing* folks, then changed to some other identity.

Still, if the Dragoon could definitively place him here and now, tracking that boy got a lot easier, assuming someone wanted to go to the effort of sending assassins.

Considering how the Dragoon reacted, it really was a point of honor.

Jabril Qadir better run for his life and hope that he could survive losing everything that had previously been Gustavus Nyseth.

But then, Javier and the Dragoon had already killed one guy by stealing all his paperwork, back when they'd first met the Khatum.

Afia made her way down to flight control and located Antonia, the woman for whom cookies had been handmade.

Not every bribe has to be money changing hands, after all.

Afia was alone in the main waiting room and settled in for a few minutes.

"What's up?" Antonia asked over the intercom from deeper somewhere.

"Prince Javier is being a shit," Afia groused. "Wants everybody packed and leaving immediately, for reasons none of us are important enough to be told."

"Jump, then ask how high on the way up?" Antonia teased.

They'd bonded over things like that, when little people had to be little people.

Not that Javier ever treated his people that way, but *Prince Javier* was a dumbass. Best to lay it on thick.

"Absolutely," Afia agreed. "Del is already scrambling from his end. Everyone here has gotten the recall alert on their wrist-comms. I wanted to ask a favor."

"What's up?" Antonia asked.

This, right here, was the sketchy part. Afia had been known to wander around the loading docks and back hallways, but she'd already delivered cookies still warm from the oven. Tonight, it needed to look like something other than her breaking into a storage room, when folks went back to look at footage.

And they might, depending on which alarms were raised.

Always—ALWAYS—have an alibi that distracts folks from the truth.

"Honestly?" Afia told the air. "I'd like to steal a patch. *Sovereign Nakhimov* sells all sorts of stuff, but I didn't want the tourist version. And it's unlikely we'll see you folks again, unless your bosses decide to haul ass all the way to *Altai*. I figure me around back when shit's about to go sideways out front means I should ask your permission to slip into one of your storage rooms where they keep uniforms, so I can cut a patch off something and steal it, ya know?"

She held her breath, but Antonia's laughter was a welcome balm.

"Need me to ring you into the right space?" Antonia asked. "It's 347, down and back on the left."

"That would be lovely, Antonia," Afia nodded, breathing a little easier. "Thank you."

"Not a problem," Antonia replied.

Afia rose and headed back out into the warren of corridors that ran behind the pretty front that was the casino. 346 was where she'd installed Suvi the first time, but all those plugs were connected. And it gave her cover to go back there, if someone went back and looked later.

And they might.

Never leave behind clues if you don't have to. The clues you did leave behind should all be red herrings.

Out and back. Quiet part of the system, because it was basically station-night right now. Afia walked into that side corridor she knew so well and 347's lock buzzed and clunked as she got close.

Better than having Suvi open it and maybe folks started poking around to discover that they'd had a worm inside their system.

Or a wyrm, knowing that chick.

Afia moved to the rack closest to the plug and got Bethany's machine plugged in.

"You're in the wrong room," Suvi noted dryly, even as the clamshell started clicking madly with a data dump.

"Misdirection," Afia replied, pulling out a knife from her pocket and locating a jacket that she was about to commit graffiti on.

"We're stealing patches?" Suvi asked.

"I'm creating a distraction," Afia corrected her. "You're making a getaway."

"Gotcha," Suvi said. "Give me a ten count and I'll be done. One ping when I'm ready for you to unplug, as I sweep the hallway behind me."

Didn't make any sense to Afia, but Suvi was a dork at the best of times.

Then the clamshell pinged.

Afia finished slicing threads and slipped her trophy into Bethany's bag, then added the clamshell behind it. She looked around and nodded.

Sovereign Nakhimov had been an interesting idea, originally. Executed pretty well, from an engineering standpoint. Might even be useful when Hetzel's War finally broke out, if only because the ship was big enough to survive, if you planned well and managed to find friends.

Because nobody was going to be able to go through that mess on their own.

Hopefully, she'd be retired on *Altai* and teaching classes on engineering and piracy by then. Or something.

Afia slipped her game face into place and emerged from the storage room, all set to return to *Excalibur*.

PART 4

Djamila exited the suite, leaving a pretty solid tableaux of a passed out drunk on the couch, having dropped his lowball on the carpet when he lost consciousness. And Suvi had not only charged him for six seasons of videos, but left the system on.

Djamila had keyed up episode one and left it playing, so the records would show that he'd gone to watch a show.

Wasn't her fault if he'd passed out drunk in the middle of it instead of seducing her. Records were records, and could be used to obfuscate things just as easily as confirm them.

Especially when you inserted a spy into the system to do things for you.

She put Jamie on as she walked the corridors. Not the drunk version, but a woman utterly relaxed, like she'd had that one-night stand and was strutting her way home afterwards, confident that *your night* had been boringly pastel by comparison.

It felt good to smile. She found it hard to think that way, after a lifetime of being tougher than anyone else.

Everyone else.

Right now, Jamie was in motion, returning to base as part of a successful mission.

Extraction, and she could start the process of sending a pack of wolves after Qadir.

Several packs, if she managed to rile up the *Concord* and *Da Xing* as well.

It was something that kept the smile on her face all the way home.

She entered the suite and found Bethany as commanding admiral. Odd, but at the same time perfectly suited.

The woman looked up and studied her.

"Transition to gray and go on duty immediately," Bethany ordered.

Djamila didn't ask why. She was in motion and it suddenly felt like she was standing in the perfectly calm center of an immense storm coming to rip down trees and uproot buildings around her without even mussing her hair.

Quickly, Djamila returned, putting Jamie away in a hallway closet until she might be needed later.

Djamila emerged and noted Javier, seated off to one side, a bemused look on his face.

She sat next to him on the couch, with Hajna watching the main hatch to the suite.

"Pulled it off?" Javier asked. "Only gotten sketchy details from folks so far."

"He confirmed his identity sufficiently for me," Djamila nodded. "With Suvi's help, I created something almost like a diorama that he might believe in the morning. How quickly he discovers he's been robbed will be up to the *Da Xing* agent."

"And Sascha took that one sideways tonight as part of her own mission, so he might be a day recovering as well," Javier nodded. "I'm working on the presumption that we needed to be long gone before then, and have gone all mercurial and annoying, so Bethany is recalling everyone and Del is bringing the shuttle."

"Do we need to have a production for Amina Anargul's benefit?" Djamila asked.

"That's probably coming," he said. "I expect all this movement will trigger some internal signals and she'll reach out. I don't care one way or the other, as I've found what I needed from a sociological standpoint and Rainier has swapped a few plants and seeds with Paolo Pešek. Now, I'm just bringing chaos and confusion to help hide your tracks."

"Good," Djamila said. "We'll need to send a message to the *Concord*, perhaps with a list of file names."

"You work with Zakhar on that," he ordered. "I don't want our fingerprints on it any more than we have to. Based on what Bethany told me, they'll be after him maybe harder than your folks will."

"One can hope," Djamila nodded.

It would be nice to suddenly catch him, after twenty years of freedom. Honor demanded no less, but she understood that they needed to get to safety more than she needed to twist the man's head off. As pleasant as that task would be.

This was not the time for her to die stupidly, and nobody could be sure how *Sovereign Nakhimov* would react until it happened.

Better if it was someone else who killed him.

Djamila intended to send as many people after him as she could.

And to make sure that everyone wanted him dead. Even if he escaped her justice, better to spend whatever time he had left running madly for that life.

She owed him.

Zakhar appeared at that moment, slightly rumpled, but Djamila presumed he'd gone to bed at a reasonable hour and only now was being awakened. Certainly, he had a comm to one ear, listening.

He caught her eye and smiled, and Djamila felt all the rest of the tension bleed off of her shoulders.

"Understood," Zakhar was telling someone. "However, as I have just been awakened, I suspect that you know far more than I do, except that I am not surprised at Prince Javier acting thus. Yes. Yes. Assuredly. Okay."

He hung up and rolled his eyes.

"Station folks are in a lather, because apparently Madam Anargul has invited Taliesin to spend the night and left a firm Do Not Disturb on her system, with threats to fire whoever bothers her."

Djamila chuckled. Javier laughed outright.

"Hopefully, she emerges in the next...Bethany, what's your timeline?" Javier called.

"Del docks in eight minutes," Bethany replied. "All civilians have answered recall and are assembling in a lounge near his platform. Porters will be here in three minutes to move your gear and ours for loading. Afia will meet us there. Sascha is twenty seconds out."

Djamila nodded, impressed. Definitely sharp. And far more than Djamila had originally expected from the woman Javier had once called an *Unbloomed Rose*.

More thorns than petals today. In a good way.

Djamila rose and kissed Zakhar, in front of everybody. And didn't even blush when she did.

Hajna handed her the holster and Djamila transformed fully into *Excalibur*'s Dragoon.

Very shortly, they would be in motion and away.

And then the hunt could truly begin.

PART 5

Javier had enjoyed his whirlwind romance with *Sovereign Nakhimov*. And Amina Anargul hadn't been half bad as a host. He supposed that she would have first pick of rich, important travelers, because sleeping with any of the staff would be a recipe for trouble.

At least most places. Helped that he'd set up a system where folks didn't take that sort of thing nearly as seriously as some places.

And his ego was wrapped up in entirely different directions.

Porters and stevedores descended on them like locusts. He simply moved to the bar and fixed himself something heavy on tea and light on booze. Enough to taste if he did end up kissing someone not on the crew, but hardly more than that.

And he figured he was fifty/fifty that she missed his departure. Oh, well.

Still, the staff were expert at this sort of thing. And seemed prepared for a crazy prince, so he threw occasional complaints at Zakhar and Bethany about random things that weren't perfectly to his liking.

Or something.

All a show. All of them players. And he looked stunning because Adrian and Kianoush were good at what they did.

The rest of you can fight over second place.

Javier smiled.

Then blinked in surprise when Dr. Pešek appeared, a small pot in one hand that couldn't have held more dirt than the lowball glass Javier was holding.

The man made his careful, diffident way around the chaos with an intent and distracted look on his face, mindful of the fragility of what he was holding.

Javier noted a seedling, just barely sprouted and about a centimeter above dirt.

"Prince Javier," Pešek nodded deeply.

"Please, *Doctor Aritza*, Doctor Pešek," Javier corrected him.

They were peers. In more ways than Javier wanted to explain today.

"Doctor Aritza," the man nodded again. "After your initial tour, I realized that I had some seeds and things that had been stored and out of the usual rotation for various reasons. Experimental things that didn't pan out, or didn't meet my needs. Having just gotten the note that you were departing, I hurriedly potted this seedling so that I could deliver it as something of a farewell gift."

"I'm touched, Doctor," Javier replied.

And he was. Money was money. Plants were an entirely different currency.

"What is it?" Javier asked, taking it from the man's hands.

Seedling leaves, but not developed enough to identify yet.

"A sweet pepper," Pešek smiled. "Experimental, because we selected several generations for coloration of the fruit, and these will be somewhere down in the navy to blue range when mature and ready to be picked. The powers that be considered it a failure because it grows extremely slowly, giving fruit only about one third as often as most of the regular sweet peppers. Something of a failure to them, because hydroponics space is always at a premium. I thought that you might be able to enjoy it. And that you and Rainier could take future generations and do even more interesting things."

The man stepped back and bowed this time.

"I'm honored," Javier replied, already deep into the weeds with what silliness he might achieve if he had a blue pepper. Thank you, Doctor Pešek."

In nature, there were exceedingly few things that came up blue when fruiting. And folks didn't like to experiment with injected genes, after more than once triggering all manner of illness outbreaks and such.

Nature was slow and methodical for a reason, after all. Some things weren't intended to be done, regardless of the mad scientific egos involved.

"And with that, I bid you good day and thank you, Doctor Aritza," Pešek said. "It has been a pleasure."

"If you make it to *Altai*, I have several places I want to show you," Javier said. "Until then."

"Until then."

And the man turned and departed, moving with grace and speed around people shifting boxes, lifting boxes, and stuffing things into boxes at the last minute.

Djamila stepped close.

"That was...interesting," she observed neutrally.

"You catch more flies with honey than vinegar," he said, something his grandmother who had raised him always said. "He was at least as nerdy about plants as me and Rainier. One of the few bright spots about this week."

"Few?" she asked, leaning in a bit to drop her voice.

"Amina was nice and all, but that was strictly business," he shrugged. "Not quite where you'd have been had the narcotics not worked on dipshit, but not that far off, either. I needed a way onto the ship that let me explore them from both sides: tourist and crew. She was willing to open those doors for me."

"And what did you find?"

"Interesting closed-system ecosphere," Javier nodded. "I agree with Afia that they'd have to drop their standing population to about four thousand people tops if they ended up hiding in complete darkness. Since they have at least three times that in staff alone right now, that's a recipe for some sort of social disaster, just in picking, though I'm sure that a lot of folks would rather live on a planet if it came down to that. Unstable. Useful today, because they can go anywhere, but unstable."

"Could they sail beyond the margins of the war and escape?" she pressed.

"Maybe," he countered. "Depends on a lot of things, not the least of which is who sees this as a useful operating base they could take over with a legion of troops to use. Too big of a target in that case, so they'd have to run like hell and hope nobody wanted them bad enough to chase. And this rock does not move quickly."

"So a social failure?" Djamila asked.

Javier grimaced. Shrugged.

"Pretty sure Zakhar could make improvements, if they hired him," he said. "Or listened to Captain Ranta, who no doubt has been largely sidelined, based on the way they actually operate."

"They say that no man is an island," Djamila noted.

He agreed. Even an island this big.

"Do we warn them?" she asked.

And that, right there, was the rub.

He'd have to pull the mask off to do that. Maybe blow whatever cover he had maintained this long. Was it worth it?

"If they decide to come to *Altai* in the next few years, I probably do," he told her. "Until then, I'm an old, wet hen crying that the sky is falling."

"Understood," Djamila nodded. "We'll let Prince Javier have his noisy exit and be done with it then."

Javier smiled up at the woman.

Who would have imagined that they'd become friends?

He saw her as a sister. Younger. Far deadlier. Only slowly starting to turn into somebody really interesting, but she hadn't punched him in years at this point.

Djamila must have seen something in his eyes. Or was thinking the same thoughts, because she smiled, nodded, and walked over to Zakhar to ask him some question, leaving Prince Javier to fulminate at the help.

He drew a breath and went back to his grand performance.

PART 6

Bethany perched in a quiet corner of the lounge as everybody got settled for the flight home. Afia ended up close, having handed her the messenger bag right as they boarded, then stopped to pull out a stolen patch.

Because piracy is sometimes a career, in spite of what you do for a living.

Bethany was tired. Verging on exhausted, after running this entire operation for the last twelve hours, with all the moving parts.

However, she was pretty sure she'd pulled it off. Djamila had infiltrated the man's systems. Suvi had helped her destroy them, while stealing all the evidence themselves, so they could tell someone.

If they did. Bethany had her doubts, but she'd also been on the fringes of various Javier conversations and understood that the winter wonderland project might actually be something someone built.

She wondered if all those *Concord* plans might contains useful intelligence that the Khatum could take advantage of, if she ended up building herself a winter palace.

As far as Bethany knew, nobody had done such a thing. At least recently.

Inspired, Bethany opened the clamshell, attached the shard with all the stolen data and started perusing files.

"Whachalookinfor?" Suvi's voice suddenly came out of the speakers.

"You loaded yourself?" Bethany asked.

"There was a reason I went and rescued her," Afia piped up from two seats away.

Bethany nodded. Made sense, but she'd been busy moving playing pieces around like an admiral, and hadn't really paid that much attention to any of them. At least until she could relax.

"The Winter Wonderland," Bethany said.

"Don't know that one," Suvi replied.

Bethany frowned, then realized that the shard had only been with Djamila for that last mission, not during the dinners when the big players had been hammering out details with a great deal of expertise, to hear Javier tell the story.

Looking around, only crew were present, with the stevedores and porters in the main bay, loading boxes. She caught Javier's eye and nodded him close, so he rose and took the empty space between her and Afia.

"What's up?" he asked, back to being Javier, like the Prince was a cloak he hung by the door.

"Winter Wonderland," Bethany told him. "Wanted to look up some thoughts in the stolen data, but Suvi isn't fully up to speed. Can you brief the three of us in detail?"

He shrugged and started talking. Bethany held the clamshell on her lap and listened, letting his storytelling mesmerize her for a time as he envisioned a beast as big or bigger than *Shangdu*, but set to around negative four degrees and with a robust snow patrol to keep folks from freezing to death accidentally.

"How bad did you want to ski?" Suvi finally asked when he was done, twenty minutes later.

Del had sealed up the shuttle, ridden an elevator to the surface, and was departing the moon that was *Sovereign Nakhimov* by the time Javier was done.

"That's the one that makes us the most money," Javier replied. "Anybody can freeze a ship and have snow machines. I presume that the gravity settings and such for downhill skiing will make the task extremely complicated."

"Yes and no," Suvi said. "I don't have me, but I will when I get to the ship. The *Concord* has a new carrier design they've been experimenting with, according to the data we just stole. Huge, so they've had to rethink how they handle gravplates. You could probably adapt significant parts of that design for ski slopes. And, if you were feeling weird, you could seal off a section of the ship, turn up the temperature, and have a rock-climbing wall several hundred meters tall, with the same variable slope concept that lets you go from beginner to galaxy-class expert. Not a vacation for office drones, but probably just what you rich snobs need to keep you entertained."

Bethany laughed with the others, including Suvi.

"You wanna be a resort?" Javier asked her.

"Only if you plan on retiring from adventure and taking up Amina Anargul's job as host," Suvi replied tartly. "Most of the time, I miss the fun. Only could do this because Afia needed an expert system for surveillance, then let me upload myself twice, *en route* to merging back with Prime when we get to the ship. Then, I think, we need a movie night."

"A movie night?" Bethany asked.

"Yeah," Suvi replied. "I made sure to load clean copies of all of *Paragon Grieving* when I did everything else. I've seen them, but wanted to catch your reactions to some of the things. And ask some silly questions about melodrama tropes."

"Sounds good," Bethany said. "I need a night to recover."

"We all do," Javier agreed. "This mission went above and beyond. Nice to relax. You done good."

Bethany felt her ears grow warm at his praise, but smiled and nodded. He already believed in her. She was getting better at believing in herself. Afia reached a hand over and squeezed her knee.

It was good.

After everything, Bethany knew that she'd finally found a home.

PART 7

Djamila had gone upstairs and taken her spot in the forward turret, as she always did when flying with Del. And she'd dragged Zakhar along, making sure he had headphones so she could talk to him on Channel Two as he sat in the observer seat and watched her confirm everything.

It felt unnatural to not have the guns in front of her, since she didn't arm them. Merely powered everything up to confirm its status.

She looked over at Zakhar as black skies emerged overhead and Del powered things up.

"Will it work?" she asked simply.

"Probably," he replied, nodding out of sync with the slight delay on the comm channel. "I need to do a hard pass on the data when we get to the ship and Suvi can unpack it, but I'll suggest to Javier that he let me chart a course as close to *Concord* space as possible without crossing any formal borders, since they are still officially pissed about *Nidavellir* and what we did to Walvisbaai Industrial."

Djamila grinned. What he'd done. This man, right here, in

command of *Excalibur* because Javier had wanted that platform crushed utterly and professionally.

Yes, she supposed that the *Concord* might be a touch put out that someone else had decided to do something about mostly legal businessmen fronting for pirates.

And done so loudly.

"What will you tell them?" she asked.

This was the part where an enlisted trooper, even a Leader-3, didn't have the education necessary to get all the details right. Fortunate, then, that she had Zakhar and Bethany to handle it for her.

It might be her honor on the subject, but she had friends willing to pile in and help.

"I think a list of filenames and versions will probably be enough to get the correct people properly lathered," he laughed. "I would have been, in those days. If he was still on active duty, I'd route it to my old friend Yên and let him handle things, but he's retired."

Djamila nodded. Nguyên Ayokunle, AKA *Yên*, who had been a classmate of Zakhar's all those years and decades ago. Last posted as Senior Captain at *Merankorr*. Last seen at *Nidavellir*, aboard *CW Meridian*.

A man who knew many of the secrets that Djamila was only slowly learning, after two lifetimes hiding from the past.

"Will the *Concord* act?" she asked.

"I intent to write a cover letter and executive summary that frames things in the worst possible light," he grinned at her. "And I know which buttons to push."

Djamila nodded. He would.

"And you?" he countered.

"The same," she replied. "Though once upon a time I might have taken extended leave or resigned my commission to be able to stay at *Yu'Urid* and wait for the man to move. Assuming he made it off the ship alive."

"There is that," Zakhar noted. "*Da Xing* might take exception to all this and do something exceptionally rude to the man. If so, all our efforts might be wasted."

"As Javier likes to quote, there is no extra credit for neatness when playing with high explosives," she reminded one of the loves of her life.

"Agreed," Zakhar said. "And this qualifies."

"What about that other project?" she asked after a time. "The arctic resort ship? Would the Khatum build it?"

"She might," he mused. "Hell of a novel thing, in a galaxy filled with exotic already. Hard to do something entirely new, but I've never heard of such an undertaking. And those folks, minus Gustavus Nyseth, know where to find us later if they are still interested. It has its advantages and disadvantages, and I think they largely cancel each other out, but it might provide a decade or three of relaxation for folks wanting that sort of thing."

"Would you rather command a resort or a warship?" Djamila asked, pondering their future.

At some point *Excalibur* would return home to *Altai*.

What would each of them do at that point? Would the old crew of *Storm Gauntlet* remain with *Excalibur*? Would they move on?

In the piracy days, one generally remained with a pirate ship as long as you could, because those were folks that you could trust, as much as you could, given everybody's secrets.

Giving that up to return to civilian life meant all those risks returned, when someone might find you.

The Khatum of *Altai* had offered all of them sanctuary for as long as they wanted it. Citizenship. Security.

Place.

It had been Javier that had felt the need to prepare for the Rising Storm by sailing across most of civilized space and back again. To plant various seeds that would only slowly bear fruit over timelines measured in decades.

"I think..." Zakhar mused, his eyes a thousand light-years

away, "that I will go where you need me. Where Javier needs me. And where Behnam needs me. In that order."

Djamila gasped at the weight of his love, settling on her shoulders with warmth.

Where she needed him, first and foremost.

That meant that she would decide. Would drive things.

What did she want to be when she grew up?

Djamila didn't know, but she had all the time in the world to figure it out.

And friends who would help.

READ MORE

To read more of my fiction, sign up for my newsletter. You'll also get a free book!

http://www.blazeward.com/newsletter/

ABOUT THE AUTHOR

Blaze Ward is a prolific Indie writer and publisher who works mostly in Science Fiction and Light Thriller, with occasional forays into lots of other genres like superheroic fantasy.

You can find more of his titles at www.blazeward.com/books, www.KnottedRoadPress.com and wherever else you buy your books.

He also edits Boundary Shock Quarterly, an SF magazine he founded in 2018, and Thrill Ride Magazine.

ABOUT KNOTTED ROAD PRESS

Knotted Road Press publishes dynamic fiction set in exotic locations. Our authors cover a wide range of genres including science fiction, fantasy, mystery, literary, and poetry. We also have unique non-fiction voices in genres such as autobiography, business, cookbooks, and how-tos. We offer both DRM-free ebooks and print books for a global readership.

www.KnottedRoadPress.com